Praise for .

"*Abandon Not My Soul* is an incredible story of a journey from despair to hope, betrayal to risk, fear to trust, and panic to rest. Sherye Green weaves a beautiful tale of grace, reconciliation, purpose, and hope. Anyone who has experienced the jolts of rejection, betrayal, and fear will find a source of encouragement and strength seldom witnessed in our chaotic and entitled world. Once you start this book, you will not be able to put it down."
—Dr. Ron Mumbower, Counseling and Congregational Care Pastor, Founder/Director of Summit Counseling Ministry, First Baptist Church, Jackson, Mississippi

"With graphic, poetic words, *Abandon Not My Soul* carries the reader through the struggles of life that are necessary, if one is to experience God in a deep and fulfilling way. At some time in life, we have all traveled to the Resting Place for soul searching, gone to Camp 4Ever to escape, and joined Loose Threads for healing. So often we discover ourselves as we seek to understand others."
—Dottie Hudson, author of *He Still Stands Tall* and family counselor with Summit Counseling Ministry, First Baptist Church, Jackson, Mississippi

"Life is full of tragedy. How do we cope? What language is the language of faith? Many books and television shows express life's tragic events, but few reveal the heart of Christ's own disciples as they face the disappointments and brokenness. Sherye Green takes us there in the life of Abbie Richardson, her son, and her friends. Leaning on her own walk with God, Sherye takes us into the soul of a journey with Christ."
—Dr. Sam Morris, senior pastor of the First United Methodist Church, Columbus, Mississippi

"Author Sherye Green has tapped into the heart of every person who has ever carried a heavy burden or experienced the overwhelming circumstances of life. *Abandon Not My Soul* will take you on a journey with Abbie, a heartbroken, middle-aged woman who is struggling to find life anew after walking through personal pain and despair. You will discover hope in the midst of her crisis and joy in the midst of her journey. This compelling story will lead you to an awareness of God's abiding presence in the darkest moments of life."

—Cindy Townsend, director of the Global Leadership Institute
Jackson Preparatory School, Jackson, Mississippi
Former Director of the Women's Missions and Ministry of the
Louisiana Baptist Convention

Sherye Simmons Green

Abandon Not My Soul

The Timothy House Chronicles: Book One

For Andrea —

You have blessed my life!

His love and mine,
Sherye Simmons Green

iUniverse, Inc.
Bloomington

Abandon Not My Soul

The Timothy House Chronicles: Book One

iUniverse books may be ordered through booksellers or by contacting:

iUniverse
1663 Liberty Drive
Bloomington, IN 47403
www.iuniverse.com
1-800-Authors (1-800-288-4677)

ISBN: 978-1-4697-6128-2 (sc)
ISBN: 978-1-4697-6126-8 (e)
ISBN: 978-1-4697-6127-5 (dj)

Library of Congress Control Number: 2012902029

Printed in the United States of America

iUniverse rev. date: 3/15/2012

"Scripture taken from the NEW AMERICAN STANDARD BIBLE®, © Copyright 1960,
1962, 1963, 1968, 1971, 1972, 1973, 1975, 1977, 1995 by The Lockman Foundation
Used by permission." (www.Lockman.org)

Author photo courtesy of Lisa Leilani Patti Fine Art Photography, Jackson, Mississippi

For Mark
My husband, best friend, champion, and the love of my life

Do not abandon me nor forsake me.
Psalm 27:9

Author's Note

The story you are about to read is a simple one. The characters may resemble friends and acquaintances in your own life. Their experiences might be similar to ones you are going through even now, like grappling with the numbing malaise of mind and bone-dry weariness of the soul often left behind like storm debris, once the hurricane-force gales of difficult times subside.

Have you ever had a time in your life when you couldn't see the rest of today, much less tomorrow? Does it ever seem like life's circumstances conspire against you, preventing you from making further forward progress? Have you ever wrestled with God in a dark night of your soul? Have you ever shaken your fist in the face of heaven?

Throughout my walk with the Lord, He has patiently endured my lamentations, allowing tirades of frustration and doubt to run their course like the tears of a petulant toddler. He has allowed me, without criticism or judgment, the freedom to ask honest, probing questions. Does God hear me when I call? Where is He in the midst of human suffering? How do I tie a knot in my faith and hang on in those seasons when it feels like God has abandoned me? What do I do when I'm not sure about the purpose for my life?

These honest, gut-wrenching questions and the search for their answers lie at the heart of Abbie Richardson's journey. Abbie is a teacher, but she could also have been a cardiovascular surgeon, a ditch digger, or an engineer. If a life storm has left doubt, fear, discouragement, and disappointment in its wake, I pray Abbie's story will cause you to take heart and find the courage to place your confidence in Him who is a strong watchtower and refuge.

Successful navigation of the Christian walk requires great diligence, a variety of which can only be cultivated through great trial. How easy it is on Sunday morning to sing bravely and cheerfully of God's love and care. All too often, however, in the stark light of Monday's morning, we cannot hear His voice or even sense His presence. I take great comfort in the fact that scripture records questions posed by many giants of the faith such as Abraham, Moses, and David. Even Jesus posed a few of His own. These personal accounts remind me that we serve a loving God who understands and indeed welcomes such inquiries.

Many days I wonder whether what I do really makes a difference. Perhaps, like you, I'm not always so sure. In those seasons of life when God is silent, it is easy to fall into the trap of thinking He has forgotten all about you. Those dark times require the exercise of great faith. I believe God doesn't mind our questions so much. What gets us into trouble is when we look in the wrong places for the answers.

For the past nine years, I have been working on and living with this story. During that time, I had the fortunate opportunity to interview author Josephine Haxton, better known in literary circles as Ellen Douglas, for a profile I was writing on her for the book *Proud to Call Mississippi Home*. Besides agreeing to the interview, Mrs. Haxton graciously allowed me to return to her home and ask a few questions about the writing life. The nugget gleaned from her on the second visit was priceless. "Write about what moves you. If it moves you, it will move someone else." Her words continually rang in my ears, serving as an inspiration and a guide. How grateful I am for her generosity and openness in sharing herself with me.

This story is known intimately to me. Its characters are old friends. I am moved every time I read it. My prayer is that it will move you, too.

Acknowledgments

Writing is like polishing a stone. The process begins with an object that initially shows very little promise but over time is refined into a lovely and functional gem. My heart brims with thankfulness for all who have smoothed away the rough edges of my words. I owe four individuals a great debt of gratitude: Terri Blackstock, Troy Carnes, Martha Stockstill, and Ellen Tarver. Without them, this book would not be a reality.

Author Terri Blackstock graciously shared with me her experiences of the writing life and offered prudent business counsel. Her direction and godly wisdom have been sure guideposts for me. Like Ellen Douglas, Terri threw down a gauntlet, "What have you got to lose?" Her words spurred me on. Thank you, Terri, for your love of the Redeemer and for always pointing the way back to Him. Most of all, thank you for your friendship. I am blessed indeed.

Enormous gratitude goes to my dear friend, Troy Carnes. He has been a constant encourager throughout the years. His unwavering support as a fellow writer has kept my spirits afloat on more days than I can count. Among the gifts he has given me are his generosity in sharing his sage advice and his tireless patience in answering my myriad questions. He has always challenged me to be a responsible steward of the gifts God has given me. Thank you, Troy, for believing in me and for believing that God has a plan for this story.

Martha Stockstill is a rock in my life, a wise mentor, a trusted friend, a ready traveling buddy, and an encouraging sister in Christ. Unselfish with her time, she was always eager to help. Alone, she spent untold hours reading, refining, and revising the manuscript. Together, we spent countless more hours developing book proposals, marketing plans, and the like. Her superb skills as a grammarian and her masterful command of the English language put the finishing touches on this story. Martha, your belief in the story was a bright light for my path. You are truly a friend who sticks closer than a sister.

Ellen Tarver is a gifted editor with whom I had the privilege to work. She has become a trusted friend and guide. Ellen taught me my first lessons in the craft of writing fiction. Ellen, your confidence in me gave me the courage to see this journey through to completion. I look forward to learning many more lessons from you.

The four friends who have graciously endorsed this book—Dottie Hudson, Sam Morris, Ron Mumbower, and Cindy Townsend—have all had a tremendous impact on my spiritual journey, each serving as a role model for how to live an authentic Christian life. There is no way to adequately tell each of you how very much you mean to me. I treasure all of you.

A special thank you goes to Margaret Clark, Lisa Leilani Patti, Elizabeth Travers, Amanda-Paige Whittington, and Amy Wiandt. Margaret, your many notes of encouragement and your shared belief in the power of words to change lives has fed my soul and fueled my pen. Lisa, your beautiful photography is above and beyond anything I could have imagined. Elizabeth, your early copy edit of the book and belief in the viability of the characters and story have meant more than you will ever know. Amanda-Paige, your steady blanket of prayer, your bright enthusiasm, your dogged belief in me on days when I didn't believe in myself, and your refusal to let the dream of this story die have been the wind beneath my wings. Amy, your enthusiasm for this book has touched me deeply, and your willingness to share your technical expertise has been invaluable.

A trustworthy group of friends served as my informal editorial board. These include Claudia Brice, David Bruce, Courtney Carnes, Norma Ferrill, Gayle Ford, Charlotte Hudson, Nancy Jones, Susan Lindsay, Charlotte McMinn, Rhonda McRae, Jan Miller, Alice Nicholas, Donna O'Neill, Duane O'Neill, Shirley Petkovsek, Trudy Powers, and

Lee Stockstill. For your priceless gifts of time and encouragement, I am deeply humbled.

I am most grateful to the following friends who provided a sure and steady blanket of prayer: Barbara Boyd, June DePriest, Malcolm Saxon, and the ladies of Hallowed Hearts.

Kudos go to the superb team at iUniverse, especially Kim West, Senior Publishing Consultant; Jessica Barringer, Editor; William A., Jade Council, Jan, Krista Hill, and Rebekka P., Production; Amy McHargue and Cara Neal, Publishing Services Associates; Shawn Waggener, Publishing Services Associate, and the members of Team London; Michelle Almeida and Hannah Evans, Customer Support; and Cherry Grant, Account Representative. Each of you shepherded me through this publishing process with great care and professionalism, and polished this story until it sparked. I am grateful to you all.

Special appreciation goes to my developmental editor, Diana S., whose insightful comments pushed me to dig deep within my writer's soul and to leave no stone unturned. I am particularly indebted to you for your valuable contributions to this story.

None of this would be possible without the unwavering love and support of my family. A sincere thank you goes to my parents, Sister and Heber Simmons, for your steadfast devotion. A special thank you goes to my brother, Heber Simmons, III, whose legal expertise greatly aided me in the writing of this book. My deep appreciation goes to my husband, Mark, to my son, Mark, and his wife, Abigail, and to my daughter, Lauren. Thank you for your extravagant love and for inspiring me to fulfill this dream. A heartfelt thank you goes to my late grandfather, Dadee, for his generous gift given long ago, a legacy tucked away for the future that has now become this present.

Finally, my utmost gratitude and praise goes to my Lord. You planted this story in my heart long ago. May it draw others close to You.

Chapter One

As surely as if he had pointed a gun at her and grabbed her purse, Joe had robbed Abbie of her trust, shattering her belief that God might have a purposeful plan for her life after all.

Joe is gone, but where does that leave me? Abbie thought.

Her husband's death had come without warning. Focus, direction, and purpose were all taken away the moment Joe exhaled his last breath.

Two weeks to the day after Joe's death, his law partner and best friend paid Abbie an unexpected visit and delivered a stunning revelation, a tale of embezzlement and financial malfeasance beyond her wildest nightmares. In the days that followed, a dark fog of doubt and aimlessness rolled in on the beach of Abbie's life. Persistent and pervasive, its thick, stagnant mist could not be dispelled. Now four years later, the beachhead that Joe's betrayal had established still undermined Abbie's ability to trust.

Perfect. That's the term that came to mind when most people first encountered Abbie Richardson. Tall and willowy with a head full of luxurious shoulder-length hair the color of dark toffee, Abbie was definitely a woman people gave a second look to, though she seldom noticed. Perhaps to the outside world Abbie appeared to have her act together, but inside her soul lay an abyss, a dark and deep inky chasm, whose depth she doubted could be plumbed by heaven's grasp. Regardless of how polished and put together Abbie looked on the outside, she was all too aware of how far from perfect her life was.

The twin sisters, Doubt and Despair, were hot on Abbie's trail. The mutterings of the diabolical duo constantly silenced the sound of her sanity. Their collective dirge, a hypnotic siren song, had captured the attention of her spirit, drowned any glimpses of joy, and stifled any of hope's attempts to peek its head over the horizon of her soul. Some days, Abbie felt utterly desolate. This particular Tuesday was such a day.

A difficult parent-teacher conference started the morning. Thankfully, due to the fact that the Gleasons' reputation had preceded them, Abbie requested that Winnie Jeffers, the junior high counselor, sit in on the conference as a third party. What a wise choice that had been. Winnie was just the ally Abbie needed in a conference such as this one. Abbie and Winnie understood each other's ebb and flow, having worked together for the past ten years.

Johnna Gleason was an academic puzzle. Articulate and intelligent, she usually made As and Bs in Abbie's class. Now she struggled to make Ds. Several conversations had taken place between the student and teacher, but all to no avail.

"Yes, ma'am," Johnna would say respectfully to Abbie every time she pulled the girl aside. "I'll work harder." Still, she never made any progress.

Johnna was on the junior varsity basketball team, quite an accomplishment for an eighth grader. Dipping into the lower grades was sometimes necessary when piecing together a team, as Kent Academy had a small student body. Abbie was all too aware how low academic performance could have athletic repercussions.

Now, in the middle of the last term, time was of the essence. Abbie had sent a letter to Johnna's parents, notifying them of their daughter's low marks, and today's conference was the result. These parents were known for antagonistic outbursts toward school personnel who didn't cater to their every whim. Abbie was now the Gleasons' target. Their what-have-you-done-for-me-lately attitude amused her.

Winnie's obsession with power walking and aerobics classes kept her slight frame well toned and in shape. Her habit of pulling off or pushing up a pair of horn-rimmed reading glasses into a tangled jumble of blonde, wavy hair that more closely resembled a wire scrub brush than a well-tamed mane usually set a certain rhythm in parent-teacher conferences. Abbie had come to recognize Winnie's assessment of how well a conference was going by how quickly and forcefully Winnie pushed her glasses up onto her head or pulled them down onto the bridge of her nose. Today, the glasses had only left Winnie's nose once, a sure sign she'd listened to quite enough from Johnna's mother.

The meeting spiraled downward as Abbie stood her ground. When it became clear that Abbie wouldn't give Johnna an extra credit assignment to make up for numerous zeros on homework and low test grades, Mrs. Gleason's voice ratcheted up a few octaves.

"We'll be calling the principal about this, Mrs. Richardson. Our family is not accustomed to being treated this way."

"I'm sorry you feel that way, Mrs. Gleason." Abbie mustered all the civility she possibly could. Her green eyes were flashing. "Johnna knew the expectations of the class when we began this term, and she has not fulfilled her obligations."

The Gleasons rose to their feet. "You have not heard the last of this," Mrs. Gleason barked.

"You obviously do not know who we are" were the last words Abbie heard as they left the conference room.

"I obviously do not," mumbled Abbie. She looked back to check Winnie's expression.

"Let's do ourselves a favor." Winnie giggled as she rose from her seat. "And go to Mr. Patterson's office right now." She nodded toward Abbie and pushed the glasses back up into the waves of gold. "We'll head them off at the pass."

Chapter Two

Abbie was a well-regarded English teacher at Kent Academy, one of several private schools in the area. A twelve-year veteran on the faculty, Abbie taught junior high students from McHenry, Tennessee. The town of some twenty-two thousand was nestled in the foothills thirty-three miles northeast of Chattanooga.

Four years ago, Abbie's husband of twenty-one years dropped dead of a heart attack in his office one morning in April. Nothing Abbie had ever read, heard, or personally experienced before prepared her for the horror of dealing with his death. Joe and Abbie's son, Drew, who was seventeen and nearing the end of his junior year of high school at the time of his father's death, was devastated. He was usually a good, solid student, but his grades dropped off precipitously after his dad's death. During his senior year, Drew skipped school and failed to turn in assignments to the point that his graduation from high school was in grave jeopardy.

The saving grace in the whole situation during his last year in high school had been that the school truly took care of its own. Drew's diploma was salvaged through the combined efforts of Abbie's prayers, gentle prodding, and the firm, yet positive encouragement of Drew's teachers. If he had failed to graduate from high school so soon after Joe's death, it would have been almost too much to take.

The summer following his high school graduation, Drew bussed tables at a local eatery. It wasn't the best money, but it was clean, honest work, and it kept him occupied. That fall, Drew entered a local community college. He told Abbie he just wasn't up to the pressures and fast pace of a four-year university.

Now twenty-one, Drew was about to begin his senior year at a small, liberal arts college that had provided a nurturing academic environment for the struggling student.

Abbie thought back over those days when being a single mother had been almost more than she could bear. In that first year after Joe's death, she had wrestled daily with the concept of God never giving one a burden heavier than one could bear with His help. Many nights, she had lain awake on her tear-soaked pillow and prayed, "Lord, You promised me in Your word that You are the husband to widows and the father of the fatherless. I need You to be all that and more for my family."

The Lord had held up His end of the bargain, although the searing pain of grief didn't always allow Abbie to recognize His provisions. Today, however, she had caught a glimpse of how divine intervention worked. Winnie's able presence at the conference this morning had certainly been God's sustenance for this day.

As if today hadn't already been bad enough, the answering machine's blinking signal irritated Abbie even more. She almost didn't check it. Finally, curiosity got the best of her. *What if it were Drew?* she thought.

She quickly deleted the first message, a telemarketer's scripted pitch. Next was the voice of her best friend Lane. "Hi, Ab. Listen, I know this is really late notice, but Eric and I were hoping you'd join us for dinner tonight. The weather's perfect, and the table on the screened porch is already set. Call me soon." Click.

Abbie puttered around the house for a minute, contemplating the offer. *I'm definitely not in the mood to see anyone, especially after today,* she thought. But after looking over at the stack of ungraded papers lugged home from school, she knew immediately that her decision was made. The papers could wait until after she'd eaten.

In less than fifteen minutes, she was navigating her way to Lane's house. She turned off the ignition of her SUV and sat in front of the Wyatt's sprawling ranch-style home for a few minutes. *Lord,* she thought,

I need a smile to wear. I seem to have misplaced mine recently. You know how tired I am, but You also know how much I need time with these friends.

An uncoiled hose in the front flower bed caught Abbie's eye, and Joe's face passed briefly through her mind. *Even casual disorder like that,* she thought, *would never have passed muster with his standard of perfect.* Abbie shook her head as if to dislodge a cobweb that had entangled itself in her hair. A flash of anger rose within her, but she quickly checked it. *Not today, Joe. Not today,* she thought.

Abbie squared her shoulders as she headed up the walk, determined to salvage the remains of the day.

Chapter Three

"Hey, you!" Lane's wide grin beckoned Abbie inside. She closed the door and wrapped Abbie in a warm hug. She pulled back, reached for her friend's hand, and pulled her down the hallway. "I'm just putting the finishing touches on dinner. I could use your help."

The two friends were often mistaken for sisters, though not necessarily because they resembled one another. Lane was a few inches shorter than Abbie was, but built with a stockier frame. Her olive-toned skin was a contrast to Abbie's peaches-and-cream complexion. Lane's blonde hair gleamed with highlights the color of summer wheat; Abbie's was dark and mysterious, the color of well-oiled mahogany. Lane's eyes were a smoky charcoal gray; Abbie's were a soft peridot, the color of summer ferns. But the two of them possessed a similar countenance, a calm, collected inner spirit that shone through to all who met them. Most strangers mistook this connectedness for a familial bond.

Abbie followed her best friend back to the kitchen. From across the room, Lane tossed her an apron. After donning it, Abbie carried a large bowl of salad out to the porch.

"How was school today?" Lane placed a large, steaming casserole on a brass trivet on the table.

"Don't ask." Abbie rolled her eyes. "It's been one of those days."

"Well," said Lane as they headed back to the kitchen, "my mom's chicken spaghetti is guaranteed to take your troubles away. Promise!"

Abbie grinned. *Who could argue with logic like that?* she thought.

Lane popped a French loaf into the oven and then filled the glasses with ice. "I know you said you didn't really want to talk about it, but what was so bad about today?"

"I don't really know what to tell you specifically." The last rays of the setting sun streamed in through the paned windows. "I can't really put my finger on it." Lane handed her two glasses of ice. Abbie filled them with tea. "Sometimes I think I've outgrown this job. I've been at Kent twelve years. Maybe I need a change."

"What kind of change?"

Abbie looked up, a bit surprised as Eric's voice filled the room. His six-foot-two frame towered over his wife's as he reached for Lane and gave her a quick kiss. He then tossed his briefcase underneath the room's built-in desk.

He headed over to Abbie and hugged her. "Hey, Abbie girl."

"Hey, yourself."

"Let me get out of this suit." Eric loosened the knot in his tie. "And then I want to hear about what kind of change you need." He smiled conspiratorially at Abbie and then disappeared through the doorway.

Eric, Lane, and Abbie sat around the table long after the sun went down. Candles flickered, their collective brightness piercing the dusk. As darkness deepened, the twinkle of fireflies danced just beyond the screens. Eric had Abbie laughing in no time. His dry wit never failed to amuse her.

At length, Eric pushed back from the table, folded his cloth napkin, and set it beside his now empty plate. "Listen, Abbie girl. Lane and I have been talking, and we know this year, in fact the last four years, have been really hard. I wish there was some way we could undo all the damage Joe caused."

Abbie stared silently at Eric from across the table, but even in the twilight's dimness, she knew he could see the sadness that hooded her velvety green eyes. After a long while, she said softly, "Eric, I'm so ashamed of what Joe did to you and the firm. Joe couldn't have asked for a better friend than you."

Lane reached over and gave Abbie's hand a reassuring squeeze.

"Abbie, we were victims just like you. There is no way you could have known what he was up to."

Abbie swallowed hard, as if to clear some unpleasant taste from her mouth. "As much as I miss Joe sometimes, I'm still so angry about the mess he left us in financially and the fact that he was so dishonest. I've never told you this before, but about six months before Joe died, I was taking some clothes to the cleaners. I always checked pockets before going, and I found a printed napkin and a plastic poker chip from the Diamond Mine casino in the breast pocket of one of Joe's suits." Abbie took a long sip from her glass of iced tea.

"When I asked him about it, he just brushed it off, saying he had gone to meet a client there. I never thought any more about it."

"There's no way you would have known what he was up to." Eric spoke encouragingly, trying to bolster her confidence. "None of us suspected a thing."

"I know. It's just that now it all seems so clear when I look back." Abbie brushed away some strands of her dark hair that had fallen around her face. "About two weeks before Joe died, a check bounced. He always took care of paying the bills. Again, when I asked him about it, he covered his tracks and said his secretary had forgotten to make a deposit. I believed him."

"Ab," said Lane, "you told me you were going to talk to Winnie about all this anger you're still dealing with. What does she say?"

"Well, to be honest, there's just not been any time lately to visit. Seems like the only time I do get to talk with Winnie is about students who aren't doing their job or parents who want me to do theirs." She proffered a slight grin.

"I'm still trying to deal with anger over how Joe pretended to be one person while living in our home and then turned into someone else when he left our front door. Just when I think I've gotten a handle on it, the anger comes out of nowhere and swallows me whole. It's as if someone has thrown a black hood over my head. I can't see anything."

Abbie took another sip of tea. "If I knew what triggered it, maybe I could figure out how to keep it from paralyzing me. I'm not there yet. I'm definitely going to find some time to talk with Winnie before the end of school. I sure hope she can help."

Lane reached over and patted her friend's hand again. "I'm sure she can. Winnie's one of the best counselors around." Lane looked across the table at Eric and grinned. "You tell her, Eric." She nodded to her husband.

Abbie looked in surprise at both of her friends.

Eric leaned forward. "Abbie, you need a break," he said in a firm tone that the widening grin spreading across his face immediately softened. "We want you to pack up and go hide out in the cabin for a week. It's yours the first week in June. Just say yes." He looked at her expectantly. His deep brown eyes begged her to accept the offer.

"Come on, Ab," chimed Lane. Her soft blonde hair gleamed in the candlelight. "You know you could use an escape. A week alone on Johnson's Mountain would be the perfect tonic for what's ailing you."

Abbie hesitated for a split second. "A week in the woods would be a great time to sort through lots of things I've not really had time to deal with lately." She held up her hands in mock protest. "That's so generous, you guys, but I don't know. What about Drew?"

"What about Drew?" Lane's gray eyes narrowed. "He's twenty-one, almost a college senior. He can fend for himself. You'll only be gone a week. It's not like you're moving to Montana."

Abbie grinned. "You're probably right, but I still want to run it past him." She fell silent as she brushed stray strands of hair behind one ear, a habit that surfaced when Abbie was nervous or in a contemplative mood.

"Well, young lady." Eric put on his stern face. "I refuse to take no for an answer, so call Drew and let us know something by tomorrow."

"Thanks, you guys. Give me until tomorrow night to get back with you."

Once home, Abbie called Drew. She knew her need to confer with her son about seemingly routine matters was yet another consequence of Joe's betrayal of trust, one she was working to overcome. The short conversation gave her the answer she needed. Fifteen minutes after leaving Eric and Lane, Abbie called back and accepted their offer.

Chapter Four

"I'm delighted she said yes," Eric said as he and Lane cleared away the remnants of dinner. "I'll never in a million years understand what got into Joe and how he could have done what he did to Abbie and Drew."

The stack of dishes in his hand hit the countertop with a bang. Indignation rose in his voice. He stopped himself before saying any more. *How many times have we been through this same conversation?* he thought.

Lane turned off the faucet and dried her hands. She walked over to where her husband stood. His face was taut with emotion.

"Let it go. We'll never get an answer to that question."

"How did I miss it? Joe and I were best friends. Surely I would have noticed something."

Lane stood beside Eric and rubbed his back for a long while until she could feel the tension in his muscles relax a bit. He continued looking out the window into the night.

"Even if you had known, I don't know if there's any way you could have prevented Joe from doing what he did," she said softly. "You've been such a support to Abbie and Drew since Joe died. Don't blame yourself. We were all duped."

Eric grasped Lane's hand. He squeezed it gently, brought it to his lips, and kissed it tenderly. "You're right, Laney. We were all duped. The least I can do is to make sure Abbie is taken care of." He placed her hand back on his shoulder.

"You always do, Eric. You've been a terrific friend to Abbie." Lane massaged his shoulders a few minutes more before returning to the sink. She sprinkled powdered cleanser into it and scrubbed away her frustration. "Right now, we can pray for Abbie to have some job direction. I think she's really tired of the routine at Kent. It's too late now to look for other work since she's already signed a contract for this next year, but at least a week at the cabin will give her some time to think about options."

The two finished their kitchen duties.

"Sweetheart, you go on up." Eric turned off the last of the lights. "I'm going to check the doors one more time. I'll be up in a minute." He disappeared through the darkened kitchen out onto the screened porch as Lane headed upstairs to get ready for bed.

This was his favorite spot in the house. Eric did some of his best thinking under the eaves of the house, safe within the shelter of the screens that kept more than the bugs at bay. He sank down onto the large, padded sofa and stared out into the night.

Thumbing through old memories like he was searching through his briefcase to find a particular file, Eric tried to go back in his memory to a place where Joe had been a guy he admired. He could hardly find such a recollection. *If I'm really honest with myself*, he thought, *I've got quite a bit of my own anger to temper.*

Eric remembered how he, Lane, Joe, and Abbie had met at church soon after each couple had moved to McHenry. The two couples instantly became best friends. The guys discovered an easy camaraderie in each other. Both were a few years out of law school and eager to tackle the world. The wives had likewise found a kindred spirit. The Wyatt's two sons, Jason and Jonathan, became fast friends with Drew. Jason was a year older than Drew was. Jonathan was a year younger. The boys weren't even in school when Eric and Joe, along with Chad Reynolds, an older attorney whom they had both met after moving to town, established the law firm of Richardson, Reynolds, and Wyatt. A local magazine had even named Joe best attorney in his field of law.

When was it that things had begun to change? he thought.

Eric had been stunned when the firm's accountant had called him one week after Joe's death regarding discrepancies in the firm's books.

Never in a million years would he have believed that Joe was responsible for the missing funds. The proof, however, was irrefutable.

Probably a good thing the poor guy died, thought Eric, *or he'd have had to answer to me.*

He immediately felt chagrin for his ill feelings. A quick glance at his watch told him it was time to turn in. As much time as he'd already spent trying to unravel this mystery, he knew that staying up late wasn't going to change anything. Joe was dead. Abbie, on the other hand, was alive and still reeling from all the debris left in Joe's wake. Eric knew instinctively he'd better serve his anger by channeling it constructively to help Abbie and Drew continue to put their lives back together.

Automatically, Eric reached up to massage a knot that had now developed at the back of his neck. *I need a good night's sleep. I've spent enough time thinking about Joe tonight,* he thought as he slowly climbed the stairs.

Lane was turning down the sheets as Eric came into the bedroom. "Solve all the problems of the world?"

"Hardly," he said wearily.

"I'm glad Abbie agreed to spend the week at the Resting Place." Lane sat on the side of the bed.

"Me, too. I just hope she can find a way to put the past behind her and really get on with her life." Eric pulled his shirt off over his head and tossed it on a nearby chair. "Joe has been gone for so long. You'd think she'd have made more forward progress than she has."

"Honey, give her time. From what Abbie's said to me lately, I know she's working hard to do just that." She followed her husband into the bathroom and joined him at the double sink.

As they were brushing their teeth, Eric's face lit up. "You remember last week's board meeting for Timothy House?"

"Ye—" Toothbrush gargle drowned the rest of Lane's reply.

"Well, don't you remember Don talking about the need for an English teacher, someone who could also live at the school? What about Abbie?" Eric looked very pleased with himself as he toweled off the toothpaste foam from around his mouth. "You said yourself she's tired of the job at Kent." He followed his wife into the bedroom.

"Let's just pray about it." She turned off the bedside lamp. "It's too late tonight to do anything else."

Chapter Five

Once home, Abbie shrugged out of her workday attire and slipped into her comfort clothes, a faded pair of navy sweatpants and a well-worn gray sweatshirt with "Vandy" printed across the front. The way they made her feel was as potent as any medicine. She thought about piling up in her bed to watch a late movie but instead headed downstairs to tackle the stack of papers waved off earlier in the evening.

Dinner with Lane and Eric was definitely worth it, she thought, smiling to herself.

She settled into her favorite spot in the den, a club-type armchair upholstered in an old-fashioned floral pattern. By 11:30, Abbie placed a rubber band around the last set of papers. Not a bit sleepy despite the late hour, she reached down into a nearby wicker basket and retrieved her dog-eared, leather-bound Bible and her journals. Her regular journal contained the typical chronicles of life: events of the day, thoughts, feelings, and prayer requests concerning myriad topics for both others and herself. The second book, however, held a different record altogether. This was her blessings book.

Most days, if Abbie were brutally honest, she had a difficult time finding things to thank God for, other than Drew. The difficulties of the past few years had considerably altered her usually positive perspective. She now saw life in shades of gray, as if through a filtered lens. In her first year of being a widow, she thought that, once she discovered she wouldn't die from the grief of her loss or the embarrassment of the scandal he had caused, things surely would get better, but they hadn't.

She had hoped this recent malaise of spirit was due to the busyness that often marks the spring of a school year, but lately she wasn't so sure. Something deep within nagged at her constantly, just underneath the surface, like a forgotten thought one struggles to remember.

Abbie was realizing that she needed to search out what this something was. She definitely needed a new lease on life but couldn't seem to get any traction on a plan of action. She knew she might be at a turning point on the road of her life.

Recently, one of her closest friends, Audry, had encouraged Abbie to record five things a day for which she was grateful. "Gratefulness is a choice of the heart and will always draw you closer to God."

Abbie wasn't so sure, but for Audry's sake, she was willing to try it.

Tonight's impromptu dinner with Lane and Eric had certainly lifted her spirits, but now back in the comfort of her own house, she revisited the more serious part of the dinner conversation. Her revelation to Lane and Eric about her discovery of Joe's gambling addiction brought to mind Audry's support of her during those difficult and dark days.

She remembered having almost fallen apart when Joe's crimes became public. For days on end, Audry had stayed with her, answering the phone and cooking meals for the family, as Abbie could hardly function. Audry had prayed for Abbie, begging God on Abbie's behalf to make Himself known to this brokenhearted believer in a very real way.

The striking of a mantle clock announcing midnight brought Abbie back from her musing. She picked up her blessings book and opened to a clean page. She ran back over the events of the evening and thought how the unexpected offer to use the mountain cabin was certainly a plus. She opened the journal and began to write.

Thursday
1. Lane and Eric's friendship
2. Not having to cook dinner tonight
3. Didn't focus on Joe today
4. The magic of fireflies
5. A week at Lane and Eric's cabin

There, she thought, *that wasn't so hard.*

She drew out her Bible from underneath the blessings book and ran her fingers across its dark, bonded surface worn smooth as a stone. She opened it to a particular passage that she had been mulling over for a few days. "Come to Me, all who are weary and heavy-laden, and I will give you rest."

The verse continued, encouraging the believer to "take up" Christ's yoke. Abbie had heard this verse all her life, but lately she found the verse bouncing around in her mind quite a lot. *What had I been taught about a yoke?* she thought. *Wasn't it a collar for a beast of burden that enabled the animal to more efficiently shoulder the load it was carrying? Hadn't it been handcrafted to specifically fit that particular animal?*

Abbie looked back down at the verse and noticed she had written the word "purpose" next to yoke. *Wonder what is God's purpose for my life?* she thought.

Even before Joe's death, Abbie grappled with this question, its answer always just out of reach. Too tired to wonder much more, Abbie returned her Bible and journals to safekeeping in the basket.

She remembered she had forgotten to look through the day's mail and quickly flipped through the stack she had tossed on the den sofa earlier. A letter addressed to Joe in an unfamiliar handwriting astounded her. The postmark read "Robbinsonville, Tennessee." She glanced at the unfamiliar address, turned the envelope over, and quickly opened the flap with her fingernail. She pulled out a neatly handwritten letter, unfolded it, and began to read.

Dear Joe,

How many years has it been? I had quite a time tracking you down but finally managed to locate someone who had your address.

Did you ever get to law school? Have been remembering how much you talked about it. I am, oddly enough, in my second career. After you and I graduated from college, I landed a pharmaceutical sales job. One thing led to another. I looked up, and almost twenty years had gone by.

I'm now in education and coaching, of all things. My job brought me to your area. It would be great if you and I could catch up on too many years that have gone by. Hope all is well. I'll call you soon.

Keith Haliday

Abbie gently refolded the letter. *Who is Keith Haliday?* she thought.

She knew she didn't have any extra energy to spare chasing down information about some stranger. Just making it through the end of this school year was going to take all the focus she could muster. She placed the letter in the top drawer of her desk and put the bills in the cubby where she kept monthly receipts. After turning out the lights, she headed upstairs.

While getting ready for bed, Abbie smiled to herself as she remembered the offer of the cabin. *A whole week alone! Just me! Thanks, Lord,* she thought.

Long after turning out the light, Abbie was still staring into the darkness. From somewhere deep within, snippets of a Bible verse came to mind, "Neither death, nor life … shall be able to separate us from the love of God." Death, Joe's death, had appeared as an eclipse in her life, totally blocking Abbie's ability to hear God's voice or feel His touch.

Abbie was tired of living life feeling defeated and broken. She longed for the abundant life experienced at other times in her Christian walk. Abbie was not so sure of God's final destination for her, but she was definitely ready to dislodge herself from this quagmire in which she was stuck.

Chapter Six

The humming office radiator lulled Keith Haliday into a drowsy bliss. The quiet of his new office was a welcome change after a busy morning of getting acquainted with the Tuesday class schedule, even though the unpacked boxes across the room clamored for his attention. Since his arrival in Robbinsonville five days ago, Keith had only managed to establish some semblance of order in the home provided for him, located across campus from the office where he was now seated. Strategy for tackling the office was yet in the developmental stages.

Thankfully, Keith thought, *this chair has good back support.*

He reached back instinctively to momentarily massage his lower back. Long, well-developed limbs and broad shoulders bore evidence of the exercise discipline honed over the years as an athlete. Those same years had contributed to nagging back pain.

Keith picked up a pencil and scribbled a few notes on a sticky pad, reminding himself of what needed to be done during this first full week on the job: purchase file folders, organize desk drawers, and talk with Beverly Taylor regarding camp. He stopped for a moment and gazed around his new office. The lack of organization totally arrested his train of thought. He put down the pencil when he realized his mind refused to stay on task. *Who am I fooling?* he thought.

A partially crumpled map of the campus in the middle of the desk caught his eye. Keith had twenty minutes before he was to be at the trailhead leading up to Windy Ridge. Josh Hastings, the cross-country coach and outdoor skills instructor at Timothy House, was leading the thirteen-year-old boys on a three-mile hike, and Keith was to accompany them. He considered himself in pretty good physical shape, so he only hoped he could keep up with a gaggle of energetic youngsters. *Maybe fifty-three isn't so young after all,* he thought. A wry grin played around the corners of his mouth.

Keith made the most of the fleeting minutes, so he turned on his computer and waited for it to boot up. *Man,* he thought as he watched the machine come slowly to life, *I am too old to have to be learning new technology.*

Timothy House was the recent recipient of an anonymous donor's generosity in the form of new computers for the administration offices. Since Keith brought computer skills with him from his former job, he was given the dubious task of mastering the system. The company whose software the school was using had sent a representative out late last week. Keith considered himself a bright guy, but at the moment, the program was a foreign language he was having trouble mastering. Lately his mind felt like a thick rubber band that hadn't been stretched in a very long while.

"Where is that guy's card?" muttered Keith to himself as he rifled through his desk drawers. A knock on the door of his office brought his head up.

"How's it going?" Don Fielding leaned against the doorway.

"Oh, you know. Trying to look like I know what I'm doing." Keith managed a smile for his new boss. Keith shuffled together a jumbled pile of papers and closed the drawers.

"Equipment a bit frustrating?" Don asked.

"I'll say. I'm going to call the rep and see if I can get this sorted out."

"You're a better man than I am." Don reached up to run a hand through his crew cut, silvered hair. "I'll look forward to gleaning wisdom from you once you have the system mastered."

"Right." Keith grinned.

"Listen, once you get settled, I want us to make a day trip. There's a great young couple, the Tidwells, who live about an hour from here. Very creative people. They've just agreed to come on board as partners in a student mentoring program called the Tentmaker Project. They're well connected within the East Tennessee arts community. They'll be a great resource for our visual art students."

"I'll look forward to meeting them." Keith leaned back in his chair. "I've been using my evenings to read through the notebook on the program. Quite a unique concept, persuading individuals from the local business community to share their business know-how with students. It's great that the kids also gain some work experience. I've learned quite a lot reading the program plan. Do other schools utilize this concept?"

"A few. Mostly up East. We could arrange a conference call sometime with my old friend who lives in Pennsylvania. He's been really successful at building bridges within corporate circles in his little corner of the world." Don stuck both hands in his pockets and stretched his stocky frame. "He'll know how to help us get a Tentmaker's Project started here."

Keith looked at his watch and stood up. "I hate to leave good company, but it wouldn't look good if I stood up Josh and the cross-country team. I've got five minutes to change and be at the trailhead."

Chapter Seven

"Hey, guys, listen up." Josh Hastings' voice commanded attention, and the young men gathered around him gave theirs adoringly.

Not an eye strayed from his tanned face. His sandy blond hair glistened like a soldier's helmet in the afternoon sun. "I want you all to give a warm Timothy House welcome to Mr. Keith Haliday."

A rowdy throng of "Hi, Mr. Haliday" and "Hello" sounded throughout the group. A few of the fellows even clapped their hands. One of the boys came forward to give Keith a high-five slap.

"Mr. Haliday has just joined our team as assistant to Mr. Don," Josh continued. "Some of you may have him for science in the fall. Others of you may be playing for him on the basketball team."

Heads nodded, and eyes widened at the images conjured up by these comments.

"Hey, fellows." Keith stepped forward just a bit. His well-toned frame towered above the group gathered around him. "Glad to be here at Timothy House. I guess you already know that I only arrived here last week. I'm still getting settled in at Stone's Throw. If you see me somewhere on campus with a lost expression on my face, it's probably because I'm in need of some direction."

Keith looked around at the group of young teens. One looked amazingly like David, his son. This kid was a little taller than David was but had dark brown hair like David. He fought back a wave of emotion. *Not now,* he thought.

He swallowed hard. "I look forward to getting to know each and every one of you." He looked back to Josh for further instruction.

"Okay, guys. Let's get going." Josh checked the time on his watch and looked up to meet Keith's gaze. "We've got to be back to get cleaned up for dinner by five. Lead on, men."

The group broke trail and headed toward the ridge above. Towering maples and elms lined the well-worn trail. A palette of sage, olive, pine, and moss green leaves embellished the branches that danced on the light breeze. Birds calling from somewhere high above in the canopy warbled a greeting to the group below. Animated chatter filtered through the mountain air as the hikers continued their ascent.

Keith could see the redheaded mop of one of the boys sticking up above the others. *Wonder if the kid likes basketball,* Keith mused to himself.

He could hear the boys laughing. Around a bend, Keith found Josh waiting for him.

"How's it going?" the younger man inquired.

Struggling to talk and walk at the same time, Keith proffered a response, "As well as can be expected." His words tapered off as the trail continued to rise. The concentration demanded by walking forced conversation to the backseat.

"You're doing great." Josh's voice was reassuring. "This trail is a good one to get started on."

"You're kind." A bead of sweat rolled slowly down the left side of Keith's face. He rubbed it away with a forearm. "I'm a bit out of shape right now," he said sheepishly. "My goal is to be back in the saddle by the time summer camp rolls around."

"Sounds like a plan to me. This is a great group of guys. Lots of needs, but also lots of heart."

Keith heard an obvious commitment to the young men in Josh's voice. Josh's maturity greatly impressed Keith, especially in light of the fact that he was almost thirty years Keith's junior.

Josh slowed his pace and then came to a stop. Keith stopped alongside.

Josh looked Keith squarely in the eye. "For what it's worth, I'm very sorry for your loss. I hope working with these guys and the older ones will ease some of the pain." Josh reached over and lightly squeezed the top of Keith's shoulder. "Glad you came with us today, Keith. Welcome again to Timothy House."

Keith could see the sincerity and compassion in Josh's eyes. However, he was grateful for the shadows created by the filtered light streaming in through the canopy as he felt his eyes fill with tears that threatened to flow. A look of silent understanding passed between the two.

Laughter and snatches of conversation from the boys broke the solemnity of the moment.

"Let me go catch up with these yahoos. We're only about ten minutes from the summit. The turnaround won't take us long at all."

Josh's solid frame swung effortlessly up the trail ahead as the golden light of afternoon glistened all around. Keith squared his shoulders and continued up the path. The crunching of twigs and small particles of rock underfoot were his only companions.

Chapter Eight

By the time Abbie got all her bags settled in one of the downstairs bedrooms and ate the salad purchased from a fast-food drive-thru, it was 8:00. In the mountains during summer, darkness falls slowly. Daylight lingers until about nine in the evening. Eastern Tennessee is especially beautiful this time of year, robed in the full splendor of early summer.

Abbie left a lamp on in the bedroom, wandered out to the screened porch, and settled in a large oak rocker. The rustling whirring of a gentle breeze stirred the branches of the hardwoods and the scattered pines surrounding her. She gently swayed in the rocking chair and watched the last fingers of the bronze June sun slip into the lake below the cabin. She could almost hear the sizzle as fire met water. Abbie thought wistfully about Joe, the old Joe, and how much he had loved this place. The gentle bass hum of frogs accompanied the fireflies' dance.

The journey up Highway 165 from McHenry to Johnson's Mountain had taken about two hours. Lane and Eric's cabin was called the Resting Place, and Abbie had visited many times before. Built in the 1940s as a summer home by a family from Knoxville, Lane and Eric had purchased it about seven years before. Modest but strong and well built, the rugged structure was safe and secure.

As Abbie rocked, her mind wandered back over the events of the last four years: Joe's untimely death, the shame and embarrassment concerning his actions, Drew's struggle to complete high school, and her own search to find satisfaction and meaning in her life. Relaxed as she was now, she also knew she had some very serious soul searching to do in this week at the Resting Place.

A recent conversation with Winnie ran through her mind, one in which Abbie had finally gathered the courage to broach a very difficult subject with her friend. She let her thoughts wander back.

Abbie knocked softly on the open door of Winnie's office. "Do you have time for a quick visit?"

Her trusted colleague looked up from a sheaf of papers scattered across her desk and pushed her glasses up into her tousled hair.

"Sure, Abbie." Her warm smile was all the confirmation Abbie needed.

"Would you mind if I closed the door?" Abbie asked a bit hesitantly. "I have a huge favor to ask."

"Be my guest." Winnie replaced the cap on her pen and set it on top of the papers as Abbie closed the office door.

Abbie sat down in front of Winnie's desk and pulled the chair closer. "I know your counseling is usually related to school, but I need some help, and at the moment, I really don't know where else to go."

"Go for it, girlfriend. You know I'll help you in any way I can."

"I know this is going to sound a bit childish." Abbie reached up and brushed back her hair, tucking the long strands behind each ear. "It's just that, ever since Joe's death, I seem to be stuck." Abbie stopped talking for a minute and tried to stanch the tears that threatened.

Winnie sat silently as her friend regained her composure.

"I felt like a stick of dynamite exploded inside my heart when Joe died. His death, as you know, was unexpected and caught me completely off guard." Abbie rubbed the palm of one hand with the thumb of the other. "Once the details of what kind of man he'd really been came to light, I almost lost my mind. I find I still can't seem to make even the simplest of decisions. Am I just totally being a baby about all this?"

Winnie pulled the reading glasses off her head and held them in her hand. She looked over at Abbie. "Absolutely not." She paused. "I've been wondering how long it would take you to start dealing with all you've been carrying around inside of you."

"You have?" Abbie looked back at her trusted colleague and friend. A look of puzzlement was on her face. "It's been so long. Why didn't you say anything?"

"Because, dear Abbie." A grin slowly spread across her face. "You would not have been able to hear what you needed to until you were ready." She threaded the temples of her glasses through her curly hair before placing them back atop her head.

"Losing a spouse would have been bad enough for anyone to deal with, but you've also had to deal with his betrayal of your trust. The psychological term for what you're dealing with is 'emotional trauma,' and its effects are as real as if you had suffered broken bones in a car wreck." Winnie reached up and fiddled with her glasses. "The seemingly invisible nature of your wounds make them all the more difficult to cope with."

Abbie stared back at Winnie from across the desk. Bewilderment was written all over her face. "Well, where do I go from here?"

"Where do you want to go?" Winnie sat quietly as her words sank in.

"I … I'm not sure," Abbie stammered. "All I know is I have to get out of this limbo. Parts of my life simply don't make sense anymore."

"What parts specifically?" Once again, Winnie fell silent.

"Well, like my job here at Kent." A long, shuddering sigh escaped from Abbie as she made this latest declaration.

"Wow," said Winnie, "that's pretty huge. Has another school made you an offer?"

"No."

"Have you said anything to Mr. Patterson about this?" Winnie nodded in the direction of the principal's office next door.

"No, I haven't." Abbie looked down and rubbed her hands together once more. "Maybe I'm just making more of this than I should. After all, I have a really great job here." Abbie looked back at Winnie.

"Abbie." Winnie pulled her glasses from her head and settled them just short of the bridge of her nose. "You are absolutely not blowing this out of proportion." She leaned back in her chair. "I suggest you follow the Patriot Plan."

"The Patriot Plan?" The look on Abbie's face said how puzzled she was. "What's that?"

"You ever see the Mel Gibson movie, *The Patriot?* It's one of my favorites. You know that Gibson plays the part of a Revolutionary-era patriot named Ben Martin. Well, there's a scene, right after the British murder one of his sons and kidnap another, that he takes his next two oldest sons with him to ambush the British patrol and free his son. Martin positions the younger boys in a stand of trees on a wooded point high above the roadbed and gives each of them a rifle. They are to shoot at the British soldiers who have taken their oldest brother. Martin reminds his sons of what he has taught them in the past about shooting a gun and advises them to, 'Aim small; miss small.'" Winnie leaned forward and looked over the top of her glasses at Abbie. "That's what you need to do, Abbie. Start small."

"Like deciding if I want to look for another job?" Abbie still looked confused.

"No. Aim smaller than that. Right now, why don't you just take some time and decide if you still enjoy teaching as a profession?" Winnie pushed up her glasses back up into her hair. "If you decide you do, then you can go on to the next step, deciding whether or not to stay here to do that teaching."

"I think I can do that." Abbie didn't sound very convinced, but the light shining in her eyes said otherwise. "Would you be willing to talk with me again? I don't have the money to go to a private counselor right now." Tears once again glistened in Abbie's eyes.

Winnie stretched out her hands across the desk toward Abbie. "You know I will. I'll help you in any way I can."

Abbie grasped Winnie's hands in her own. "Thanks, Winnie. This means more than you will ever know." She squeezed her friend's hands and then released them.

As Abbie opened the door to leave the office, Winnie spoke, "Remember, Abbie. Aim small."

The hoot of an owl nearby sounded through the night and brought her back to the Resting Place. The moon had risen by now and cast a milky gleam through the woods. Abbie pulled her sweater close and wrapped its bulky warmth around her.

"Dear Lord," she whispered, "thank You so much for the kindness of friends. I've needed lots of quiet time with You. I know You're here, Lord, but I can't feel You, and I need so badly to be able to do that. I'm not sure what to do anymore or what direction to take. Please guide me out of this fog that surrounds my life. Please speak to my heart as only You can do. Please do not abandon me. Let me see Your face and the light of Your love. Amen."

A gentle fragrance wafted through the screens as the wind picked up slightly. Abbie rocked for a few minutes more until sleep began to overtake her. She rose and went inside. After lifting the window next to the bed and turning on the ceiling fan, she settled into the smooth, clean sheets of the old cannonball poster bed.

Abbie uttered one last prayer of the day after fluffing her pillow. "I'm so tired, Lord. Please still my mind tonight. Grant me rest and peace."

Sleep, for the first night in many, came immediately. Standing as sentinels in the dark night were the oaks and maples and silver moon hanging over the Resting Place.

Chapter Nine

By the time Abbie woke up the next morning, the sun was almost overhead the cabin. Abbie reached over and groped the surface of the bedside table until she located her watch. Its metal surface was cold against the warmth of her hand. The dial read 11:37. Abbie grinned and rolled over. *How long has it been,* she thought, *since I've allowed myself this luxury?*

After a few more minutes burrowing in the warmth and comfort of the sheets and handmade quilts, Abbie roused herself, pulled on her robe, and wandered into the kitchen. She found a note she hadn't noticed the night before, left for her under a pitcher of flowers on the kitchen table. Its cheery message welcomed her to the Resting Place. It also contained an invitation to dinner with Lane and Eric on Thursday evening. Abbie smiled as she placed the note back on the table and thought of her friends, yet another sign of God's love to her. *Where had the time gone?* she thought. *It seemed like only yesterday when Joe, Eric, and Chad established their law firm, Richardson, Reynolds, and Wyatt.*

She shook her head and said aloud to herself, "Joe, for at least one day, I'm not going to think about you."

Abbie crossed the small kitchen and inspected the refrigerator and pantry cabinet. Both brimmed with a variety of edible delights. Considering the late hour of the morning, she decided on a breakfast bar. She washed it down with a glass of cold milk and then rinsed her glass in the old porcelain sink, leaving it to dry in the wooden rack on the counter.

She returned to the bedroom and pulled on her favorite jeans and a T-shirt. She gathered her shoulder-length hair into a ponytail. She grabbed her tennis shoes and socks, a favorite baseball cap, and her sunglasses and then headed out to the porch to complete her ensemble. Grant Lake glistened in the noonday sun, beckoning Abbie.

An hour later as she made her way back from the shore, she noticed leaves and small branches that had fallen from the trees had littered the path, evidence it had been a while since visitors ventured this way. Abbie also noted monkey grass springing up indiscriminately around the river stones bordering the trail to the cabin. The variegated sprigs reminded her of work awaiting her in her own yard. Abbie dismissed the thought as quickly as it had appeared. *I have weeds of a different sort to pull this week*, she thought.

She pulled open the door to the screened porch and headed inside. Suddenly ravenous, Abbie fixed herself a sandwich and headed in to the great room of the cabin. She settled on the sofa and looked around, taking in the details that made this particular room so inviting. On one end of the room rose a great stone wall made of individually set pieces of river rock that formed a wandering pattern some twenty feet up to the pitch of the ceiling. An old rifle sporting a polished walnut stock hung over a large pastoral oil painting. Both presided over the cedar log mantel's planed surface like guardians of time. A deep-set fireplace beckoned beneath.

A massive, worn, Oriental rug covered the heart pine floor, having mellowed over the years to a deep shade of golden honey. A plump wingback chair sat next to the hearth. The shade of a wrought iron floor lamp peeked its head like an inquisitive child over the left wing of the chair. To the right of the chair lay a multicolored, woven Indian basket, brimming with old magazines and paperback novels. Two smaller club chairs, an ottoman, and an old barn table completed the sitting area. Across from the chairs was the comfortable sofa on which Abbie sat.

Bookshelves that ran from floor to ceiling underneath an upstairs walkway lined the wall opposite the fireplace. Lane and Eric were voracious readers, and their residence had long ago run out of room for their expansive literature collection. They had moved the overflow here to the Resting Place.

Abbie felt pampered, having this week alone in the cabin, a gift of time in which to reflect and do some serious thinking. She reached behind her to the back of the sofa, pulled down a worn Ohio Star quilt, and spread it over herself. Muted shades of red, brown, and blue rippled across the top of the old coverlet. Abbie settled back against the cushions and burrowed under the soft texture of the fabric until she was warm and still. Despite her best efforts, memory commandeered all present thought, forcing Abbie to remember the events that had turned her world upside down.

The day was surreal. The April sky had been as blue as a robin's egg. The look on Mr. Patterson's face was a bit odd as he opened the door to her fourth period class on that spring day. Abbie knew instinctively something was wrong.

"You have a phone call holding for you in my office, Mrs. Richardson," said the principal. "I'll handle the rest of this class for you. Perhaps you should take your purse with you."

Abbie hurriedly gathered her grade book and purse. She mouthed a silent "thank you," quietly left the room, and headed down the hallway. A strange sensation of dread gripped her as she turned the knob of the junior high office door.

Rosie, the office secretary, looked up. "Abbie, line one is holding for you. Mr. Patterson said to take the call in his office."

The tingling sensation at the back of Abbie's neck became very pronounced.

A voice said, "Mrs. Richardson, this is Crosspoint Regional Medical Center. Your husband has been brought to the hospital. Please come to the emergency room. Dr. Phillip Rollins will be waiting for you."

"Uh, thank you. I'll be right there." Abbie gently placed the receiver back in the cradle.

She knew Joe recently had a physical and appeared to be the picture of health.

As she opened the door to Mr. Patterson's office, the bell rang, signaling the end of the class period.

"Rosie, I've got to go to the hospital to check on Joe. It seems he got sick and was taken to Crosspoint Regional. What should I do about my fifth period class?"

Rosie glanced up. "Mr. Patterson said he would handle it. You hurry on."

As Abbie left the office, she told Rosie, "I'll call you when I figure out what's going on."

Abbie made the drive across town in seventeen minutes. "Please, Lord," she whispered, "please let Joe be all right. Help me remember that You are in control of our lives."

The emergency room had been packed. Abbie checked in and squeezed herself into a seat between a family with two crying children on one side and a middle-aged man holding a dirty rag to his head on the other. Mercifully, she was not forced to wait long until a staff nurse called her name.

Abbie followed the woman down a series of artificially lighted corridors. The pair finally arrived at their destination, a dimly lit conference room. After asking if Abbie would like anything to drink, the nurse left Abbie to wait alone. Minutes seemed to drag by like hours.

At last, a trim, balding man in a white coat knocked softly and entered. Dr. Rollins gave the news as swiftly and as mercifully as possible. "Mrs. Richardson, I am so sorry to inform you that we tried everything humanly possible. We were never able to revive your husband. As far as I can tell, the end was immediate and virtually painless."

Abbie sat stunned by his pronouncement, as tears made their way slowly down her face.

"Would you like to see your husband?"

Abbie nodded softly. She felt as if she were in a movie theater, watching this scene of her life from a distant balcony. Dr. Rollins led her from the conference room to a bank of elevators. After a short, silent ride up two floors, the physician left her just outside an exam room near a nurses' station.

Once Abbie entered the room, she discovered a nurse who stood near several monitors. After making a notation on a chart, the woman patted Abbie's shoulder and quietly left the room. The only sounds in the room were the beeps and mechanical whirring noises of the machines. A pungent, sterile odor of a cleaning solution pricked at her nostrils. Sparse furnishings made the small room seem even more austere.

Abbie stood near the door, watching her husband for the longest time. Joe looked so relaxed, just like he did when he took his Sunday naps. She couldn't quite comprehend that he was dead.

She walked over to the bedside and gently stroked Joe's cheek with her hand. His face was still warm and soft as Abbie bent down and gently kissed his lips.

"Oh, Joe," she whispered.

There was no answer. Her knees felt as if they would buckle beneath her. Abbie grasped for the chair and sat down. Her entire world had just come crashing down.

The sound of the door opening caught her off guard. The principal, who had driven Drew to the hospital, stood behind Drew in the hallway. She rose and engulfed her son in her arms.

"Mom …" Drew pulled away. "Is Dad—" He couldn't finish the sentence.

"Oh, son," Abbie tightened her grip on Drew's arms. "He's gone." Her voice broke as she looked away from Drew to glance back at her husband's body.

Again, as if in an out-of-body experience, Abbie watched as Drew closed the small distance toward where his father lay. Abbie could see a host of emotions play across Drew's face as he wrestled to maintain his composure. After a long while, he walked over to the other side of the bed and placed one hand on his father's shoulder. Suddenly, the little boy in Drew won out, and he fell across his father's chest, hugging his neck tightly. Wrenching sobs filled the room for a long while.

Drew finally stood up and reached across the bed, searching for comfort from his remaining parent. Mother and son clasped hands across Joe's chest. Both wept for a husband and father now gone.

Chapter Ten

Gradually, Abbie became aware of warm tears on her face. The moist sensation broke the spell that memories of Joe always produced. Abbie reached up to wipe the tears and noticed the time on her watch, 5:33. The last time she had checked, it was a little before five. She could hardly believe over thirty minutes had passed. She emerged from underneath the quilt and found the room felt much cooler than earlier. Up on the mountain, even in summer, the temperature could drop quite a bit in the evenings.

Abbie went to the bedroom in search of a sweater and then padded into the kitchen to make something for dinner. She looked through the fridge and settled on lake trout. She pan-broiled it, fixed a fresh green salad, and chose sliced strawberries with whipped cream as a dessert.

After dinner, Abbie returned to the bedroom to retrieve a book bag containing her Bible and her journal. She placed the bag on the couch and headed back to the kitchen to make a pot of coffee. A delicious aroma produced by the hazelnut-flavored grounds soon wafted toward the beams in the old lodge.

Careful not to spill the brimming cup of liquid, Abbie returned to the den. Once again, she pulled the hand-sewn blanket over her legs and settled back onto the couch. She opened her Bible and thumbed past various notes she had written in the margin throughout the years. A practice adopted from Audry, Abbie frequently marked dates and details of important life events next to Scriptures claimed. These notations served as visual reminders of God's faithfulness in keeping His promises.

A verse of Scripture especially meaningful to Abbie was Psalm 34:18: "The Lord is near to the brokenhearted, and saves those who are crushed in spirit." In the dark days immediately following Joe's death, God multiplied the promise of this verse many times over.

Abbie's mind wandered back to the day Joe died.

Lane, Eric, Audry, and Beulah Tanner, another close friend, were already there at the house answering both the door and the phone by the time she and Drew got home from the hospital. Dr. Carter Franklin, their pastor, arrived around seven that evening to help them tackle the task of planning the funeral. The minister had been at Oak Hills ever since Abbie and Joe had moved to McHenry and had seen them through many scrapes and storms.

The service was held on a Thursday and was what Abbie thought Joe would have been pleased with. *Funny*, she thought to herself, *I'm sure Joe never thought about his own funeral.*

People came in droves. Many remarked they had never seen Oak Hill's sanctuary so filled. In the days that followed, many friends and acquaintances showered the Richardson household with savory home-cooked meals and beautiful bouquets of fresh flowers. Lane and Miss Beulah helped Abbie begin the enormous task of recording visitors, memorials, gifts of food, and the like.

Two weeks after Joe's funeral, the phone rang early on a Thursday morning.

"Abbie," Eric's voice sounded on the line.

"Hello, friend," said Abbie. "It's good to hear your voice."

"Would it be okay if I dropped by for a minute? Murphy Gates is with me. We just have a couple of loose ends that need tying up concerning Joe's affairs." Eric's voice sounded strained, as if those lines had been rehearsed several hundred times and still hadn't come out right.

"I'd be happy to see both of you. The house is a little quieter these days than I'm used to."

Eric had gently and carefully began the conversation, as if completing some terrible task and not knowing quite how to begin.

"Abbie," Eric said, "thanks for letting us come by. I'm afraid we have a problem we need to discuss with you." He glanced over at the heavyset older man, as if looking for courage to continue.

A five-alarm warning bell began clanging somewhere inside of Abbie.

The story Eric and Murphy told her was unbelievable. Apparently, Joe had a gambling habit that no one knew about. He had embezzled funds from clients of his firm. He'd even pilfered monies from their joint savings account and a savings fund set up years ago for Drew's education. The tale they told her had stunned Abbie, making the twenty-one years of her marriage rise up like bile in the back of her throat.

Perfect. It was a word often used by many to describe Abbie. Perfect. The word held no relevance for her. Everyone thought Abbie and Joe had the perfect marriage. Abbie never had a model of what a healthy marriage was supposed to look like. Her parents' union had been a farce at best.

Her mother had lost the battle with the bottle when Abbie was a little girl. Her father had been Abbie's champion but had died young. He was a godly man, but his body finally succumbed to the enormous pressure of trying to maintain a rigorous work schedule as a paper supply salesman while at the same time attempting to keep his family from falling apart.

Over the years, as her own marriage slowly unraveled, Abbie put on a bright face and tried to make the best of it. No one would have believed her anyway. Joe had mastered the fine art of wearing a believable mask at work and with their social acquaintances.

At home, Joe was a different character altogether. He constantly goaded Abbie about making sure the house was spotless and demanded she look the part of the perfect wife. Drew also never measured up to his father's impossible standards. Joe often belittled the boy, hurling derisive comments like darts in a board game.

To the outside world, Abbie and Joe's life did look perfect: handsome husband in an upwardly mobile career, a healthy, bright young son, a teaching position at one of the most respected schools in the area, a third-row seat at Oak Hills Community Church. What more could one want? It was perfect.

❧

Here in the quietness of this room, she heard the sounds of her own soul, restless and afraid, confused and bewildered. The realities of her inner life, kept hidden from most, were definitely not perfect. Perfect in no way related to the chaos that bubbled and hissed just below the surface of her soul, yearning to erupt and flow, wild and uncontrolled. Even four years later, the chaos spilled over, finding fissures in the carefully crafted veneer of her life.

The ringing of the telephone broke Abbie's quiet reverie. It took her a few seconds to determine where it was located.

She picked up the receiver. "Hello?"

"Abbie, hi!" Lane's welcome voice sounded over the line. "I just wanted to check on you to make sure you were okay."

"Oh, Lane, I'm great." The cheerful tone in Abbie's own voice surprising her. "The cabin is wonderful. You and Eric were dear to have gone to so much trouble for me."

"I'm glad you're settling in. Did you find the note? Can you go to dinner Thursday night?"

"Definitely. I'll be glad for company by then. I've been so hungry for time to myself, but now, seven whole days seems quite indulgent. Have you talked to Drew?"

"Matter of fact, I have. He came over for dinner last night, and then he and my guys went to the late movie. I woke up around three this morning and found them all talking in the den. I don't know how Drew got up for work this morning, but he assured me he didn't need much sleep. He's a terrific young man, Abbie!"

Abbie beamed. "Thanks. He's overcome a lot these last few years. I'm very proud of him. I appreciate you keeping an eye on him. He may be twenty-one, but he still needs lots of love and attention."

"Well, he's welcome to all the love and attention he wants at our house," said Lane. "Look, I'll let you go. Get some rest. We'll see you at five thirty on Thursday."

"Goodnight, Lane. Thanks for calling."

Abbie got up and turned off all the lights. She was barely in bed when she fell asleep.

Chapter Eleven

On Wednesday morning, Abbie considered her options, endless possibilities of the freedom of a day spent solely at her own leisure. She could crawl back under the covers to finish the novel thrown in her bag, she could work on a Bear Paw quilt top she'd been piecing together off and on for the last six months, or she could venture into the town of Craggy Bluff to discover its charm for herself. The click of the seat belt across her slender waist announced Abbie's decision.

Her SUV made its way down the winding drive out to Meadow Lane Road. Once on the main road, Abbie pushed the power button on her cell phone. *No messages*, she thought. *Perfect!*

Ten miles and fifteen minutes later, Abbie arrived in town. Established in 1863, Craggy Bluff had developed during the Civil War as a settlement of families fleeing the Union Army's determined invasion of southern Georgia. Many of the old-timers still referred to the Civil War as the War of Northern Aggression. She made her way into town and pulled into a parking space in front of The Nail's Head, Craggy Bluff's hardware store, general merchandise store, find-just-about-anything-you-can't-find-anywhere-else store.

Abbie reached up to adjust the rearview mirror and leaned forward to catch a glimpse of herself. She patted a few loose strands of hair and then repositioned the mirror for driving. As she unbuckled her seat belt, she silently admonished herself, *This is a day for me to enjoy! No thoughts of Joe allowed.*

A bell jangled against the glass as Abbie opened the front door of the store. A man inside dressed in worn Levi's and a red plaid shirt tipped the brim of his Atlanta Braves ball cap toward Abbie as she entered the establishment. He was thin as a fence rail, yet moved with a light spring in his step.

"Mornin'," he said in a distinctive East Tennessee drawl. "My name's Gurney Tompkins, and I own this here store."

"Good morning." Abbie reveled in the quaintness of Craggy Bluff and the friendly nature of her people.

"Can I help you?" Gurney swished a cloth over the top of a glass counter.

"No, thanks. I'm just looking around." Abbie smiled at Gurney and headed toward a shelf stocked with handmade pottery and blue-speckled enamel dishware.

The Nail's Head carried an eclectic inventory, everything from chainsaws and drill bits to cleaning supplies to old-fashioned toys to hand-loomed table linens and handmade pottery.

The bell jangled several more times as Gurney's business picked up. The thin man worked his way down the entire length of countertop, alternating between splashes of Windex and swishes of cloth.

"From around here?" he asked as he continued wiping.

"No. Actually, I'm from McHenry, but I'm staying in this area for the week." She picked up a small bowl from the wooden shelf. "Craggy Bluff is a lovely town."

"Thank ya, ma'am. We like it." Gurney, having completed his task, now moved to the hardware shelf to restock the peg board displaying packages of nuts, bolts, and drill bits.

Abbie brought her purchases up to the front counter, having settled on a small pitcher made of local clay and an enameled colander. The counter's main fixture was a huge, old brass cash register located just inside the front door. Turned with its keys facing out toward customers, the vintage machine was clearly a remembrance of an earlier time. Its burnished surface gleamed in the midday sun, which streamed in through the front windows. A smaller, modern electronic register was nestled beside it, its sleek design evidence of the encroachment of the modern world on Craggy Bluff. A Radio Flyer tricycle, suspended over an adjacent counter, swayed gently on an airflow created each time the front door was opened.

Gurney joined her at the counter. He nodded toward the pitcher as he entered its price in the register and commented with obvious pride, "My cousin made this. She's a right good potter."

"That she is." Abbie reached for her credit card. Gurney swiped it through the reader. "Please tell your cousin that I certainly will enjoy her pitcher."

Gurney carefully wrapped both of her purchases and placed them in a large brown paper bag. He tucked the receipt between the two items and then slid the bag across the counter toward Abbie.

"Thank ya kindly, miss, for stoppin' by. Hope the rest of your stay goes well here in Craggy Bluff."

"Thank you." Abbie smiled warmly at the man's comments. She picked up the sack containing her purchases. The bell jangled against the glass as Abbie opened the front door. She stopped and turned to look back at the owner. "Have a nice day."

Gurney tipped the brim of his Braves cap to Abbie once more. "You, too, ma'am."

Warm summer sun glistened on the windshield as Abbie made her way to the back door of her SUV. She placed her purchases inside and then turned to look up and down Commerce Street, one of Craggy Bluff's main drags. Posie's, an art gallery specializing in local and regional art and mountain crafts, was two doors down to the left of The Nail's Head. It was her next destination.

Chapter Twelve

Abbie stood just inside the front door of Posie's for a few moments to get her bearings, not sure if anyone were in the store. The soothing aroma of some unusual spice she couldn't quite identify filled the air.

A flaxen-colored, ponytailed head peeked out from behind a whitewashed folding screen constructed from old building shutters standing near the center of the shop.

"Welcome to Posie's." The woman's voice was relaxed and upbeat. "I'll be with you in just a minute. Just let me finish with this."

The woman stepped back far enough that Abbie could see she was in the midst of hanging a lovely framed watercolor. The large picture just obscured the slogan adorning the T-shirt that the woman wore.

"Take your time," Abbie replied. "I'm just browsing."

"Make yourself at home," the voice called out from somewhere behind the screens. The whacking sound of hammer upon nail promptly followed.

Abbie moved around the front of the gallery. Warm earth tones of terra-cotta and sandstone adorned the walls of the studio-style shop. Soon, a group of five sixtysomething women entered, laughing as one remarked to another, "Look, Lucille, blown glass. I told you we could find it here."

As Abbie moved toward the rear of the gallery, the pungent odor of cedar shavings made her nose wrinkle. Through an open doorway, she could see a slender man sporting a ponytail unpacking a box. He nodded to Abbie as their eyes met. His appearance was identical to the woman's, complete with garb of worn T-shirt and jeans.

The woman appeared around the corner of a wooden display shelf, her T-shirt slogan now in full view. *Save the Forests and the Trees.*

"Now," she said with a smile, "I've maneuvered that painting up where it needs to be. How can I help you?"

"This is a lovely shop. Is it yours?" Abbie ventured.

"Why, yes, it is." The pride of ownership was obvious on the young woman's face. "I'm Summer Tidwell." She thrust her hand toward Abbie. "And that ..." She nodded her head toward the open doorway. "Is my husband, Elton."

He offered another nod Abbie's way. His rust-colored ponytail swayed slightly.

"I'm Abbie Richardson." Abbie firmly shook the hand extended to her. "How nice to meet you."

"We're both potters." Summer looked around the shop. "We moved to Craggy Bluff about a year and a half ago. We named the shop for Elton's grandmother. Posie taught him the basics of the wheel and throwing clay when he was just a little fellow." Summer smiled at Elton.

"Take your time looking around. We have a really large assortment, much of it made by local craftsmen. If you need any help, Abbie, just holler."

Summer's easygoing manner made Abbie feel right at home. Abbie mingled among the other tourists, browsing Posie's handcrafted offerings. One entire wall of the shop, covered in a rich shade of mocha burlap, displayed a handsome collection of watercolors, acrylics, oil landscapes, and still-lifes. Abbie, lost in the beauty of the landscapes, barely even heard the tinkle of the front doorbell. Soon two male voices joined Summer's in conversation.

"Hi, Don," Abbie heard Summer say.

"Hello, Summer. Thanks so much for letting me run by today." The voice was confident and friendly. "I wanted you to meet my new right-hand man, Keith Haliday."

More pleasantries. Although the exact words were lost amid cackles of laughter erupting from the sixtysomethings, the other man's voice mesmerized Abbie. Low and relaxed, its rich timbre captivated her. Abbie strained to make out his words.

Some inner sense of self-awareness alerted Abbie to the fact that she was on the verge of eavesdropping. Mustering self-discipline, she attempted to concentrate on the paintings before her. She toyed with the price tags of several that caught her eye, but practicality got the better of her. Instead, she walked back across the gallery to select a small, shallow bowl made of fruitwood for Drew. It could hold change on his dresser.

She walked toward the checkout counter and heard the older man say, "Summer, I have some friends in McHenry, the Wyatts, who'll be at camp with us in July."

At the mention of the name Wyatt, Abbie stopped dead in her tracks.

The man continued, "They're big supporters of Timothy House. They'll love getting to meet you at camp and hearing about how you and Elton are showcasing some of our students' talent."

Abbie stepped quickly behind a large, hanging rack.

Summer's voice was the next one Abbie heard. "I'll look forward to meeting them, Don."

Abbie peered through the display rack hung with hand-woven textiles and strained to get a better look at the men. *No one that I know,* she thought.

The older gentleman appeared to be in his mid-sixties with close-cropped, salt-and-pepper hair. The other man was somewhat younger and much taller with dark hair and deep-set eyes, although Abbie couldn't quite determine the color. *Sad eyes,* she thought.

The sixtysomethings rounded the aisle, erupting in another wave of laughter. *I hope life will be that hilarious,* Abbie thought to herself, *when I get to be that age.*

The conversation between Summer and the men was over. Abbie moved to get in the checkout line behind the women. As the men turned to leave, Abbie stepped aside to make room for them to pass. She met the taller man's gaze and was captured momentarily by eyes the color of blue-gray slate that were rimmed with dark lashes. *Sad eyes,* she again thought.

He smiled as he passed her and then was gone.

As Abbie purchased the bowl for Drew, she considered asking Summer who the men were but decided against it. A bit too shy for her own good, she never wanted to be perceived as a busybody.

"Is there a bookstore here in Craggy Bluff?" she asked instead and folded her receipt.

"Yes." Summer closed the register drawer. She pointed out Chapter's End through the shop's front window. "It's located just across the intersection a few doors down on Franklin." She handed the packaged purchase across the counter. "It was a pleasure meeting you, Abbie. Please come back to visit us again soon."

"Thanks, Summer. I will."

The front door of Posie's created a slight breeze that set a wind chime in motion just outside the shop. Its pleasant metallic sound mingled with the rumble of passing traffic as Abbie stepped out onto the sidewalk. She noticed that the visitor foot traffic had picked up on the sidewalks of Craggy Bluff as she walked the short distance to the bookstore.

A pleasant, older gentleman greeted Abbie warmly as she entered Chapter's End. "Good afternoon, miss." His starched khakis, paisley bow tie, and crisp button-down shirt were the perfect complement to the tidy shelves surrounding her. "Anything I can interest you in today?"

"Not actually," said Abbie a bit hesitantly. "I'd really just like to browse, if that's okay."

"Certainly, miss. Just call for me if I can be of service." He then disappeared into another room. His manner reminded Abbie of a butler in an English novel.

Her gaze followed row after row of books crammed neatly into every nook and cranny of the bookstore's front room. The faint scents of well-worn leather and paper hung in the air.

At some point, Abbie glanced down at her watch and drew in a sharp breath. *4:15. Good heavens! Where has the time gone?* she thought.

On the walk back to her car, she made a mental note, *I have to remember to ask Lane and Eric about the Tidwells and Posie's.* The conversation she had overheard earlier was a puzzle.

Abbie sipped the remnants of a sugar-free caramel latte on her drive back

to the cabin. Craggy Bluff's newest retail establishment, the Steamin'
Mug, had been the last stop on her outing to the mountain village. The
sun was just making its slow decline down the backside of the sky toward
twilight, Abbie's favorite time of the day. After ferrying in her purchases
from the day's excursion, Abbie rummaged through her suitcase until
she found her favorite sweatshirt. She headed out to the screened porch,
pulled the worn, fleece-lined garment over her head, and freed her long
hair from the neckline. She settled onto a canvas chaise in a corner of
the porch and pulled a blanket borrowed from the den over her long,
slender legs.

The sun, now a deep golden red, hung just over the tree line behind
the lake. Without warning, it was gone, leaving behind a dim, rosy glow
that slowly faded into the deep, velvety gray of dusk. For the longest time,
Abbie willed herself to lay aside all thoughts and concentrate only on the
symphony of creation being performed all around her. Relaxed and warm
under the soft woolen coverlet, she soon nodded off.

Abbie couldn't actually remember what woke her, but she realized
she had been dreaming of Joe, the Joe she first fell in love with all those
years before. She scooted up on the chaise and brushed strands of hair
back from her face. She sought to chase away the dregs of sleep and the
dream that disturbed her. Quickly, the old memories were replaced
with newer ones, memories accompanied by pangs of resentment and
indignation, now constant companions to Abbie's soul. Ignore them as
she might, the emotions of anger, doubt, and bitterness clouded her every
thought where Joe was concerned.

"Oh, no, you don't, Joe Richardson," said Abbie aloud to herself in a
very cross tone. "There's no way I'm going to let your problems become
mine. Not now, buddy. Not today."

She headed back into the cabin to salvage the rest of what had
otherwise been a very lovely day.

Chapter Thirteen

All throughout Thursday, Abbie looked forward to the dinner ahead. Now with only an hour left to get ready, she began her preparations. The spigot in the old cabin's ball-and-claw bathtub gurgled with steaming hot water as the tub filled. Abbie poured in three capfuls of a new bubble bath, and the floral fragrance of freesia rose in the air. Thirty minutes later, she stepped from the tub, rejuvenated. She headed back into the bedroom to decide what to wear and settled on a dark navy print sundress. After dressing, she grabbed her makeup bag and headed to the porch to enjoy the natural light.

At 5:30 sharp, she heard the crunch of gravel and the friendly toot of the Wyatt's horn. Eric and Lane got out of the car and greeted her with hugs. Eric put his two dates in the car, and the trio pulled away from the cabin.

"You look fabulous, Abbie." Eric looked back at her in the rearview mirror. "How do you like the cabin?"

"I love it. I feel extremely pampered with all this room to myself." She pulled a white summer shawl closer around her shoulders.

"Good." Lane smiled. "That's exactly how we want you to feel."

The three friends caught up on the latest news from McHenry during the trip to their destination, a quaint town that lay an hour away, some thirty miles across the state line in North Carolina.

"The Butterfield Inn is a real treasure, Abbie." Lane's voice carried into the backseat as the travelers pulled into Ford's Gap. "The décor is understated. Navy blue checked tablecloths, white linen napkins, pewter flatware, and blue and white ironstone china. You feel like you've been transported to a cozy English cottage."

"Sounds enticing. I'm starved."

Eric arranged for a table in front of a large bay window overlooking a fern-banked ravine complete with a waterfall and babbling stream. Candles set around lent a warm, intimate glow to the room. After dinner, the threesome enjoyed a fresh pot of coffee, accompanied by warm slices of chocolate truffle delight, the house favorite.

All throughout the evening, Eric and Lane would look at each other, look over at Abbie, and then glance back at each other.

Finally, Abbie couldn't stand it any longer. "Okay, you two. What's up your sleeve?"

"Is it that obvious?" Eric laughed. "You tell her, hon." He nodded to his wife.

Lane took a big breath. "Well, you know how you've been feeling lost at sea this year, questioning your job at Kent?"

As Lane was talking, Eric slid a color brochure across the table toward Abbie.

"Is this a setup?" A grin crept across Abbie's face.

"We have a proposition for you." Lane's eyes glistened with excitement. "Our Sunday school class has gotten involved with a very special school up in Robbinsonville called Timothy House. They host a weeklong camp for area elementary kids the last full week in July."

Eric joined in. "Lane and I are going for the week as counselors, and we want you to join us. There's an application process, but I don't think there'd be anything to worry about. You could ride with us, so travel wouldn't be a problem. The camp gives free room and board to counselors as a thank you."

Eric uttered a deep sigh as if he had just completed a long anticipated assignment. He sat back in his chair and looked at Abbie. "What do you think?"

Abbie sat silent for a while. "You know, that sounds like an adventure, perhaps one I need to go on. I'm not sure of the date, though. I'll have to check my calendar."

Eric hesitated for a moment. "I might as well be completely honest with you. We do want you to come with us for the week. Our class has such a great time together, and helping the kids will be really special. But there's another reason we'd like you to go.

"The headmaster, Don Fielding, is an old friend of mine. We've been involved in mission projects together for years. He and his wife, Doris, don't come any finer. They called me in late February to ask me if I knew of a really good English teacher, preferably a woman, who might also serve as a house mom for some of the junior high-aged girls. You'd be perfect for the job."

"You guys." Abbie gasped. She pushed her chair slightly back from the table and adjusted her shawl.

"Oh, Abbie." Lane leaned forward. "At least pray about it and give it some thought. It may be just where God needs you to be." Her bright eyes sparkled with genuine concern for her dear friend.

"Gee," Abbie replied, "you really know how to pressure a girl. You're talking about a move, uprooting and starting over. Mr. Patterson has been terrific to me. I'd really hate to let him down."

"Just promise us you'll think about it." Lane settled back into her chair. "First things first. See if you can make the trip in July. If you want to, that is. We'll have the camp mail you an application early next week. Maybe being there and meeting some of the kids and the staff will give you more to think about."

Thinking aloud, Abbie said, "I brought my calendar to the cabin. I'll call you tomorrow and let you know about the week. That's all I really can commit to right now."

Eric and Lane smiled conspiratorially. "That'll do for now."

Chapter Fourteen

The sun was perched high in the sky by the time Abbie awoke on Friday. The late hour of the previous evening, the richness of the superb meal, and the intriguing proposal made by Eric and Lane added to her fatigue. Besides, she was on vacation. *What did it matter if I slept half the day away?* she thought.

After a quick bite of bagels and cream cheese, Abbie donned her jeans, a turtleneck, and an old Woolrich plaid shirt Drew had outgrown.

It was time to tackle the upper trail around the lake. Abbie grabbed her backpack and threw in her Bible, her journal, a pen, and the Timothy House brochure. From the kitchen, she added an apple, a Ziploc full of wheat crackers, and a thermos of ice water. The porch's screened door sounded its good-bye as she bounded down the steps. Two ducks floated serenely on the lake. Abbie walked along the bank to the far side, smiling to herself, content to be alone.

The path up to Summit Ridge, the top of Johnson's Mountain, wound slowly upward, taking the hiker over small rock outcroppings and through a delightful profusion of towering hardwoods and fragrant evergreens. Sunlight filtered through the canopy, piercing the forest floor with shafts of light bright as cut glass. Sounds of falling water greeted Abbie as she rounded a bend in the path. The trail afforded her a view that brought a joyful exclamation to her lips.

On up the mountain, a clear, cool stream tumbled over boulders, smoothed and worn by the falling water. A pool formed at the base of the falls. The water waited patiently to continue its gravity-driven journey down the mountain. Drinking from the pool was a white-tailed fawn. Abbie stopped for a few moments and took in this rare gift from nature. The fawn looked up at Abbie with eyes dark and bright as polished black marbles. Flicking its tail, the creature leisurely ambled away into the brush.

Abbie headed on to the summit. A weathered marker noted Summit Ridge's elevation, 3,249 feet. Near the marker was a large, flat-topped boulder. Abbie decided this would be a perfect stopping place. She dropped her pack and climbed up onto the smooth ledge. The massive surface was large enough for her to lie down and stretch out.

Abbie thought back over her conversation with Winnie.

"Aim small."

She was to decide if teaching were really a job she wanted to stick with. In the weeks since the meeting, Abbie had concluded that she indeed did love working with children. Bull's-eye! Now all she had to do was figure out if staying at Kent Academy were the right decision.

Warmth from the sun radiated off the rock and seeped into Abbie's tired body and deeper still into her depleted soul. A gentle breeze stirred as rustling sounds from the trees lulled her to sleep.

A rumbling in her stomach awoke Abbie two hours later. It was almost three. She hungrily ate the treats packed earlier in the day and washed them down with the cold water from her thermos. Abbie took out her Bible and journal and placed them on the surface of the boulder next to her. She hugged her knees to her chest and closed her eyes. Here alone on this rocky point, she could shut out the world and bring all the broken pieces of her heart to the throne of heaven.

As the afternoon sun wrapped a golden cloak around Abbie, she poured out her thoughts and feelings to God. "Oh, Father," she began, gently whispering as she prayed, "thank You for Your patience with me. I do thank You, Lord, for providing for Drew and me in so many ways. My job, the friendship of Eric and Lane, even this beautiful cabin to enjoy have all been gifts from You that I don't want to take for granted. Lord, I need direction, Your direction. I love teaching, but most days at Kent, I don't feel like I make a difference. Is there something else You want me to do? Is there somewhere else I'm supposed to go?"

Abbie stopped and listened to the song the breeze sang as it wound its way up Johnson's Mountain. The verse, "Cease striving, and know that I am God," came to her. This word of God woven long ago into Abbie's heart and mind now provided solace. After a while, she opened her eyes. She grabbed her backpack, reached inside, and fumbled around until her hand located the slick paper surface of the Timothy House brochure. She drew it out.

Four colored pictures of smiling children and energetic teens grinned back at her. She gently ran her finger across the pictures of their bright, happy faces. The copy explained the school's mission and ministry and highlighted the work of Don Fielding. Suddenly, the conversation she overhead in Craggy Bluff at Posie's came back with startling clarity.

Abbie turned a page and read the description of the summer camp. She smiled as she thought about Eric and Lane's invitation to join them there. Called Camp 4Ever Adventure, the weeklong program exposed elementary-age children in the Robbinsonville community to activities such as hiking, canoeing, and rock climbing. An array of crafts, including whittling, painting, and quilting were also taught. Bible groups provided spiritual exercise and growth opportunities for the campers.

Abbie clutched the brochure to her chest and bowed her head again. When she lifted her head, a quiet peace settled over her, one she hadn't experienced in a very long time. She was reminded of a verse of Scripture that had guided first-century Christians, and she knew this was the peace that was beyond all understanding. As Abbie made her way down Summit Ridge and back to the shelter of the Resting Place, she reveled in the reassurance of God's presence in her life this day.

Chapter Fifteen

Abbie awoke on Saturday morning feeling more rested than she had in a long time. After making a pot of coffee, she poured a cup and headed out to the screened porch to enjoy the June morning. Birds chirped and called. A pair of feisty squirrels played tag up and around a hickory tree not far off the porch. Their claws made a crisp, scratching noise against the bark of the tree. Abbie smiled at their amusing game.

Another sound tickled her ears. She sat forward in her rocking chair as she heard a car pull up the driveway. Abbie instantly recognized the sound of her son's older-model GMC Jimmy. With a squeal, she leaped out of the rocker, pushed open the porch door, and bounded down the steps.

"Drew!"

"Hi, Mom," said Drew, climbing out.

Abbie reached up to put her arms around his strong shoulders and enveloped him in a hug. "I hope you don't mind me coming without calling, but I thought you might enjoy a little company, at least for a little while."

"Joseph Andrew Richardson," Abbie exclaimed. "Don't be ridiculous. Mind? This is the biggest treat I could imagine. I've missed you terribly." Abbie linked her arm through Drew's. She looked up adoringly at this son of hers who had somehow become a man.

What a handsome fellow, Abbie thought to herself.

Drew's chiseled features looked somewhat like his mother's, but his eyes, unlike hers, were a light shade of brown, almost the color of caramel candy. A well-proportioned physique built like a runner's was topped with thick, sandy brown hair, a lighter-colored version of her own.

"What have you got in that sack?" Abbie grabbed for an aroma-filled bag tucked under Drew's arm.

"No fair peeking, Mom." He snatched the bag away just beyond her reach. "I stopped by Dessie's Bakery and bought their breakfast special. You don't want to spoil it, do you?"

Once inside, Abbie set out plates, silverware, and napkins. She poured milk into a small saucepan and set it on the stove to warm. Ever since he had been a little fellow, Drew had adored hot chocolate with his breakfast. Today was not the day to break that tradition. Mother and son enjoyed a leisurely, laughter-filled breakfast. She made enough hot chocolate for both of them. They were now on their second cup.

"Son, I need your opinion on something. The Wyatts drove up Thursday night and took me to dinner. They asked me to think about coming with them to a youth camp in July at some place called Timothy House. What do you think?"

"That's cool, Mom. I might be going, too. Jason told me about the camp this week. He's been a counselor for the past five years and said it's really fun. He said the food's not bad either." Drew grinned.

Abbie put down the mug she had been cradling between her hands. "That would be really special, Drew, getting to be there with you."

"Jason said the kids who come to Camp 4Ever have really big needs. We stayed up late Sunday night talking about how much he had learned at camp. Sounds like God is definitely moving in that program."

Abbie picked up her hot chocolate, and after taking a sip, she held the warm pottery in her hands. She stared down at the leaf design worked in muted shades of blue.

"Mom," he said gently, "is that all you wanted to tell me?" He reached over and put his hand on her shoulder.

His touch snapped Abbie out of deep thought. "Uh, no, Drew. The camp isn't all. Eric and Lane also told me that the school is looking for an English teacher who would also serve as a house mother. They want me to consider the job."

Drew looked surprised. "Leave Kent? Wouldn't that mean you'd have to leave McHenry? That's a really big step."

"I know. I don't actually know what to think. Eric said the school's headmaster would be willing to wait a year in order to find the right person." Abbie pushed her chair back from the table and folded her arms.

"I've been doing a lot of soul searching lately, trying to make sense actually of all we've been through these past few years. Your dad hurt both of us pretty badly." Her eyes roved over Drew's face, searching for his reaction. This was the first time that Abbie had been so frank with her son about the past. She wasn't sure how he would react to her words.

Drew looked down at the mug he had been sipping from and stayed silent for a long while. When he finally looked up, the hard, painful glint in his dark eyes cut Abbie to the quick and mirrored the anger and hurt feelings that she herself worked so hard to hide from her son.

"Mom," said Drew in a dull, flat tone, "ever since I was about twelve or so, about the time I accepted the Lord, I noticed a real change in Dad. It was as if he looked right through me most days, like I wasn't even there.

"At first, I thought he was just busy or preoccupied with some case he was working on. After a while though, it became obvious that I wasn't the son Dad wanted me to be. The harder I tried, the more I felt like I didn't measure up. Dad was always on my case about something, especially about what I wanted to do when I grew up. Once I told Dad I was interested in becoming a minister, he seemed to make fun of me even more. Knowing he had a secret life on the side, gambling away all our savings, makes me madder than I can even tell you."

"Oh, Drew." Tears welled up in Abbie's eyes as she reached over and pulled her son to her in a hug. She let go, settled back in her chair, and wiped her eyes. "I pray that someday the hurt and pain your dad caused you will lessen. I guess that's something both of us will need God's help in dealing with. Have you still been talking with Dr. Franklin about all of this?"

"Yes, ma'am." Drew pushed his chair back a bit from the table. "He usually calls me every few weeks or so to check on me, especially since I don't get to see him at church as often. He even took me to lunch a few weeks ago."

"I'm glad." Abbie reached over to brush away a lock of sandy blond hair that had fallen down over her son's eyes. "You just keep talking to me, Dr. Franklin, your friends, and God. I'm trusting God to bring something good out of this awful mess for each of us. I don't pretend to understand everything that happened with your dad. I'm so sorry his bad choices have cost you so much."

"Cost me?" Drew's face got red. "Look at what those choices cost you. You had to go back to work full time, and you had to beat the bushes to find money for me to go to college. How could Dad do that to you?"

"I don't know." Abbie sighed. "I just don't know. I've asked myself that same question a thousand times. I'm coming to know that gambling is an addiction, just like alcohol or drug addiction. And someone who is sick with it doesn't think rationally the same way that you and I do.

"We can't change what your dad did to us, but we can make a decision about how we deal with the impact of his actions. Miss Audry taught me years ago that, when you hit a pothole in life's highway, you have two choices. You can let the experience make you bitter or allow it to make you better. I'm praying God will help me to be better. I'm not there yet, son, but with God's grace, I hope to be. That's also my prayer for you."

Drew reached across the table for his mother's hand and squeezed it. "We're going to get through this together."

Abbie was touched to see a protective spirit in her son.

"We already are getting through." Abbie looked proudly at her son. "I'm so thankful we've had solid friends to lean on, people like Eric and Lane, Miss Audry, Miss Beulah, Jason and Jonathan, and Dr. Franklin. I don't know how we would have made it through these past few years. I'm just trying to determine which path God wants me to take next. I'm not really sure if I make a difference anymore at Kent."

"Mom!" exclaimed Drew. "You know you're one of the coolest teachers they've got. Everybody who's ever been in your class says what a great teacher you are."

"Oh, honey, you're so sweet. I'm not looking for praise. It's something deeper. I'm really struggling, trying to determine what God wants me to do now with my life. It's not a decision I have to make right now. I covet your prayers, Drew. I also trust your opinion. Give me five minutes to throw on some clothes, and we'll go for a walk." Abbie turned back to glance at Drew as she left the room.

A few minutes later, she tapped Drew on the shoulder as she headed out the porch door. "Last one around the lake is a rotten egg!"

Chapter Sixteen

Sunday was a day of quiet reverie for Abbie. The week at the cabin was quickly ending, like a chapter in a favorite book nearing its end, and Abbie was determined to savor every last minute of it. Even though the calendar said June, the temperature said early March. High on Johnson's Mountain, the air was cool, crisp, and invigorating. Abbie built a fire in the old stone fireplace and then opened her Bible and her heart before its warming brilliance.

The fire crackled and popped, the scent of burning wood wafting its earthy aroma into every nook and cranny of the Resting Place. Abbie savored this quiet, uninterrupted time. Her soul hungered for it. Befittingly on a Sunday, this span of elastic hours was God's grace supplied to her. Every hour or so, Abbie got up to add new wood. She was amazed how something as simple as a flickering flame could comfort her wounded spirit.

Abbie readjusted the soft coverlet over her legs. She ran her fingers across the various pieced squares and smiled as she thought of her quilting group, the Loose Threads.

She'd been a member since Drew was in elementary school. Joe worked late a lot during those years, and the gals of Loose Threads convinced her that a night activity such as this one would be worthwhile.

The women of the group—Beulah Tanner, Audry McCormick,

Gladys McLaren, and Muriel Wilson—were all at least thirty years older than Abbie was, yet she felt perfectly at ease when she was with them. Their warm camaraderie and friendly, playful banter gave her a sense of belonging she felt nowhere else. Beulah and Audry, in particular, touched a place in Abbie's soul that was still healing, having been scarred many years before when her own mother deserted the family. Besides Audry, Beulah was one of Abbie's dearest friends.

By the time Drew reached the age of ten, life with Joe was beginning to unravel. Abbie could almost see the rifts appearing in the fabric of their family relationships but was never quite sure what to do about them. The more she worked to repair them, the larger they became. Joe pulled away from both Abbie and Drew and poured himself into his work. He still attended church with them but never made an effort to get involved or to build deeper relationships within Oak Hill's congregation.

The monthly gathering of Loose Threads became an anchor in the midst of a storm for Abbie. She confided once to Audry about it.

"I call it the tranquility theory of quilting," she commented while sewing the binding on a quilt of red calico.

"How's that?" Audry asked.

"So much of my life seems chaotic and totally beyond my ability to control. But when I'm holding these pieces of cloth in my hands, I feel like I can make some sense out of all these different pieces of fabric. There's a real sense of completion after I get a quilt put together."

"Funny you should say that." Audry pulled her reading glasses down from her nose. "That's the very idea that gave us the name for our group, Loose Threads. If we try to make sense of all the loose ends in life, it's always a jumble. But when we give those same loose ends to God, look at the beauty He can make of them in our lives."

A verse that had been present in Abbie's mind for weeks now surfaced. "'For I know the plans that I have for you,' declares the Lord, 'plans for welfare and not for calamity to give you a future and a hope.'"

The week in the woods allowed Abbie time to sit and think, time to consider the path her life had taken over the last four years. Since Thursday, when Eric and Lane extended the invitation to join them at the camp at Timothy House, Abbie had pondered the possibility of a new course that God might be charting.

In the flickering firelight, she looked over the Timothy House brochure one more time. "Lord," she prayed, "if this is the path You want me on, make Your will known to me very clearly. I'm tired of stumbling in the dark. Please don't abandon me. Shed Your light on my life. Amen."

Later that afternoon on the drive home, Abbie flipped open her cell phone and pressed the speed dial button for Lane. After two rings, she answered. "Hey, I'm about an hour out from town. I can't thank you guys enough for letting me stay at the cabin this week." Abbie smiled and thought of how much she had enjoyed the much-needed time alone.

"Oh, Ab, it was our joy to share the place with you. Eric and I only wish we could do more for you."

"You two do too much as it is. Listen, dinner was great Thursday night. That was such a special evening. Thanks for introducing me to Ford's Gap. The Butterfield Inn was so enchanting. I didn't want to leave."

"Eric and I didn't either. We loved being with you. We've really missed seeing you. In fact, we've talked about little else but our conversation with you about Timothy House. Have you thought any more about the teaching job?"

"Yes, I have." Abbie brushed a stray strand of hair behind one ear. "Drew surprised me on Saturday and brought me breakfast. I told him about it."

"Well, don't keep me in suspense," Lane responded in a plaintive tone.

"Drew felt like it was something worth looking into. Making a move like that would be a life-changing decision. Let's just take one step at a time. I don't even know if Timothy House will accept me as a counselor for Camp 4Ever."

"You'll be a natural. I called our friend Doris on Friday morning. You should be receiving the packet of information from camp any day now." The exuberance in Lane's voice radiated through the phone.

"You did not," exclaimed Abbie, an air of excitement rising suddenly within her. "I don't even know these people, and I've never been a part of a program like Camp 4Ever before. I'm sure I'm not what they need."

"Listen, Abbie." Lane sounded a bit more serious. "This camp thing may be more about what you need at this point in your life than about anything you can do for any of the kids. Eric and I have been asking God to open a door for you. This could well be it."

"Well, friend, let's just hope that, if God opens the door, I don't trip going over the threshold."

Chapter Seventeen

The sound of running water emanated from the kitchen. A muffled voice uttering "Blast!" could be heard, accompanied by the clank of ceramic mugs and followed by the slamming of a cabinet door. More sloshing liquid sounds. This was Thursday night, and shortly the gals of Loose Threads would be arriving.

"Don't knock yourself out in there, Beulah," Audry called in the direction of the kitchen.

Her statuesque form leaned over as she plumped up pillows on the plaid sofa in Beulah's den. Although almost eighty, Audry was still a very attractive woman, elegant and refined. The lessons of civility and common courtesy learned at her mother's knee had served her well in the years since. Her auburn hair now shone like burnished bronze when the intermittent strands of gray caught the light. Audry had stubbornly refused to cut her locks at an age when many had done so, choosing instead to pull her hair back at the nape of her neck in a style that was both youthful and mature.

A few seconds later, Beulah's silver-crowned head popped through the doorway. "Glory be, Audry. Are they here yet?" A bit breathless, Beulah joined Audry in the den. "All that grabbin' around in the cabinet for coffee mugs wore me out."

"Sit down, sister." Audry pat her hand on the seat of Beulah's favorite chair, an upholstered rocker. "And rest a spell."

Beulah was as plump and round as Audry was reedy and tall. Perfectly formed pearl-colored curls, only produced by regularly scheduled appointments with an experienced hair stylist, framed her dimply face. Deep brown eyes, turned velvety soft by the passage of time, greeted everyone she met with genuine warmth and sincerity.

Audry and Beulah had been friends for close to two decades. Such close friends, they were practically sisters. They'd been the best older sisters in the Lord Abbie ever had. Soon after Joe's death, Audry recognized the hopelessness and prolonged despair in Abbie's spirit and took it upon herself to invite the younger widow to join her and Beulah to a weekly time of fellowship and prayer in addition to the night they shared each month in the Loose Threads group. Every Wednesday after her departure for school, the pair of friends resumed conversation with their Heavenly Father, claiming His goodness, protection, and guidance in the life of their younger friend.

Beulah was familiar with the difficult road Abbie was on, learning to move forward after the devastating loss of a spouse. Beulah had been down it herself thirty years before when her beloved Walter had died suddenly from a ruptured aneurism at age forty-one. Even though Beulah had two married sons, they lived out West and only came to see their mother about once a year. Abbie's friendship filled a tremendous void in Beulah's life.

About the time Beulah got settled, the doorbell rang.

"Stay put, sweetie." Audry motioned from across the room for Beulah to remain where she was. "I'll do the honors."

Gladys and Muriel followed Audry back into the den. Gladys' hands were full with purses and bags stuffed with quilting projects that she carried in for Muriel and herself. One could easily see how organized Gladys was. Her quilting bag was packed with the efficiency of a military training force. She was the self-appointed marshal of the group, always peering through her gold-rimmed reading glasses at each Loose Threads member as if she were a quality control inspector. Her hair was always perfectly styled, but unlike the other seniors in the group, she refused to give in to the gray. Over time, her brunette tresses had been transformed into a lighter shade of brown, which Beulah called chocolate swirl. Gladys' cheerful spirit perfectly complemented the bright highlights in her hair.

Muriel followed close behind, cradling a plastic cake container against her with one hand and pulling an oxygen tank behind her with the other. She looked like a pixie, a geriatric Tinker Bell if ever there were one. Her once-black hair, now peppered with varying shades of gray, was cut close like a cap around her small, angular face. Black eyes shone like finely polished jet buttons. Lips adorned with Revlon's Love That Red, her signature color for almost thirty years, completed her jaunty look.

Diagnosed a few years ago with a chronic pulmonary disorder, Muriel cheerfully accepted the thin, clear plastic tubing now worn constantly just beneath her nose. The two friends walked over to where Beulah was seated and greeted her with hugs and kisses. Muriel headed into the kitchen to deposit the sour cream pound cake she had made for their snack, the tank thumping behind her. Gladys settled in an armchair across from Beulah.

"Where's Abbie?" Gladys pulled a partially pieced quilt top out of her sewing bag. Alternating patches of rose and mint green calico billowed across her lap.

"She'll be along shortly." Beulah untangled her reading glasses from their neck chain. Almost as if speaking to herself, she muttered, "These things are more trouble than they're worth."

Gladys politely overlooked her friend's exasperation. "I have really missed that girl. She brightens my day every time I see her."

"Same here, Glad." Now Beulah was trying to wrestle a round lap quilting frame onto a red and green Christmas quilt she was making. "Abbie's just gotten home from her week in the mountains. I can't wait to hear all about it."

At that moment, the doorbell sounded again. As Audry headed into the kitchen to help Muriel cut the cake, she could see that Gladys was smothered in quilt top.

Audry nodded her head toward Beulah. "Be a dear, and get that for me."

Beulah raised her softly rounded frame on the arms of the worn rocker and headed for the front hall.

"Look who I found!" Beulah entered the room with her arm around Abbie's shoulders. "Our girl has arrived!"

The next few minutes were a jumble of "Hello" and "How are you" and warm hugs all around.

As Audry bustled around the kitchen, she remembered when Abbie first joined the group. Drew was about six. Not only had Abbie learned the intricacies of quilting, but she also became part of a process as old as time itself. The monthly meetings of Loose Threads provided a mechanism where these women of an older generation passed down their wisdom carefully and lovingly to this younger sister in the Lord, life lessons tucked innocently among scraps of soft fabric and shared through the years over countless cups of coffee or hot tea and bites of cake or pie. The ministry of mentoring, occurring naturally through the camaraderie of friendship, bound them all—Beulah, Audry, Gladys, Muriel, and Abbie—like many strands coming together to form a thick cord that could not be broken.

There's nothing loose about the Loose Threads, Audry thought as she headed back into the den.

Once everyone was settled with her individual projects, Beulah prodded Abbie for conversation to relieve their curiosity. "So, tell us. How was the week?"

Abbie tried to talk with three straight pins held between her lips. Not able to manage coherent speech, she reached up to remove them. "It was fabulous! I almost didn't want to come home."

Audry smiled as she listened to Abbie's stories of her week on Johnson's Mountain. Muriel seemed especially captivated with descriptions of Craggy Bluff. Laughter and nods accompanied threading of needles and placement of stitches.

"Did you make it up Johnson's Mountain, up to Summit Ridge?" asked Muriel.

"Yes, I did." Abbie continued to piece her quilt top.

"My family vacationed for years on the mountain," said Muriel. "My brothers and I used to think the summit belonged just to us. My younger brother Jake still does."

The constant gentle droning of Muriel's oxygen compressor tank hummed cheerfully just underneath the conversation. The machine pressing air into the tubing, whooshing it up Muriel's nostrils, broke the constancy of the sound every few seconds. The plastic tubing was fitted around Muriel's ears like a lasso, fastened together just under her chin.

Audry worked to push her needle through several layers of a

patchwork square. She looked across the room at her younger friend and wondered if Abbie would open up tonight and share with these trusted friends of Loose Threads about the chance to volunteer at Timothy House.

At that very moment, Muriel gently steered the conversation to a deeper level. "How was this school year at Kent? I've been praying about direction for your work, like you asked me to." Her dark eyes watched Abbie intently.

"Thanks, Muriel. This year was all right, though it probably won't go down as one of my better years in the classroom." She placed a few more pins along the seams of the pieced fabric squares.

"What exactly isn't working for you?" Muriel pulled a few more stitches through her quilt and waited patiently for Abbie's answer.

Audry looked down at her quilting, trying not to grin. She knew how determined Muriel was and knew instinctively that she was not going to let Abbie off the hook that easily. Audry wasn't sure how Abbie would handle making herself vulnerable and opening up to this group. *This is going to be interesting*, Audry thought. Her head shot up when she heard Abbie reply.

"I wish I knew that myself." Abbie sighed deeply and put down her quilting hoop. "Some days, it feels like I'm slogging through mud." She looked into Muriel's bright eyes. "The students at Kent are really good kids. Many of them, though, don't seem to care about their work. It's as if they've lost their sense of awe and wonder about learning."

Muriel pressed forward again. "What do you think is causing this?"

"Maybe it's the level of affluence of Kent's families. There's a great deal of entitlement." Abbie reached up and brushed a few strands of hair behind one ear. "Many of these parents want their kids to succeed at any cost. Instead of looking at themselves, their schedule, or their own child's lack of responsibility, too many think the school should bend to accommodate their lifestyles. I'm not sure those are battles I want to keep fighting." Abbie sank back into her chair.

"Abbie," said Muriel in a quiet tone, "have you ever thought of teaching at another school?"

Audry felt like an onlooker at a fireside chat as she watched this healing interchange take place between Abbie and Muriel.

"Funny you should ask that." A slight grin broke across Abbie's face. "Lane and Eric took me to dinner one night the week I was at the cabin. They've invited me to join them in July as a volunteer for a program called Camp 4Ever. I think I just might apply."

Abbie's expression grew more radiant the more she talked. "Timothy House is the school that sponsors the camp. Lane and Eric are good friends with the couple who run the school. The week would certainly provide me a look at another academic program."

Muriel reached for the quilt top on her lap. "Well, you let us know about how that turns out. We'll certainly be praying for you. Won't we, girls?" Muriel nodded toward the other Loose Threads members seated nearby.

Audry, Beulah, and Gladys all bobbed their agreement in unison. Muriel located the needle tucked into the fabric and began stitching again.

A great sense of pride for Abbie filled Audry's heart. She knew what a huge step her dear friend had taken tonight. Audry was also grateful for the fact that Muriel had followed her instinct and provided Abbie with an opportunity to share her thoughts. *Winnie's advice is certainly yielding great dividends*, Audry thought to herself.

Gradually, the conversation drifted from one topic to another. Gladys was holding forth in this latest discussion about a new quilt pattern she had recently discovered. By the time she had described the project, every member of Loose Threads had asked for a copy.

About 8:45, Beulah looked up. "Glory be! Look at the time. Audry, come in here and help me get this cake on."

After a short time in the kitchen, Audry leaned through the doorway and exclaimed, "Come and get it!"

Sounds of industry ceased as the ladies began to make their way toward Beulah's kitchen table.

As Muriel entered the kitchen, she held the extra feet of tubing in one hand while pulling the oxygen tank with the other. When she crossed the threshold onto the kitchen's rolled linoleum floor, she whipped the length of tubing out beside her. "Ladies, don't trip on my tail!" she said with a laugh. Her cheerful spirit, in spite of many medical difficulties, had always amazed and inspired Audry.

As Abbie drove away from Beulah's house later that evening, she reveled in the glow of love and acceptance that the women of Loose Threads constantly lavished on her. Their strong circle of friendship had sustained her over the years when others, less sincere, had failed. Unlike many people Abbie knew, these women weren't interested in her social connections or what advantages her association with them could garner. Beulah, Audry, Muriel, and Gladys loved Abbie purely for herself.

The quilting group provided a safe refuge for her, a place like no other. "Thank You, Lord," she prayed, "for a glimpse of Your love that I see in the lives of these dear ladies."

Abbie turned in the driveway of her house and stepped out of her car, invigorated and sustained by the secure knots of friendship tied by the gals of Loose Threads.

Chapter Eighteen

A week later, Abbie spent most of Wednesday morning working in the flower beds bordering her back patio. Assorted pots and planters scattered around the scored concrete expanse desperately needed attention. Almost two weeks had passed since she had returned from her trip to the mountains, and despite Drew's excellent job of watering both the yard and planted containers during her absence, the plants seemed to clamor for Abbie's special touch.

Just as Abbie began unearthing the remains of a wilted begonia, her cell phone began to jangle, demanding her immediate attention. She slipped off one gardening glove as quickly as she could manage and flipped the phone open just before the fourth ring sent it to message mode.

"Hello." The bright summer sun was already beginning to rise in the sky on this Friday morning.

"Hello, dear girl," Audry's cheery voice sounded over the line. "How's your week gone?"

"Fast, Audry." Abbie tucked the phone under her chin as she worked to free her other hand from its protective shield. "It's great to hear your voice. Sorry I've been hard to track down. I've been busy trying to reclaim order here at home."

"I really hate to bother you." Audry paused for a moment. "I was wondering if you could possibly run me around for a few errands later this morning."

"I'd be happy to." Abbie dead-headed a bougainvillea that threatened to overtake her garden trellis.

"That's perfect, dear. Thanks ever so much." Audry sounded greatly relieved.

"In fact, I need to run by the post office myself." Abbie held her phone with one hand and retrieved gardening tools scattered around the patio with the other. "Think I'm going to exercise a little courage and faith and mail the application form back to Camp 4Ever. Sounds like a really fun program."

"Good, Abbie girl. I've already told you what I think," Audry said with a bit of bravado in her voice. "God's got something really special for you up His sleeve. You just have to keep watching for it. Camp 4Ever will be such a blessing. You just wait and see."

Abbie dropped the tools in a box located underneath a window on the patio. She opened the back door as she stamped her feet on the patio doormat and headed into the house toward the kitchen. The cool of the air conditioning enveloped her.

Abbie balanced the phone between her shoulder and right ear while reaching for a clean towel from the pile of laundry scattered across the kitchen table. She listened to Audry and began folding.

"That's what I'm hoping. That He has a plan for me. I think taking this leap of faith with the summer camp program may be the first step toward that plan."

"Good girl, Abbie. You won't be sorry. I'll see you soon, my dear friend."

"Can you give me about thirty minutes? Say about eleven?" She glanced down at her watch. "That'll give me time to tie up loose ends around here."

"Great. I'll see you at eleven." As Abbie heard the click signaling the end of the call, she smiled and thought of how much Audry's support meant. She dropped her cell phone into her purse, picked up a hand towel, and continued folding. Soon she was headed for the upstairs master bath, folded linens stacked high in her arms.

Audry's bright red front door swung wide open as soon as Abbie turned off the ignition in her SUV. She bounded up the wide brick steps of Audry's front porch. Her friend's familiar face grinned out at her from the doorway. She crossed the wide planked floor in three steps, reaching out for the older friend, who already held her arms open. Audry enveloped the younger woman in a bear hug and held her tightly like a mother welcoming a daughter home from a long journey.

"Come in this house, dear," said Audry.

"Good morning," said Abbie brightly as she stepped past Audry into the living room, pausing to take in a deep breath. How she loved the scent of Audry's house! It smelled like home. She smiled to herself as she looked around the front room of Audry's house. Abbie realized just how much Audry's decorating style had influenced her own. The room reminded her of her own living room in her house.

"Good morning, yourself," replied Audry, a smile evident in her voice. She headed back toward the kitchen with Abbie following close behind. "Thanks ever so much for picking me up." Audry gathered a stack of posted letters scattered in a loose pile on the kitchen counter and stuffed them in a brown leather purse. "I don't think these errands will take very long." She stepped over to the kitchen table to retrieve a steel blue woolen sweater. Abbie helped her put it on.

"There now." Abbie straightened the neckline on Audry's sweater. "What else can I help you with?"

"Well, I just need to pick up a sack of mulch out by the garage." Audry picked up her purse. "I don't know where my mind has been lately, but it seems I picked up the wrong kind the last time I was at Lowe's. If you could just help me put the bag into the car, there's a nice, young high school student who always helps me with my gardening items. I'm sure he'll be able to lift it out when we get there." She headed toward the front of the house.

As they left, Abbie closed the front door and checked to make sure it was locked securely. She then followed Audry, who was already halfway down the sidewalk. Once they reached the car, Abbie opened the passenger door and helped Audry get into the vehicle. Audry's agility and spry movements always amazed Abbie, especially considering that she was well into her seventies by now.

"I'll just be a minute," she told Audry as she closed the door and headed down the driveway to pick up the bright green and brown bag of mulch.

As Abbie headed back up the short driveway, she looked longingly at the generous front porch of the old ramshackle house. Various pieces of faded white wicker furniture were grouped in the shade of the wide porch roof. Her favorite spot was the south end of the porch where a swing hung invitingly, just past a bank of paned windows.

Now at her SUV, Abbie opened the back door and swung the mulch up onto the vinyl floor cover. As she shut the door, she glanced back at the porch. How many countless conversations had she and Audry shared over the last twenty years or so out on that porch, talks about the joys and struggles of life like marriage, child rearing, faith, doubt, and God. Her heart was full of gratitude for this dear friend.

Abbie had first met Audry at church shortly after she and Joe had moved to McHenry. From the first moment the two women met, they had been close. Abbie yearned for a mother figure in her life. Over the years, God had provided not one but several older women, including Audry, who had mentored Abbie and lent moral support on many occasions.

Abbie knew the story by heart of how Audry had been engaged to a dashing young fighter pilot, Bill Norris. He popped the question in the fall of 1942, barely three weeks after they met. Two days later, his naval air squadron was called up for a secret mission. He never returned.

Audry had been inconsolable. Her parents initially feared she might attempt to take her own life. A few months later, however, on a bright, crisp day in January, Audry woke up a new person. She emerged out of her cocoon of mourning, determined to go on with her life the best way she knew how. After attending a tent revival that year, Audry's conversation soon turned to talk of a foreign mission field. Shortly afterward, she was approved for service in England and spent the next forty years in a little town there, laboring to soften many a hardened heart. Never having married, she had now been stateside almost twenty years and had continued those labors of love.

The motion of Audry adjusting her seatbelt caught Abbie's eye. *I know,* she thought, *how rich my life has been through the friendship shared with this dear woman.* She smiled to herself as she opened the driver's side door and got in. *Audry always points me back to God, no matter how off track I get,* she thought.

The trip to Lowe's didn't take very long, and true to Audry's word, Brad, the "nice, young high school student," was as helpful as Audry said he would be. The exchange was over and done with in a matter of minutes. Abbie headed out of the parking lot of Lowe's and onto a main road bustling with traffic. Three blocks later, Abbie turned onto an avenue and into the post office parking lot. She stopped in line two cars behind a sleek black, late-model Infiniti, whose owner was loading several letters into the mail drop box ahead.

Audry looked over at Abbie and reached out her hand. "Let me see that envelope."

Abbie handed the sealed paper across. Audry took it and peered carefully at the address scrawled across the front in Abbie's beautiful cursive script. She held the paper close to her nose as if inhaling a hint of fragrance.

"I've been praying about this day for a long time," Audry said almost reverently. "A time in which God would open a door for you to walk through, one through which you'd find the rest of your life waiting out in front of you. This just may be the catalyst that jump-starts that process." She grinned and handed the letter addressed to Timothy House back to Abbie.

When her turn came, Abbie eased her SUV up to the postal drop box and rolled down her window. "I'm ready to find out what the next step is, one way or the other. My radar is tuned to heaven. I just pray I'll recognize the signal when God delivers."

As they drove off, Audry said with a chuckle, "Don't you worry, Abbie. God uses all kinds of ways to get our attention, but I suspect He'll whistle a tune that's already familiar to your heart."

Chapter Nineteen

A week later, Abbie and Lane were engrossed in a phone conversation, and at this specific moment, they were discussing their sons. Abbie headed through the kitchen to the laundry room. She opened the top of the washing machine and poured in liquid detergent, switching the cell phone to her left hand. A silvery metallic sound reverberated from the laundry room as the water filled the tub.

"Yeah, I know what you mean," said Lane. Abbie loaded a large pile of white clothing into the machine. "I'm working to cultivate some domestic expertise in Jason and Jonathan. Look, I know this is last minute, but could you break away this afternoon for a movie?"

"That would be great." Abbie closed the laundry room door behind her. She walked over to the sink and reached for the glass of tea she had poured earlier.

"There's a matinee at two thirty. How about if I pick you up around two fifteen?"

"I'll be ready."

"Look, I've got to run." Lane sounded preoccupied and distracted. "A repairman from Sears just pulled in the driveway. Our icemaker's been on the blink. I'll see you this afternoon."

Abbie smiled to herself as she closed her phone. She walked out to the patio. She pulled her gloves on and returned to the task of planting a fresh begonia in her favorite terra-cotta planter before the sun rose too high in the summer sky.

After attending to the patio plants, Abbie left her gardening gloves and clogs just outside the back door as she stepped inside from the patio. She glanced up at the digital clock on the oven and saw that she had about an hour, time enough to shower and check the mail before Lane picked her up for the movie.

Abbie walked out to the mailbox in front of her house and gathered an assorted stack of bills, junk mail, catalogs, and letters. Now toward the end of June, she checked every day for a letter from Timothy House. Abbie was starved for a place of ministry in her life, her own special place where she could plug in and serve others in Jesus's name. Her heart yearned for a place where she was needed, to know she really made a difference. She knew Timothy House just might be such a place.

Once inside, Abbie went out to the screened porch. She perched on the edge of a wicker sofa and sorted through the mailman's delivery. An oversized dark green envelope with the Timothy House logo caught her eye. She opened the envelope and pulled out the contents.

The first line of the cover letter read, "We are so excited to tell you that you have been selected as an adult counselor for the Camp 4Ever Adventure program."

Overcome with a sudden case of euphoria, Abbie threw up her arms and pumped both fists in the air. "Yes, Lord! Thank You so much!" Too excited to look through the rest of the packet, Abbie grabbed her cell phone and headed out to the patio. Exuberant, chatty conversations followed with Audry and Beulah.

After her phone calls, Abbie carefully folded the acceptance letter from Camp 4Ever and slid it inside the large envelope along with its accompanying literature. A copy of the now-familiar brochure of Timothy House was also included. She headed into the kitchen to read through the rest of the mail.

Abbie was practically bursting with excitement by the time Lane arrived. No sooner had she slammed the car door shut and fastened her seat belt than she let out a jubilant, "I've got a secret!"

Lane pulled her car over at the corner and slipped the gear into park. She turned to face Abbie. "You got the letter from camp, didn't you?"

"Yes, I did. But how did you know?" Abbie looked a bit crestfallen.

"I didn't know, just a good guess." Lane smiled as she moved the gear shaft into drive and turned onto the intersecting street. "Eric and I have been calling Don and Doris for days, but they said we'd have to wait just like you would. I'm so excited for you. Camp 4Ever will be a week you'll never forget."

On the way to the movie theatre, through the opening trailers, and all the way back to Abbie's house, Lane shared with Abbie past experiences from her own time as a camp volunteer. As Lane talked, Abbie listened with one ear to Lane's conversation and strained internally with the other, trying to remember something she wanted to ask Lane about. Suddenly, she remembered the forgotten conversation from the art gallery weeks ago in Craggy Bluff.

"Say, Lane, I've been meaning to ask you about something that happened to me while I was at the cabin." Abbie turned in the seat to be able to look directly at her friend. "I went into Craggy Bluff one day and was bumming around in a shop called Posie's.

"I overheard a conversation with a man named Don, who was talking to the owner about some friends, the Wyatts from McHenry, who were going to be helping with a summer camp. Could the man by any chance have been the Don Fielding who's headmaster of Timothy House?" Abbie waited for Lane's response.

"It must have been. Just last night, Don called Eric. He wants us to meet a young couple who have recently become involved with a program at the school, the Tentmakers or something like that. It certainly could be the couple you met. I'll ask Eric and call you."

As Abbie opened the door to get out, Lane reached over to hug her. "Congratulations about camp! We'll have the best time in July."

"Thanks." Abbie climbed out of the car. "Sure looks like God is up to something. I'm just not sure what."

Chapter Twenty

The days of summer flew by quickly. In no time, July 20 arrived. Eric and Lane picked up Abbie on this hot, sunny Sunday morning and headed north to Robbinsonville. Drew and the Wyatt brothers were following in a second car. Other than a quick stop at a fast-food burger chain, the three-hour journey was uninterrupted, providing time for lively conversation.

About thirty minutes out from camp, Eric's comments grew a bit more serious. "Abbie, have you thought any more about applying for the teaching job at Timothy House?"

"I have a little. It's hard to think about a decision as important as a move when I've never even seen the place."

Eric laughed. "I guess you're right. Just promise me you'll give the school a close look during this week at camp. The Lord is really using this place to change lots of lives."

The description of the campus Abbie had been given in the camp literature helped her get her bearings as they pulled through the gate of Timothy House. The buildings of the campus, she had learned, were built in the late 1930s. Covenant Kitchen, the dining hall, served as command central for the weeklong camp. The parking lot was almost full as Lane and Eric's car pulled in.

Several long tables were set up along the front porch of the building. A friendly group of camp staff was there to greet volunteers and hand out information packets. Eric, Lane, and Abbie took their packets and headed into the dining hall.

Filtered sunlight scattered through the beams of the dining hall, and the aroma of knotty pine beckoned to Abbie as she glanced around the large room. She noticed Jonathan, Jason, and Drew seated with a group of teenage guys and gals a few tables over.

After making sure Lane and Abbie were seated, Eric made his way over to an older man standing by a large river rock fireplace at one end of the room. The man and Eric exchanged a warm hug, and their faces lit up as they talked. Abbie recognized Eric's friend as the man she had seen at Posie's.

Abbie turned her attention back to her information packet and began to remove the many colored papers from the large envelope. She looked up to find Eric and his friend approaching their table.

"I'm Don Fielding. You must be Abbie." Don smiled and extended his hand to shake hers. "Eric and Lane have told me great things about you."

"Thanks, Mr. Fielding. Likewise." Abbie gripped his rugged, firm hand in hers.

"It's Don, Abbie," he said, mocking offense. "No Mr. Fielding. If you need anything, just let me or Doris know."

"Thanks, Don. I'll do that. I'm really glad to be here."

"I'm also hopeful we can find some time to visit about teaching. I want to hear about your work at Kent Academy." Don winked at Eric as he spoke.

Abbie blushed a bit. "I'd like that."

"See you folks at dinner," said Don as he walked away.

Don found his way to the front of the room and called the meeting to order. "Welcome, friends, to Timothy House. Thank you for agreeing to give of your time and talents at Camp 4Ever. Would you join me as we pray and ask God's blessing on this week? Dear Lord, thank You for hearts that are moved by what moves You. I thank You for this group gathered here. Give us strength for the many tasks at hand. Give us encouragement and joy to share with these young people. Most of all, use us to pour Your love into the lives of these kids. May all we accomplish this week honor You."

A hushed "Amen" followed.

"Gang, we're in for a great week." Don rubbed his hands together.

"Before we get started, I'd like to ask for a show of hands. How many of you have worked at Camp 4Ever before?"

The majority of hands were raised.

"And how many new friends do we have this session?"

Abbie raised her hand along with Drew and several other first-timers.

"Welcome to Timothy House," said Don warmly. "For those new to this place, my aunt and uncle started Timothy House, and it has been home to thousands of kids over the last sixty-one years. Thanks for partnering with us to continue the Timothy House tradition.

"We're expecting a group of about seventy campers. These kids have just finished first through fifth grades. The main thing you have to remember about these campers is that, in spite of their young age, many are jaded and scarred by cruel realities of life. They'll be suspicious of you as adults because sadly most of the adults in their lives are unreliable. Words like love, trust, and stability are not in their vocabulary. If we share nothing else but the love of Jesus with them this week, we will have blessed their lives tremendously."

Several heads nodded in agreement.

"Each cabin sleeps eight campers and two counselors. Campers arrive tomorrow morning at eight thirty and will leave by ten on Friday morning. That barely gives us five days to do our work. About twenty of our regular boarding students will be serving as junior counselors during the week. You will find these young men and women eager to work and to serve. This is one way they help pay their way at Timothy House.

"Area churches partner with us as camp sponsors, and that may be a different camp model for some of you. Evening activities for the first three nights beginning on Monday night will be under the direction of a different church. On Thursday evening, we have a closing camp ceremony that is held here on campus. We'll use our school buses to transport the kids where they need to go."

As Don spoke, Lane glanced over toward Abbie. The two friends exchanged a knowing smile.

"The church partnership program has proved successful in the past for several reasons. First, it involves more people. Volunteer counselors will have time off each night from six thirty when the buses leave until they return at ten. The junior counselors will accompany campers to night activities. This provides these young people opportunities to hone their leadership skills. Each of the sponsoring churches will also have volunteers helping with each function. After the kids get back, they have until ten forty-five to get ready for bed, and then lights out.

"In your packets, you'll find your cabin assignments, a list of campers, and the weekly schedule. Why don't you go ahead and look at the green sheet in your packets? That outlines the daytime and evening activities."

The rustle of papers could be heard throughout the large room.

Don continued his orientation spiel. "Our days will start at seven o'clock in the morning. There are four classes every day. A bell will ring to tell you when it's time to move to the next activity. The campers choose three activities for the week. Small-group Bible studies are held during the last period of the day. After lunch, there's an hour and a half rest time. A mid-afternoon snack is served right after quiet time.

"I know I've hit you with a lot of information all at once. Let me introduce you to some of our camp staff. After they've been introduced, you're free to find your cabins. We'll meet back here in the dining hall at six o'clock for supper. After dinner, we'll break into groups for our training sessions. You'll also be given some background info on each of your campers." He pointed to a woman in the audience.

"For those of you who don't know, this is my better half, Doris." An attractive older woman with pewter-colored hair stood to a chorus of applause and whistles. "Doris is in charge of what I call the softer side of camp: crafts, sewing, music, and camper-counselor relations. If any of you have a particular need with any of your kids, Doris is the lady to see.

"Next, I'd like you to meet a new addition to Timothy House, Keith Haliday. During this week, Keith is in charge of outdoor sports."

As the tall, well-built, dark-haired man stood, Abbie felt a vague sense of recognition and realized that he was the man she had seen with Don Fielding earlier in the summer in Craggy Bluff. *Sad eyes*, she thought, remembering her initial impression. *I wonder what that's about.*

"Another mainstay at Camp 4Ever is Josh Hastings." A stocky, towheaded young man stood toward the back of the room. "Josh attended

Timothy House. Now part of our permanent staff, he knows firsthand the struggles these kids go through. Josh is our adventure sports specialist, heading up hiking, rock climbing, and the ropes course."

Don introduced a few more staff, repeat volunteers who possessed specialized skills in different areas. "Well, folks, I guess that about wraps up our opening session. I've rambled on long enough. Thanks again so much for giving your time to these kids this week. I promise you won't be sorry. See you back here at six for dinner."

A sense of excitement washed over Abbie as she collected the camp literature and placed it back in her packet. This week as a volunteer at Camp 4Ever would definitely provide her with a bird's-eye view of Timothy House. *What was it Don had said about wanting to talk with me?* she thought.

Winnie's advice ran through her mind. "Aim small."

Perhaps this week would be a first small step toward the rest of my life, she thought.

Back in McHenry, Abbie's friends were on a secret mission. Audry finished her household chores early that morning so she would have uninterrupted time to spend in prayer on Abbie's behalf. She retreated to her guest room. In one corner stood an antique prayer kneeler, rescued years ago from a salvage store. Its mahogany frame had been lovingly restored, and a new needlepoint cushion had been fashioned for its small pew. Its soft, hand-sewn surface cushioned Audry's knees.

The weathered kneeler creaked as she lowered her tall frame into a kneeling position. "Dear Father, I ask that You take care of my Abbie girl. You know how much I love that child. She's so wounded, Lord. It's time that You lift the burden from her shoulders and give her a new direction in life. I ask You to reveal to her the next step."

Three blocks over, Beulah was settled in her den in a worn, upholstered rocker long ago christened the "prayer mobile." She bowed her head and entered into conversation with her Heavenly Father. "Oh, dear Lord, my young friend Abbie is in need of Your services and Your gifts of wisdom and guidance. I'm not too clear on all the details, but Father, it doesn't really matter because I know You already know the end of the story.

Please give Abbie the direction she's looking for. And Father, while You're at it, see what You can do about another man for my Abbie. She's so young. I know now that a second chance wasn't in Your plan for me, but maybe it will be for my sweet friend. Love her, dear Lord. She's hurting so bad. Thank You for meeting me here today. I love You, Lord. Amen."

For a long while after Beulah stopped praying, she rocked slowly and listened to her Heavenly Father, His voice accompanied by the creaking of the old rocker.

Chapter Twenty-One

A blur of frenzied activity settling somehow into organized chaos marked the opening day of Camp 4Ever. Abbie simply did as she was directed, following Lane's lead. A few times during the day, she caught glimpses of Drew and found it very comforting to know they were here together.

Abbie and Lane were cabin "mothers" for seven little girls about to enter the fifth grade. Two of the girls, Liza and Donnie Gail, had attended Camp 4Ever the summer before and immediately helped their new friends get settled into Cabin Five. Abbie was assigned to help with crafts and canoeing, two activities she always enjoyed as a camper in her own youth. With Doris in charge of the crafts program, Abbie's assignment would be to provide a friendly, relaxed atmosphere in which to get to know her. Abbie already found Doris to be easygoing and comfortable to be with, as if Abbie had known her all her life.

Abbie met the members of the Covenant Kitchen cook staff, local women hired to work at the school, at lunch. All accomplished cooks, they used the food skills learned from raising generations of their own. The girls in her cabin literally inhaled their food.

As the meal ended, Don walked over to speak to Eric, Lane, and Abbie. "Doris and I would like to invite the three of you over for dinner tonight. A small group of faculty and friends will be there that we'd really like you to meet."

Eric looked first at Lane and then at Abbie, who both grinned back at him. "We'd love to, Don. What time?"

"How about six forty-five?"

"We'll look forward to it," declared Lane.

The day's activities flew by, and before Abbie knew it, the buses were picking up the campers for night activity, and Abbie was dressing for dinner. The Fielding's residence was located on the Timothy House grounds, the other side of campus from where the Camp 4Ever cabins were located. The three friends enjoyed the leisurely walk. Abbie found Don and Doris' home, the Manse, to be elegant yet comfortable. Heart pine floors ran throughout the massive old stone cottage. Two large stone fireplaces flanked either end of the gabled structure. Lane had told Abbie how the rocks had been plucked long ago from the beds of local rivers.

After exchanging initial pleasantries, Abbie and Lane joined Doris in the kitchen to help as last-minute meal preparations took place. An attractive, middle-aged woman, Evelyn Benson, soon joined them. Doris introduced her as the head of the English department at Timothy House.

Evelyn and Abbie chatted amiably as they prepared the salad. Abbie heard the doorbell ring several times while they were in the kitchen but didn't think much about it. As she headed through a swinging door with the salad bowl in hand, she noticed Keith Haliday across the room. He caught her gaze and nodded slightly.

The home-cooked meal created a tempting buffet atop a cherry sideboard set against one wall of the dining room. Candlelight spilled across its polished surface. A massive round mahogany dining table could have easily been at home in a medieval castle. Upon Doris' request, guests gathered their plates from the table and headed over to fill them at the sideboard.

Cheerful banter echoed through the spacious room. As Abbie settled into the line behind Lane and Eric, she turned slightly and found herself looking up into Keith Haliday's warm blue eyes.

"I don't believe we've met." He disengaged his right hand from underneath his plate. "I'm Keith Haliday."

Abbie returned his firm handshake. "I'm Abbie Richardson." She shifted her weight from one foot to the other nervously. "It's a pleasure to meet you." She found Keith's gaze direct yet pleasant.

"Same here." Keith readjusted his grasp on the dinner plate. "Welcome to Timothy House. I hear you're a newbie at Camp 4Ever just like I am. Have you ever volunteered for a program like this before?"

"No," said Abbie. By this time, the line had moved, and she found herself in front of the sideboard. She ladled a spoonful of lasagna onto her plate. "I've got Lane and Eric to thank for roping me into this adventure." She turned back to filling her plate.

Keith stepped up to the buffet. "Hope your week's a winner." He smiled and turned his attention back to the sideboard and to the business of serving himself dinner.

As Abbie made her way over to the table, she was surprised to see Summer Tidwell sitting down in the seat next to hers. Elton pulled up a chair at the table just as Keith settled in one to his right.

"Hi, Summer," Abbie greeted the young woman warmly as she settled into her place. "You probably don't remember me, but I visited your shop earlier this summer." She reached for her napkin and unfolded it in her lap.

A bright smile of recognition soon replaced a look of uncertainty on Summer's face. "Well, sure I remember you. Elton, look." She called out to her husband. "You remember Abbie. She visited our shop this summer."

Elton nodded. At the comment, Keith turned their way, and his gaze held Abbie's briefly. She felt a slow flush begin its rise across her cheeks. Abbie wasn't interested in becoming the center of attention. Don's request to bless the meal ended her discomfort.

Two other faculty members, Tim and Taylor Nunley, rounded out the dinner party. By the time the serving platters had been taken from the sideboard and passed around a second and then a third time, jovial remarks and laughter were sprinkled generously all around the table. Several times during dinner, Abbie felt Keith Haliday watching her. When their eyes met, she saw a hint of the sorrow she had seen earlier that summer when they passed each other in Posie's shop.

A little after nine, Doris pushed her chair back from the table, making a remark about going to turn on the coffeepot and ready dessert. Abbie excused herself from the group to help. Once in the kitchen, Doris gave her a large, warm pan of chocolate brownies, needing to be cut into squares. As Abbie stacked the brownies on an ironstone platter, Doris filled a tray with coffee cups and saucers and a silver creamer and sugar set.

She picked up the tray and nodded to Abbie. "Let's place these goodies on the long table behind the sofa in the den. That way people will have to move around in order to get dessert."

As Doris and Abbie carried their delicacies across the room, a series of "oohs" and "ahs" greeted them.

Doris looked back at her expectant guests. "Give me a few more minutes to bring out the coffee, and then all will be ready." She went back to the kitchen and returned shortly with an old brass samovar. The delicious aroma of hazelnut coffee wafted from within its gleaming surface that reflected the flicker of candles set round the room. In groups of twos and threes, the dinner guests made their way to the den and stood or settled on sofas and chairs throughout the room, renewing conversations begun earlier at dinner.

After filling her coffee cup, Abbie slowly made her way along the edges of the den. One entire wall was composed of ceiling-to-floor bookcases. A commendable library of great reads as well as collectibles, old brass candlesticks, and family photos graced the shelves. Intent on reading book titles, Abbie missed Keith's approach.

"Quite a collection, wouldn't you say?" Keith asked quietly.

She turned around quickly. The sound of his voice brought her back to the moment. "Well, hello, Keith. I didn't see you walk over." She nodded toward the shelves. "I could spend hours poring over Don's library. I love books."

"Me, too." Keith paused for a moment. "I understand from Don that we both lost a good friend, your husband, Joe." Another lengthy pause followed.

Puzzled, Abbie looked up at Keith. Her face warmed slightly. She backed up from him a bit. "I'm sorry. I don't understand."

"I'm sorry." Keith noted her reaction. "I didn't mean to upset you. Only earlier this afternoon did Don tell me about Joe's death. Joe and I were friends in college. He was someone I really looked up to. I had written Joe a letter earlier this summer, and I was wondering why I hadn't heard from him."

Suddenly, the mysterious letter reappeared in her mind's eye. She struggled to maintain her composure. "I do remember your letter and wondered who you were. In fact, I kept it but had forgotten about it until now."

"Look," Keith said, "I know you don't know me at all, but I admired Joe tremendously. His friendship meant a lot to me. I just wanted you to know how very sorry I am."

"I'm sorry. I really don't want to discuss Joe right now," she replied curtly.

She tried to calm her racing heartbeat and took a sip of her now-cooling coffee. Abbie felt her eyes narrow, aware of how the mention of her dead husband's name turned them cold and hard like green glass.

Just at that moment, from across the room, a burst of laughter interrupted the moment, and Keith and Abbie both turned to see what all the hoopla was about.

Don waved to the pair. "Come on over, you two. I was just sharing some funny stories from my early days here at Timothy House."

The evening broke up soon afterward. Keith was one of the first guests to say goodnight and leave. As Abbie lay on her cot in the cabin that night, her last thoughts were of Keith's revelation.

Chapter Twenty-Two

Tuesday's dawn broke cool and crisp. It was unusual weather, especially for July. The morning's activities passed quickly, and before Abbie knew it, she was walking hand in hand with her girls into the dining hall for lunch. Abbie bonded instantly with one of them, Chloe Minton, on the opening day of camp. She was the smallest of the girls in Cabin Five, all a common age of nine. Chloe's brown-black hair was a sharp contrast to her indigo eyes and porcelain skin. A few freckles lay scattered across the bridge of her nose and just along her cheekbones.

The little girl had practically become Abbie's shadow since they met. Chloe often asked to sit in Abbie's lap. The child's petite, lithe frame made her look younger than she was. Abbie noticed the young girl's deep blue eyes glowed with intensity whenever she was around. From the few details Abbie had gleaned about the unkindness of her short life and the continual lack of any responsibility in either of her parents, she knew Chloe had grown up in ways far beyond the naïveté of childhood. Counselors at Camp 4Ever were given a limited family history of each camper in their cabin. From what Abbie knew, Chloe's mother was an alcoholic, and her father had deserted the family when the child was three. Abbie's eyes stung with tears as she remembered all too well many painful memories of her own mother's battle with the bottle.

Over the past two days, Abbie had been surprised when memories from her childhood sprang up to the surface like bubbles of air rising to the surface of a pond. All too familiar with the emotional pain caused by the dysfunction of alcoholism, Abbie wished her father was here to tell her what to do to help this innocent victim of abuse. He had been a rock in her life but died of a heart attack when Abbie was ten, leaving her all alone with her mother.

Abbie's mother, Tina, was a faithful alcoholic. The bottle was her one constant. After Lin's death, Tina immediately set about squandering the proceeds from his life insurance policy and somehow managed to get her hands on a small trust fund Lin had established for Abbie's education. As Abbie entered her junior high years, Tina's drinking binges became more frequent and much more destructive. Abbie lost count of how many times her mother embarrassed her, showing up drunk at school athletic events and PTA meetings.

In November of Abbie's ninth-grade year, Tina dropped Abbie off at school one Tuesday morning and didn't return home until four days later on a Friday afternoon. At 11:00 that Tuesday night, Abbie called her Aunt Caty, Tina's older sister. By 11:45, Abbie was tucked safely into Caty's front seat, speeding away from the dark, empty house.

Shortly after Tina's disappearing act, Abbie moved in with Caty and her husband, Scott. Caty, Scott, and their two daughters, Lexie and Jan, both a few years older than Abbie, provided the only normal picture of family life Abbie ever knew. This latest mishap, however, provided the ammunition necessary for Caty and Scott to gain guardianship of Abbie.

Abbie's father led her to the Lord when she was five. During the next five years before his death, Lin planted foundational, godly principles within the fertile soil of his daughter's heart and soul.

A trust fund that her paternal grandmother left to her provided the funding necessary for Abbie to attend the University of Alabama, where she received a liberal arts degree in literature. The trust also paved her way to graduate school for a master's degree in English from Vanderbilt.

Tina died of cirrhosis of the liver during Abbie's junior year at 'Bama. An enormous burden rolled off Abbie's shoulders the afternoon of Tina's brief funeral service. She tried hard to be sad that her mother was gone. But how could she miss someone she never really knew?

Excited squeals and giggles from Chloe and several others brought Abbie out of her reverie. As she watched the little girls playing without a care in the world, Abbie wondered what would eventually become of

Chloe. She had recently been placed with a foster family who were friends of the Fieldings and thought Camp 4Ever would be a good experience for Chloe. They were, however, not interested in adopting her. Abbie made a mental note to pray for Chloe. The week had certainly gotten off to an interesting start.

Chapter Twenty-Three

Abbie heard Josh Hastings' voice across the dining hall as Tuesday's lunch ended, "All right, everybody. Follow me!"

A clatter of chairs mingled with excited chatter as campers and staff poured out of Covenant Kitchen to make their way to Pasture Green. A long-standing camp tradition followed every noon meal. Counselors challenged the campers to a contest of Ultimate Frisbee. The game lasted thirty minutes until rest period began and always proved successful in readying tired youngsters for a nap.

As she headed out of the dining hall to make her way to the athletic field, Abbie noticed Don waiting near the door for her.

"Abbie, I'm so glad I caught you. I've arranged for one of the kitchen staffers to fill in for you this afternoon. I thought, if you're interested, you and I could talk about the teaching job the Wyatts mentioned to you."

They shared light conversation as they walked across the well-landscaped campus to Sanctuary Hall, the main administration building. Don's office was located in a first-floor corner of the three-story, gray stone building. Abbie smiled to herself as she recognized Doris's decorating flare. The room resembled the living room in the Fielding home. Don motioned for Abbie to sit down on a small loveseat near a large window. He settled in an adjoining club chair.

"How's the week going?" started Don.

"Oh, I'm really enjoying myself. I'm not sure if I really know what I'm doing, but I'm having fun doing it. My girls are adorable. One in particular, Chloe Minton, has really stolen my heart."

"I'm so glad she's taken to you." Don grinned. "I just knew you and Lane would both be tonic for her soul. She's had a rough go of it in her nine short years. You have to truly believe in the power of God and His transforming love or carrying the emotional load of all these children would be too much."

Abbie replied soberly, "I know what you mean. Oddly enough, I've been right where Chloe is. My mother was an alcoholic. I know all too well many of the things she has experienced. Maybe that's why God wanted me to be here this week."

"Maybe so." Don leaned forward in his chair a bit. He rested his elbows on his knees. "Doris and I are both so delighted that you and Drew decided to join us on the camp staff this week. Drew appears to be doing a fine job. We've heard so much about both of you from Eric and Lane."

Abbie felt her face redden a bit and replied softly, "Thank you. I'm glad to be here."

"I may as well jump right to the point." Don settled back in his chair. "Eric and Lane have bragged so much about you and your teaching skills. I've done a bit of checking on you and have decided to tempt you to consider joining the faculty of Timothy House."

Abbie shifted a bit on the loveseat, uncomfortable to be the focus of so much attention. "I'll admit I was totally flabbergasted when they took me to dinner in June and dropped that bombshell on me. It is a subject, however, that I've spent a lot of time since then praying about and mulling over in my mind."

"I'm glad to hear that," said Don. "Eric explained to me all that came to light after your husband died. I'm so sorry that you and your son have had that to contend with."

"Well, I am, too." She changed the subject and returned to Don's offer. "I love teaching, but this past year, I have even entertained thoughts of leaving the classroom. If I did leave, though, I'm not exactly sure what I could do. I'm forty-five now, and it would be like starting all over again."

"Maybe." Don beamed enthusiastically. "You don't have to start over. Maybe you just need a fresh beginning in a new place. Let me tell you about the job, and you can decide if it's something you'd be interested in."

Don explained that, during the regular school year, Timothy House was home to about 120 students in grades seven through twelve. "Most of these children are from the Robbinsonville area or from this part of eastern Tennessee. About a fourth of them have been living in less than ideal situations, some having been abused or neglected. Within each lies great promise, but the storms of life have threatened to snuff out any glimmer of hope or happiness within their lives.

"We're in need of a junior high English teacher. The other main responsibility for this person would be serving as a house mother for the seventh-grade girls. There would be no more than ten in the group. There are twelve cottages in all on campus: six for the girls and six for the fellows.

"The junior high cottages are in one area of campus, segregated by gender, of course." Don chuckled. "And the senior high cottages are in another. Doris and I have talked at great length, and we really feel the seventh-grade ladies are in great need of a mother figure. In fact, a young single woman from one of the local churches will be filling in this year for that group of girls, but she's not permanent. Doris and I spend a lot of time with all the twelve-year olds. I guess you could call me their surrogate father."

"Your offer definitely sounds intriguing," said Abbie warily, "but I'm afraid that Eric and Lane may have overstated my qualifications. I've never done any counseling work, and I hardly even know how things work in a residential, educational community."

Don gently replied, "Know that you have all the gifts and talents we're looking for in such a faculty member. I realize you're already under contract for this coming school year, and through some creative scheduling, we have juggled present faculty assignments to cover this year's classes. I'd like to offer you this job today and give you this school year to think it over."

"Wow," a bewildered Abbie said. "You really know how to take a girl's breath away. That's a lot to consider." She paused for a minute. "I'd be moving, and I haven't even thought about the possibility of selling my home. And there's Drew to consider, although he would have just finished college by next fall."

Don moved to the edge of his chair. "I'm game to take this one step at a time if you are. Let's walk through campus, and you could see where you'd be living. I have a packet of information on the school over there on my desk. You could take it home and digest it at your own pace. Doris and I are going to be down in McHenry for a meeting with some patrons this fall, and maybe the three of us could go to dinner and visit again then."

Abbie moved to the edge of the loveseat. "That sounds fair, Don. I just don't want to disappoint you if I decide not to take this job. You would have invested all this time and energy in me for nothing."

Don interrupted, "Abbie, in God's plan, nothing is ever wasted. I hope, regardless of your decision, that Doris and I will have you as a friend for many years to come."

Abbie smiled tentatively at him and relaxed a bit.

"There is one more thing I wanted to mention." Don's tone became quiet and serious. "Keith told me he mentioned to you last night at dinner that he knew your husband, Joe. I feel partially responsible for any hurt that may have been caused by his mentioning him. Until earlier today, Keith didn't know any of the details of the last few years of your life. He certainly didn't know last night at dinner, or I don't think he would have even mentioned his knowing Joe to you. Eric told me about what Joe did, and I told Keith. I didn't think you would mind. You should have seen the disappointment and sorrow on Keith's face when he learned of Joe's wrongdoings."

Abbie's voice broke a bit as she spoke. "Keith's revelation did catch me off guard. I just can't remember Joe ever mentioning Keith. By the time I met Joe, however, we had both been out of college a few years. I know Keith didn't intend to hurt me by bringing up the subject. You'd think the pain would have diminished some after four years."

"Keith Haliday is a man well acquainted with sorrows," Don said softly, "and I can promise you that he would be the last one to utter a careless word, especially one that caused emotional pain. A drunk driver killed Keith's entire family, a wife and two teenage children, in a car wreck seven years ago. That was before I knew Keith."

A pall settled over the office with this last declaration. Don remained silent. Tears that had been filling Abbie's eyes now made their way slowly down her cheeks.

"How very sad," Abbie whispered as she wiped away the tears.

"I know." Don reached over to grasp her hand with one of his and wipe away tears of his own with the other. After a gentle squeeze, he let go of her hand. He slapped his hands down on the top of his knees. "Enough of this serious stuff. Let me show you Timothy House."

As Abbie followed Don out of Sanctuary Hall, she thought, *Lord, is a place at Timothy House part of Your plan for me?*

Chapter Twenty-Four

Abbie thought perhaps two cats were locked in mortal combat, judging from the yelps and squeals coming from Cabin Five. She remembered seeing several tabbies and a gray-and-white striped kitten wandering around campus. She bounded up the wooden steps two at a time and opened the screened door just in time to see Donnie Gail Rogers take a swing at Liza Hensley.

The smaller girl screamed as the strike narrowly missed her. Through the blur of motion, Abbie could just see Chloe Minton huddled in a corner, wedged in tightly between two bunks, clutching a pale blue blanket close to her wide-eyed face. *Where's the student counselor assigned to these campers?* she thought.

"Girls!" Abbie exclaimed loudly. "What in the world is going on?"

Like a referee in a boxing match, she stepped in between Donnie Gail and Liza just in time to deflect what looked like a pretty experienced punch, especially for a nine year old, thrown by Donnie Gail. Abbie instinctively raised her hand, and the girl's balled-up fist landed squarely on her forearm.

"Ouch!" Abbie jumped back a bit.

In the next instant, she grabbed wildly for one of Donnie Gail's arms, which still flailed about her like a windmill picking up speed. She wrapped her fingers around the child's wrist and closed the grip tightly. With all the authority she could muster, she said, "Young lady, that is quite enough. Stop it right now."

Abbie glanced over at Liza but wasn't sure who was more surprised, her or Liza. The expression on Liza's face mirrored the uncertainty Abbie was trying to squelch within herself. Despite her years of teaching experience, breaking up fistfights between girls was not in her repertoire. A bright red whelp on Liza's lower right jaw was deepening in color. Strands of hair had been pulled out of her ponytail holder and hung around her face, limp and damp with sweat and tears.

"Donnie Gail." Abbie maintained her grip on the taller girl's wrist. "You've got some serious explaining to do."

Donnie Gail glared back at Abbie. Her eyes were dark and impenetrable. Abbie had seen the expression Donnie Gail now wore many times on the faces of her own students at Kent Academy. It was stubborn defiance, pure and simple.

She lessened her hold on Donnie Gail's wrist. "You go sit on your bed and don't move. Not one inch."

The sullen stare didn't disappear, but the child did as she was told. Abbie then turned to Liza who was now crying softly. Her arms were wrapped tightly around her waist.

"Come here, sweetie." Abbie moved toward the girl.

Liza moved tentatively toward her, all the while casting furtive glances at Donnie Gail, who sat sulking on her bunk bed. Abbie gently hugged the young girl and then began wiping away her tears.

At that moment, the screen door to the cabin flew open. A gangly, thin adolescent girl with shoulder-length strawberry-blonde hair stood in the door panting, obviously out of breath. Her eyes grew wide as she surveyed the scene of the recent scuffle. A chair was overturned, and the contents of a duffel bag lay strewn around like confetti. Nearby, a stuffed rabbit looked like a Mack truck had recently flattened it.

"Oh, gosh." The teenager looked at Abbie. "I just left them for a minute."

Abbie read the fear written on her face and stared disbelievingly at the girl. "We'll discuss that later, Melissa." She glanced over at Chloe still huddled in the corner. "Right now, I need you to help Liza get cleaned up. I'll check on Chloe."

Melissa led Liza over to her bunk. As Abbie headed across the open space of the cabin's cluttered floor to the corner in which Chloe had wedged herself, she could hear Liza laughing at a joke Melissa told her.

The space was the ideal size for a small child. Even though Abbie was slender, there was no way she was going to be able to get in the corner with Chloe. Breathing in deeply, she uttered a whispered "Help me, Lord" and then sat down on Chloe's bed, facing the corner.

She sat cross-legged and patted the space next to her. "Come here, Chloe," she said in a low, gentle voice. "Everything's okay. No one's going to hurt you."

Chloe sat motionless for a moment. Her small fingers rubbed the soft, comforting fabric of the blanket clutched to her chest. She eyed Abbie suspiciously and then shifted her gaze to where Donnie Gail sat across the room. Abbie turned to follow Chloe's stare.

"Chloe," said Abbie softly and turned back to look at the frightened girl. "Donnie Gail won't hurt you. The argument is over. Come on." She patted the space next to her once more. Abbie prayed silently, unsure of what to do next if Chloe wouldn't vacate the corner.

"She's just a scaredy cat," sounded Donnie Gail's sarcastic voice from behind Abbie. "She's just a big baby."

Chloe burrowed even deeper into the corner, if that were even possible.

Abbie whirled around toward Donnie Gail and scrambled off the bed. "Listen, young lady, I've had just about enough of you."

She crossed the distance between Chloe's and Donnie Gail's bunk in two quick strides. Abbie stood in front of the offender and leaned down toward her, positioning her face exactly in front of Donnie Gail's. "Not another word. Do you understand me?" A wave of protective nature for Chloe promoted Abbie's demonstrative tone that had washed over her. She was not going to allow anything or anyone else to upset the child.

Abbie straightened up and stepped back. She noticed that Melissa had completed her task of getting Liza cleaned up. Liza's clothes had been changed, and the teen counselor had even managed to fashion the camper's long, blonde hair in a French braid. Melissa and her young charge were now engaged in a friendly game of slaps, each taking turns to try to swat the other's upturned hands.

"Melissa," Abbie said, "I need you to go find Mr. Fielding. Please bring him back to the cabin as soon as possible." Abbie glanced down at her watch and saw only about fifteen more minutes were left in this after-lunch period before the bell would sound for rest period.

The screen door slammed once more as Melissa headed down the cabin steps to complete her mission.

Suddenly, a brilliant thought struck Abbie. "Liza," she called out cheerily to the now-calm young camper, "how about a game of hide-and-seek? What do you say?" Abbie crawled back onto Chloe's bunk once more and drew her legs up Indian style. "I need you to help me find Chloe."

Abbie smiled brightly, hoping to attract Liza's attention. Liza immediately scampered over, scrambling up on the camp mattress next to Abbie.

"You're silly, Miss Abbie." Liza giggled. "Chloe's right there." The child reached around Abbie. Her pudgy finger pointed in Chloe's direction.

Thankful Liza had engaged in the game, Abbie egged her on. "You're silly, Liza." She looked over toward the corner. She deliberately looked everywhere but directly at Chloe. Out of the corner of her eye, though, she could see Chloe watching her. "There's nothing but a big, black, long-legged spider in that corner."

At that pronouncement, Chloe shot up from the corner with a shriek like a Roman candle on New Year's Eve. She launched herself onto the bed and landed right in Abbie's lap. "I'm here! I'm here!" the child exclaimed. "Tag, Miss Abbie! You're it!" Chloe wrapped her arms around Abbie's neck and squeezed tightly with all her might.

"There you are, Chloe." Abbie returned the bear hug. "I never saw you. What a great hiding place you found!"

After a few seconds, Chloe released her hold on Abbie, settled back down in her lap once more, and turned to face Liza. The wide grin across the little girl's face told Abbie all she needed to know. The storm had passed.

"Who wants to hide next?" Abbie knew she needed to keep this ball rolling, at least until Melissa returned with Don.

Lane ought to be getting here any minute, Abbie thought, remembering Lane's prior commitment to working in the craft hut after lunch.

"Me! Me! Me!" clamored Liza. She jumped off the bed and stood straight and tall on the floor. By now, the mark on her face was looking less red. "Close your eyes, and count to twenty."

Just before covering her eyes, Abbie glared over at Donnie Gail with her sternest you-better-not-move-a-muscle teacher look. The sound of footsteps on the path just outside the cabin told her help was on the way.

Chapter Twenty-Five

Later that afternoon, Abbie made her way to Sanctuary Hall. She passed a teary Melissa on the path to the building. The girl would hardly meet Abbie's gaze. Abbie offered a quick greeting and continued toward the administration building.

Don and Doris met Abbie at the door to Don's office.

"Come on in, Abbie." Don put his arm around her shoulders briefly and gave her a quick hug. "I'm sure this has been a trying day for you."

Abbie nodded, feeling like she had been called into the principal's office. The pit in her stomach warned her that she had walked into a situation for which she was totally unprepared. Doris gave her a reassuring look as the three settled into the seating area in the office.

"Doris and I are very grateful for your quick, levelheaded actions. They certainly prevented a potentially serious situation." Don looked across at Abbie with an open and warm expression.

"I've never witnessed a fight like that before," began Abbie, "certainly not between girls. And these are so young, only nine. I'm not sure what's going on with Donnie Gail, but she certainly seems angry about something." Abbie reached up to brush back a strand of hair behind her ear.

"We're still trying to work out some kinks with this summer program," replied Don. "As you know, a portion of the Timothy House student body is comprised of what we'd call at-risk students. Donnie Gail would certainly fit into that category. She's been abused some in her young life, and as you have correctly surmised, she has a great deal of anger pent up within her. We are working to help her manage that anger. Even though Donnie Gail only came to Timothy House as a full-time student last year, this is actually her second summer at Camp 4Ever."

Abbie hesitated a bit. "I feel really responsible for what happened today. I had no idea the girls would be left alone in the cabin."

"Oh, Abbie." Doris leaned over to grab the hand of the younger woman. "Quite the opposite. What happened today was not your fault at all. Melissa is the one who dropped the ball." Doris squeezed her hand reassuringly.

Abbie smiled briefly and relaxed a bit.

Doris continued, "We're still working on how much responsibility to give to the older teen counselors. Melissa has just graduated from high school, and she should be able to handle a group of nine year olds, certainly for a period of thirty minutes or so. We're terribly sorry you had to witness Donnie Gail's temper. When it erupts in all its fury, it's not pretty to witness."

"I'll say." Abbie managed a weak smile. "That little girl packs an incredibly strong wallop." She looked down at her forearm. A bruise was now forming from Donnie Gail's sucker punch.

Don picked up where Doris' last comment had ended. "Donnie Gail, like many of our at-risk students, has some serious issues with control and setting boundaries. When she feels threatened, she reacts in a physical way. We're working hard to help her find a more appropriate way of dealing with her frustration.

"I hope you won't let what happened earlier today interfere with your consideration of the offer to teach here at Timothy House. We could certainly benefit from someone of your caliber on our staff."

Abbie bit the inside of her lower lip as she pondered a reply. "I'll have to be honest with you. Nothing in my educational training ever prepared me for what I witnessed today. The most serious offenses I've encountered have been rude remarks made by sassy, disrespectful students. I can't even tell you how I was able to gain control of the situation this afternoon."

"Honey," said Doris, "you did exactly the right thing today. You used a no-nonsense, tough love approach, and that's exactly the same tack we attempt to take with all our students. Even our regular students occasionally have issues that have to be dealt with."

Don chimed in, "As you and I discussed yesterday, we provide our faculty with specialized training. What impressed me today is that I witnessed a correct instinctual response to a very threatening situation. That can't be taught in a classroom." He paused.

"Look, I know you're probably worn out. We've assigned another teen counselor to help you and Lane in Cabin Five. Her name is Cary. I think you'll really like her. Dinner's not for another hour. Why don't you take some time to yourself?"

"That really sounds good to me," said Abbie, grateful for the kind offer and the encouraging words. She was also relieved to know she was not to blame for the violence she had witnessed.

Instead of heading back to her cabin, Abbie changed direction and headed toward Serenity Cove, the lake at the back of the campus. Once there, she paused to watch the ripples on the lake created by the warm July breeze. The gentle wind played with her hair the same way it teased the water's surface. Abbie took a seat on a large boulder near the water's edge.

Try as she might, she couldn't shake the feeling that she might not be cut out for this kind of school. She hurt for Donnie Gail, in spite of the girl's violent streak. What a shame that so much rage was bottled up in such a young life, waiting like a time bomb to explode. *But pity*, she thought, *won't help heal what's really eating up the little girl on the inside.*

Abbie knew firsthand about anger and the way it smoldered deep inside you. Ever since her week alone at the Resting Place, she'd been applying Winnie's principle of the Patriot Plan to other areas of her life. She knew she hadn't yet found a way to successfully manage the raging anger toward Joe that still burned within her spirit. *How could I possibly help students like Donnie Gail deal with their anger if I haven't even learned to deal with my own?* she thought.

The reflection of the late afternoon sky cast a dark blue sheen across the lake's broad surface. A slow-moving cloud caught her eye as it drifted overhead. As it meandered lazily across the afternoon sky, it seemed to carry off with it any hopes Abbie had entertained of joining the program at Timothy House.

Chapter Twenty-Six

The last full day of Camp 4Ever was a blur. What would remain vividly ingrained in Abbie's memory long after the week at camp was over was the closing service held that evening in Peter's Chapel. Camp staff, school faculty, family members of the campers, and patrons of the school filled the little church to overflowing. The fifth-grade boys and girls prepared a special song for the occasion, and as Abbie listened to their innocent voices, her eyes glistened with tears as she thought of the lives to which they would soon return. The words of their selection tugged at her heart.

Don's sermon was based on the Apostle Paul's letters to Timothy, his younger brother in the faith. He encouraged the campers to serve God and others right where they were in their lives: with their grades, through their chores around the house, and in the way they treated their family members and friends. He challenged the kids to stand tall in their young years and to not feel awkward because of their youth. God could and would perform mighty deeds through their lives.

Abbie sat with Eric and Lane, a few rows back from Doris, Keith, Josh, and other school faculty. As the service ended and everyone stood up to leave, Keith's gaze caught Abbie's as he was leaving his pew. Abbie returned the look, but realizing that she was reaching the stare stage, she smiled and looked away.

As the crowd spilled out onto the lawn of the chapel, Abbie found her girls, wrapped each of them in big hugs, and exclaimed excitedly about their music and how it moved her. She caught a glimpse of Keith across the crowd. He nodded slightly to her and turned, disappearing into the night.

Later that night after all her little charges were safely in their beds and after hearing Lane's breathing slow to an even tempo, Abbie slipped out of her cot and knelt on her knees beside the crude bed stand. She clasped her hands together and bowed her head.

"Dear Lord, I am amazed at all You are doing in my life. It's been so much fun to be part of camp this week and to love these little girls. Is teaching at Timothy House a part of Your plan? I'm ready, Lord, to hear what You have to say to me about serving You. I'm so sorry that I've let my anger and grief numb my heart over these past years. Thank You for not giving up on me. I've seen so much evidence of Your power during this week at camp. Give me eyes to see, ears to hear, and a heart to understand Your will for my life.

"Jesus, please protect these little girls as they go back to their regular lives tomorrow. Send with them your grace and a little touch of heaven. Help them to trust You with their hearts and their lives. Wrap us safely in Your arms as we rest tonight. Amen."

Abbie had an overwhelming sense of being held gently, yet firmly, in a loving embrace as she slid back under the covers of her cot. For the first time in many years, Abbie dreamed of days to come and not of Joe and nightmares of the past.

Hugs, kisses, and even a few tears marked the final morning of Camp 4Ever. By 10:45, the last of the children were in cars or vans, headed home to enjoy the last remaining days of summer. The faculty and staff then began to move in the direction of Covenant Kitchen to gather together for one last meal before the week came to a close.

As Abbie walked to meet Eric and Lane at the dining hall, she ran into Keith coming toward her on the path. "Oh, Abbie," he said, "I'm so glad I found you. I was trying to catch you before you left."

"Hey, Keith." Abbie was surprised at how calm her voice sounded.

"Look, I know we don't have much time before lunch, but would you take a walk with me for a few minutes? I'd really like to talk to you."

Abbie nodded. Keith turned and led her back in the general direction of the dining hall, but when the building came into view, he took a left fork in the path, leading them into the nearby woods. After a few more minutes along the path, a clearing appeared, one Abbie had never seen before. Two stone benches flanked a small reflecting pool. A mountain stream gurgled into and trickled over one side of the pond, providing a natural aeration system for the fish swimming to and fro within the cool waters.

Keith motioned for Abbie to sit down. He joined her on the bench.

"Abbie, sometimes I'm not so good with words, so I'll try to do the best I can. I want to apologize for having upset you at dinner the other night with my comments about Joe."

Abbie turned to face Keith more directly. "You didn't really. I was merely surprised. That's all."

"I didn't know about Joe's shenanigans when we met the other night, only that he had died." Keith watched her face for a minute and looked for any signs of anger or distress. He didn't find any. "Don was able to fill me in Tuesday morning about the awful things Joe did and how they only came to light after his death. Please know that I would never have mentioned him if I thought it would upset you."

Abbie looked down at her hands. "Joe's gambling addiction has caused me and my son, Drew, deep emotional pain, personal embarrassment, and great financial difficulty."

"The tears in your eyes told me all I needed to know. Believe me when I say I understand your pain. More than you know."

Abbie looked back at Keith. "I also know about your loss. I wish I knew what to say."

"Let's just say that we have both walked in each other's shoes. Look, I know we probably didn't get off to a great start, but I'd really like to know about Joe's life and your life with him. As I told you earlier, he was a straight-up guy when I knew him, and he was a great influence on my life in college."

Abbie hesitated for only a moment. Even though Keith was a virtual stranger, some quiet voice within told her he was safe and could be trusted. "I'd like that. I'd be more than happy to answer any questions you have about Joe. I would also like to know more about your family as well."

"I'm down your way quite frequently on business. Would you mind if I got your number from Don? I could call you sometime, say for lunch or dinner?"

"I'll look forward to it." Abbie smiled.

Keith looked at his watch. "Well, we'd better make a dash for lunch before the others eat all the food."

As they neared the dining hall, Keith asked Abbie once more, "Promise me you're not upset about the other night?"

"Scout's honor." Abbie grinned widely.

They entered the room just as the rest of the group was being seated. Before walking to his place in the dining hall, Keith turned to Abbie and, with a gleam in his eye, said, "Later!"

Chapter Twenty-Seven

Keith had been in his office making phone calls for the past two hours, and it was already 10:00. The morning was flying by. Although basketball season didn't officially start until the end of October, there was still plenty of planning needed during these early days of September, preparations that would ensure a smooth start to the season.

"Richard, we're looking forward to a hard game with the Johnson City Wolverines. I'll look forward to seeing you soon on the court." Keith placed the receiver back on the phone and made a mark on the list of names in front of him. *Only eight more calls to go*, he thought.

Keith closed the folder marked "Current Basketball Schedule" and slipped it into the framework of a hanging file folder in a bottom drawer of his desk. *Basketball, check*, thought Keith. *Now on to budget matters.*

He reached across his desk for a file folder. As he did, his eye fell on a pewter cross that sat on a bookshelf in his office. A flood of memories came crashing in to remind him of how that cross led him to Timothy House.

Seven years ago, after the school year ended in late May, six months after his family had died, he'd had no other employment plans after leaving his position as head basketball coach at Mountain Laurel High School. A random call from an old boss brought Keith back into the fold at Buechner Pharmaceuticals, a company he had worked for before becoming a coach. He was a rising star in their organization years ago when he left the first time, so the company was thrilled to have him back.

About two years into his sales job, Keith ran into his old friend Don Fielding at a men's retreat. That same weekend, at age forty-eight, Keith came face to face with the risen, living Savior. The life-changing experience totally altered Keith's outlook on life.

The pain from Keith's great loss still lingered, but where before it was a wound left to fester, the heartache had now been cleansed and could heal properly. God was using the purifying pain of suffering to carve out and fashion a new heart within Keith Haliday. Where he was once lukewarm and merely acknowledged God, Keith now knew beyond a shadow of a doubt that Christ was real and He wanted to perform an exciting, serious work through his life. Keith also knew that God wanted to use him to reach others in His name.

If he had been ignoring it before, he was now keenly aware that, once more, the allure of big money and the lifestyle it afforded was blinding him to the things in life that really mattered. *I've already been there and done that once with Genny and the kids,* he thought, angry at himself for getting caught up once more in the world's trap. *Why am I getting suckered into this again?*

It didn't take Keith long to figure out that he needed a change of scenery. God was gently ending a chapter in Keith's life. A few weeks later, Keith and Don had lunch together.

"I haven't been able to get you or Timothy House off my mind since you called me," Keith told the older man. "I feel that God wants me involved in partnership with your ministry, but I'm not sure how."

"Well, just putting your heart and will in the right place and saying yes to God is a start. He'll show you the rest."

"Tell me more about how Timothy House operates." Keith put down his coffee cup.

"Sure. My uncle, Roger O'Ferrall, founded the school initially. He and his wife, Marie, loved kids, yet were never able to have any of their own. Roger owned a very successful lumber business in Robbinsonville. He was a generous, kindhearted soul, and he would go visit the men who worked at the lumber mill when they got sick. He saw the pitiful living conditions many of those families endured. Most of the children of those men, if they were educated at all, attended an antiquated, dilapidated, one-room school run by an old maid. She was the meanest woman God ever made." Don chuckled.

"One of the guiding principles of Timothy House is that kids respond better to love and encouragement than they do to criticism and harsh words. Once Doris and I realized God wasn't going to send us children of our own, we decided the next best thing was to love the ones at Timothy House. We've seen God do amazing things through that school."

As Don talked on, Keith felt a certainty that somehow the ministry at Timothy House was something he was supposed to become involved with. "It's hard for me to believe that God could use me to work a miracle, but I'm sure willing to be available. I guess the rest is up to Him."

Keith reached into the inside pocket of his blazer, pulled out a signed check, and handed it to Don. "I want you to take this, Don. It's not much, but I believe God wants me to support your school."

Don unfolded the check and saw that it was for four hundred dollars. Don reached over to shake Keith's hand. "This is very generous. Thank you so much."

"You're welcome, Don. I'm going to start sending you one of those every month. You use it in any way that you see fit."

Don beamed. "God's going to bless you for your faithfulness. This money will provide extra benefits for the children of Timothy House."

As they got up to leave, Keith looked at Don with eyes brimming and full. "I don't have my children anymore, but I don't want anyone else's little boy or girl to miss out on what Genny and I tried to give ours, love and a good education."

As the two men said good-bye, Keith was touched to see the older man choking back tears of his own.

Several months later over dinner one night, Don pitched an idea to him. "Keith, I know these last six years have been extremely hard on you. I've been so moved by all you've shared with me, about your openness to God and your unwavering commitment to Christ. I have a proposition for you. Timothy House has several staff needs. First of all, we need a varsity basketball coach for both our boys' and girls' programs. It would be a much different program than the one you used to be a part of. Second, I need an assistant administrator, someone with a good head on his shoulders and a knack for numbers, someone who could look down the road, far ahead of where we are today. I think you may just be that man.

"One of the perks for senior staff at Timothy House is that housing is provided for them on the campus grounds. A two-bedroom cottage is waiting for you. It's not terribly spacious, but the tall ceilings make it feel a lot bigger than it is."

During all of this time, Keith hadn't said a word, but his heart was about to leap out of his chest. *Is this it, Lord?* he thought. *Is this the next step?*

Don delivered the last part of the offer. "The salary figure we can offer is considerably lower than what you've been making in sales. There'll be no monetary bonuses, but I can tell you there will be many benefits to working at Timothy House that can't be measured in a paycheck."

"How much lower are we talking about?"

When Don quoted the figure, Keith just beamed. It was $5,000 over the budget salary he had already set for himself.

Keith responded instantly, "I'll take it!"

The ringing of the office phone snapped Keith back from the halls of memory to the present. It was Don, asking Keith to join him in his office. Now early September, the school year was in full swing. As Keith walked down the hall, he mused over how quickly his first four months at Timothy House had passed. Keith reveled in the steady, sure routine of life at Timothy House. The yoke of responsibility, coupled with demanding mental and physical work, was custom made for him.

Keith was surprised to see Chuck Hawthorne, a member of the board of trustees, seated in the office. Don motioned for Keith to take a seat as he settled behind his desk.

"We just wanted to make sure all is going well with your work," said Chuck.

Keith found a friendly, open gaze in Chuck's clear blue eyes. Already the trustee had proven to be an ally and encourager for Keith.

Keith glanced over at Don. "I know you guys are taking a chance on me, but I'm having a ball here at Timothy House." He raked his hair away from his forehead with his fingers. "Now don't get me wrong. Most days, there's more that I don't know than I do, but all in all, I feel like I'm making progress." He glanced from Chuck to Don and back again. "I hope you'll let me know if I'm not performing up to par."

A smile broke slowly across Chuck's face. "Keith, I'm here to tell you on behalf of the board that we couldn't be happier with your work."

Keith slowly let out the breath that until now he hadn't realized he was holding.

Chuck continued, "The adjustments you've made in the budget are already reducing costs."

Don nodded approvingly, listening to Chuck's compliments.

"Camp 4Ever was the best yet. Your visits over the summer with civic clubs and networking groups have paid dividends in an increased enrollment this fall. Keep up the good work."

After a few more comments, the meeting ended, and Chuck departed.

"Congratulations." Don grinned. "Chuck and the board are thrilled with you. Sure makes my job a whole lot easier."

Keith looked at him, not sure what to say. He was still trying to process all of Chuck's glowing comments. "Thanks," he said a bit hesitantly. "I think."

After covering a few routine matters, Don leaned back in his chair and clasped his hands behind his head. "We need to start thinking about teaching assignments for next year. Have you thought anymore about Abbie Richardson?"

Keith almost blurted out his real thoughts but managed instead to utter a composed response, "A little. Tell me what you had in mind."

Chapter Twenty-Eight

As the new school year progressed, Abbie couldn't get Timothy House and the week at Camp 4Ever off her mind. As much as she enjoyed being at Kent Academy, she still felt something was missing. Abbie loved a challenge, and quite frankly, her work lately was beginning to bore her. She longed to feel like she made a difference in the lives of others, like she had felt she did during the week in July. She remembered the connection forged with Chloe Minton. She recalled calling upon wisdom greater than her own to calm the anger and frustration of Donnie Gail Rogers. She reveled in the memory of how alive and plugged in she felt, how surprised she was that her own troubles disappeared in the wake of reaching out to others with far more pressing concerns.

The severe need of the kids at Camp 4Ever appalled her and yet, at the same time, piqued her interest. They were referred by pastors or youth ministers who knew of the specialized and much-needed loving care that the children would receive at Timothy House. Abbie's special little friend, Chloe, had become a subject of frequent prayer. She'd even exchanged a few letters with the little girl, delighting in the childish scrawl scribbled on the pages.

Lane had served as one of the worship leaders that week. Abbie loved watching and listening to her best friend. She was vivacious and energetic and radiated the very essence of God. Her faith was profound and yet naturally simple. In her devotions with the female counselors, Lane challenged them to do something bold for Jesus and abandon themselves in service to others in His name. More and more in her quiet time,

Abbie's prayers drifted toward one burning question: What do You want me to do with my life now, Lord?

Another aspect of the week in Robbinsonville, meeting Keith Haliday, intrigued her. Perhaps it was because he shared a part of Joe's past. Keith's letter to Joe, having arrived just weeks before Camp 4Ever, now seemed providential. Somehow it had prepared Abbie for meeting him in July. Thoughts of Keith wandered through Abbie's mind rather frequently in fact. They both surprised and confused her.

On this Friday morning in September, Abbie told her boss of the pending offer from Timothy House.

Arthur Patterson's gentle gray eyes followed her every word. "I appreciate you letting me know. Don Fielding is an old friend of mine, and he is one the most respected colleagues I know within educational circles. I'll be praying for God's counsel and obvious direction as you seek His will. He'll let you know which way to go. Just listen."

"Thanks, Mr. Patterson. I will."

Abbie left the office with a lighter spring in her step. She headed down the hallway to her classroom. She had about thirty minutes before her next class started and had planned to use the time grading a set of papers. *The building is so quiet*, she thought. Once the next bell rung, organized chaos would erupt as students teemed like salmon swimming upstream as they made their way to their next scheduled class.

As grateful as she was for a few moments alone, Abbie also knew she'd never quite gotten used to the isolation of a teacher's life. Being in a room with a group of energetic thirteen year olds was fun and stimulating, but Abbie found she missed conversation with other adults. Her current situation made the void more pronounced. Many times, the demands of the school day left little time to visit with colleagues or sit and share a cup of coffee in the lounge.

Abbie was blessed with many female friends, women whom she admired, who cheered and encouraged her. Sometimes though, she found herself wandering mentally, imagining conversations with a handsome, rugged man. That imaginary someone was beginning to look, oddly enough, like Keith Haliday.

The loss of male companionship since Joe's death made Abbie feel like half a woman, incomplete somehow. She was wary of most men she met and often wondered if she'd ever meet one she could totally trust. A few invitations for dates had come her way over these last four years. Most were with divorced or still-single men at her church. A few awkward dinners, one disastrous brunch, and an out-of-tune symphony concert later, Abbie had all but sworn off dating.

More days than not, Abbie prayed, "Lord, what do You want me to do with my life now?" She hoped the answer would come.

Chapter Twenty-Nine

Abbie had just ten minutes before Audry was due for dinner. She scurried around the kitchen putting last-minute touches on a green salad. She peeked in the oven window to make sure the chicken and wild rice casserole was ready. *Five more minutes*, she thought.

The smell of rolls warming filled the room. A pitcher full of zinnias graced the table. The flowers were Audry's favorites, and Abbie had picked them out of her garden especially for her friend.

Precisely at 6:30, the doorbell rang.

"Come in this house." Abbie wrapped Audry tightly in a hug. "It's so good to see you."

"You, too, dearie." Audry followed Abbie toward the back of the house. "What smells so delicious? I'm famished."

"I'm glad it smells good. Let's just hope it tastes as good," said Abbie. "It's just a chicken casserole, baked fruit, and a surprise for dessert."

She smiled to herself and thought, *What would I do without Audry?* She so appreciated the many ways her older friend affirmed her, something her own mother had never done.

Once in the kitchen, Audry placed her purse on a nearby chair. "What can I do to help?"

"Not one thing. Just have a seat and visit until I get everything on the table." She reached into the lower oven and brought out the rolls. She wrapped them in a cloth napkin, put them in a shallow wicker basket, and placed it on the table. "I'm sorry I haven't talked to you much this week. It's just been nuts at school."

"No worry. I know how busy life can get."

After a few more preparations, Abbie filled their plates and served the meal. She settled into her chair at the table. She took Audry's hand in her own and asked the blessing. "Dear Lord, we thank You for this day. I thank You especially for my dear friend Audry and for all she means to me. I ask You to bless our time together. Use this food to nourish us so we may better serve You. In Your name, I pray. Amen."

"So school's been nuts this week?" Audry buttered her roll and waited for Abbie's reply.

"Yes, it's been frustrating." Abbie could feel a speck of food on the corner of her mouth and dabbed at it with her napkin. "I did step out on a limb, though. I told Mr. Patterson about Don Fielding's job offer."

"What did he say?"

"He said Don has a great reputation and is well respected in the educational world. Mr. Patterson told me to listen, that God would tell me the way to go." Abbie filled her fork with the last bite of food left on her plate.

"He'll definitely do that. God, I mean." Audry placed her knife next to her fork in the center of the plate.

"Do you have any room for dessert? I've got a lemon ice box pie ready." Abbie picked up their plates from the table and placed them in the sink. She then reached into the refrigerator for the treat she'd made earlier. She turned back to Audry and waited for a reply. Her hand held a serving knife poised above the dessert's smooth surface.

"Just a sliver." Audry grinned slightly. "I'm watching my figure, you know. Watching it expand, that is." She laughed lightly at her own joke.

Abbie set the piece of pie in front of Audry. "Coffee?" She nodded her head back toward the sink area. "It's decaf."

"Yes, dearie, that would be great."

The pair enjoyed their hot coffee and cold pie. Like most deep conversations shared between Abbie and Audry, the discussion often turned back to Joe. Audry listened patiently to this now-familiar story.

"During these last four years, I've been very angry with Joe and also with God. I've asked God hundreds of questions, including 'Why?' I've been wondering if I'll ever see the color in life again. It's as if my field of vision has turned to black and white. Some days, I feel like God's forgotten me."

"I've never been where you are in your life right now, but I can promise you that God has not forgotten you, and He definitely has a plan for your life." Audry's clear blue eyes seemed to look right down to the bottom of Abbie's soul.

Abbie smiled briefly. "I know. It's just that, right now, my prayers seem to hit a glass ceiling instead of reaching heaven. It's really strange. I can sense God's presence, but I can't hear His voice. Does that make any sense to you?"

"You're making perfect sense." The older woman reached over and patted Abbie's hand. "I've gone through many seasons in my life when I couldn't see anything, much less the Lord's face, for the fog that was present at the time." Audry squeezed Abbie's hand. "These are the times, dear girl, when you have to trust God's word and not your feelings. Otherwise, you'll feel like He's nowhere to be found."

Abbie leaned back in her chair and gathered her thoughts. "I feel like such a baby sometimes. As bad as my life's been, I realize it also could be a lot worse. I can't quite put it into words. It's like I'm out of step with the music in every area of my life. I want my life to count. More importantly, though, I want to find that place of service that God has prepared for me." Abbie stopped talking and sighed deeply.

"Wait on God." Audry patted her friend's hand. "He's got that plan, and I suspect He'll let you know what it is sooner rather than later."

Chapter Thirty

True to his word, Don called Abbie the last week in September and invited her to dinner with him and Doris. He suggested they meet somewhere that was quiet, affording some privacy for their conversation. Abbie met the couple at Weston's, an upscale restaurant that was a favorite spot in McHenry. Dark paneled walls, high-backed leather booths, and recessed lighting gave an intimate ambiance to the restaurant. Best of all, it was small and, thereby, offered limited seating. Abbie made the reservation for 7:00.

During the first part of the meal, the trio caught each other up on what they had been doing since Camp 4Ever. Once dessert was ordered and the coffee served, Don posed a question. "Well, Abbie, have you thought any more about my offer to teach at Timothy House?"

Abbie smiled. "Matter of fact, I have."

Don leaned forward with his coffee cup between his hands and winked at Doris. "Let's hear it. Tell us what you've been thinking."

"I've had so many thoughts. It's difficult to know where to begin. First of all, I just want to thank you so much for letting me be a part of the Camp 4Ever staff this past summer. The children really touched my heart."

"They have a way of doing that," said Doris as the waiter refilled their cups.

Tendrils of steam curled upward from their table. Bowls of warm bread pudding topped with rum sauce, a Weston's specialty, followed.

"Second, these last four years have been tough on me. This past summer, though, it felt like I was starting to wake up just a little from the emotional coma I've been in since Joe died. The week of Camp 4Ever was a terrific week. That was some of the hardest work I've ever done, and yet I fell into bed each night feeling satisfied, having served someone else's needs rather than my own.

"That may sound kind of silly since I teach school every day. Those precious kids at Camp 4Ever could give us nothing in return but their smiles and their love. It was very meaningful to get to be a part of something like that." Abbie took a sip of her coffee. "How is Chloe Minton doing? I've really missed that little girl."

"She's doing all right," replied Don. Even though his words were positive, the tone of his voice raised a flag of concern within Abbie. "Chloe's attending Timothy House on a partial scholarship this year. Hope and Kevin Henderson, Chloe's foster parents, are able to cover some of her tuition costs.

"Bless their hearts," Don continued pensively. "They mean well, but they're very ambivalent about their commitment to Chloe. I just hope they're helping Chloe for the right reasons. A number of children have come through the Henderson's household over the past few years. They've developed a somewhat questionable reputation in the Robbinsonville area. Hope has been overheard more than a few times bragging about the money she and Kevin make from foster parenting.

"We'll reevaluate Chloe's place in the Timothy House community at the end of the school year. I wish I knew some good-hearted couple who would adopt Chloe. She needs love and stability in her life."

"I'll add that to my prayer list," replied Abbie.

Don nodded approvingly.

"Please tell Chloe hello," said Abbie, with a big grin, remembering all the sweet times shared with the little girl and the other campers at Camp 4Ever. "She sent me a letter right after camp. It's amazing how those Timothy House kids can wiggle their way into your heart."

Don and Doris shared a knowing glance between them.

Abbie paused and took of bite of her bread pudding. Doris joined in the conversation. "Honey, several of the camp staffers and Timothy House faculty who have been with us for a long time commented on how caring you were and what a positive difference you made in the week."

Abbie beamed.

Doris continued, "I certainly couldn't have run the craft hut without your help. You have a natural creative talent. Best of all, I enjoyed being around you. You have much to give to others."

"Doris is right, young lady," chimed in Don. "I thought tonight I'd give you some more concrete information about the job offer. You can chew on that info for a few more weeks, and then we can get together again. Perhaps you could drive up to the school for a weekend visit."

The trio stayed long after most patrons of the restaurant had departed. Abbie listened as Don listed a salary and benefits package much more attractive than her present one. He also described her living accommodations. The teaching load would actually be lighter than what Abbie currently carried at Kent Academy, while the counseling aspect of being a house parent provided the counterbalance.

When Don mentioned counseling, Abbie interrupted. "Don, I have no training or experience in counseling. I'm not qualified for the job."

Don reached over to pat her hand. "Timothy House sends our faculty to an intense, three-week program at a theological seminary near Nashville. We also hold several in-service programs for faculty throughout the year. You're a parent, and you're also loving and kindhearted. God will provide the rest."

A little before 9:30, Doris looked at her watch. "Oh my, Don, we've kept Abbie out far too long. She's got to get up and teach tomorrow."

"Gracious, Abbie," said Don sheepishly. "I had no idea it was so late. Keep in touch with us and let us know what you think."

They exchanged hugs in the parking lot. Doris said goodnight, and Don helped his wife into their car. He then walked Abbie across the lot to hers.

As Don held her door open, he said warmly, "We'd really like you to be a part of the family of Timothy House. You know we'll be praying for you."

"Thanks, Don. I appreciate that. I'll let you know what God lays on my heart."

Abbie got in her car, closed the door, and started the engine. The sound of a light tapping on her window caught her attention. She rolled the window down. Don leaned into the car and said with a twinkle in his eye, "By the way, Keith Haliday said to tell you hello!"

Chapter Thirty-One

This was turning into a bear of a week for Abbie. Monday and Tuesday offered two parent-teacher conferences that were especially difficult. Monday's battle was with Linda Peterson. A divorced mother of three, Linda had a reputation for taking out her bitterness on everyone in her life: her children, her children's teachers, the daycare workers, her ex-husband, her coworkers, and the grocery clerk in the checkout line. Abbie had heard from other teachers how life had dealt Ms. Peterson a sour pill and how the woman was determined if she had to swallow it, so would everyone else. Abbie had taught a Peterson child two years ago and was currently teaching Shannon. By now, she was on to the "Peterson Strategy," as she called it.

Whenever parent-teacher conferences were held, Linda verbally attacked the teacher in question, never taking responsibility for her own child's lack of effort. Shannon was an average student whose biggest problem wasn't academic but rather a wounded heart and low self-esteem caused by her mother's childish behavior. More days than not, she was on Abbie's prayer list.

Fay and Gary Landrum were Tuesday's conference de jour. Both parents wanted their son Blake to reap the benefits of their social connections. Fay contested results of any elections in which Blake participated but did not win. Gary always found an opportunity to talk to the football coach and ask about Blake's performance. During the sports season, his outbursts—"Atta boy, son" and "Way to put on the heat"—were just louder and more frequent than other parents' comments to border on obnoxious. Blake, an athlete on the junior varsity football and basketball teams, was also enrolled in cotillion and karate classes. Active in a local outdoor hiking club, Blake was a fine example of the Landrum family motto, "Busier is better."

Abbie realized after Tuesday's conference with the Landrums that she and they would probably never see eye to eye. Both parents wanted her to bend the rules of her classroom due to Blake's "very busy schedule," allowing him extra time to take tests and turn in assignments. Abbie politely, yet firmly, held her ground during the conference. She knew Blake's schedule, not her own, was the one that needed rearranging. By the tilt of Fay Landrum's well-coifed head, however, Abbie was sure the mother didn't agree.

It was now Thursday, and things had only gotten worse. The day began hectically when Abbie slept past her alarm. Waking up at 6:52 when she normally rose at 5:00 put her in an immediate panic. She raced frantically to get to school. Her classes were rushed and out of sync throughout the entire day.

The hours after school only brought more frenzy: errands to the dry cleaners, pharmacy, and the grocery. The phone was ringing as Abbie unlocked the back door. She threw her book satchel and purse on the counter and lunged for the receiver.

"Hello." She held the phone to her ear with her shoulder as she tried to slide a plastic grocery bag off her wrist.

"Is Abbie Richardson in?" asked a firm, vaguely familiar voice.

"Yes, this is she." Abbie triumphantly slung the plastic bag onto the counter next to the sink.

"This is Keith Haliday from Timothy House."

"Oh, hi, Keith. How are you?" Abbie felt an unexpected flush rise in her cheeks.

She didn't want to admit to herself just how much she had remembered him.

"I'm fine, thanks. Look, I hope I'm not calling you at a bad time."

"Nope. I'm just walking in the door from school."

"We enjoyed having you and your friends, Lane and Eric, with us on staff at camp this summer." Abbie listened to the deep, confident tone of his voice. "You guys made a huge difference in the lives of some of those kids."

"Well, thanks, Keith. I'm not sure I knew what I was doing, but I had a great time. My son Drew really enjoyed it, too."

"I was very impressed with him. He's a fine young man."

"Thanks."

"I'm sorry it's taken me this long to get in touch with you. Look, I know this is late notice, but I'm going to be in McHenry on Saturday on some business for Timothy House. I was wondering if I could take you to lunch and have that visit we talked about."

Abbie was quiet for moment. The invitation caught her totally off guard.

"Abbie?" asked Keith.

"Uh, yes. I think that would be great. I was just thinking over my schedule for the rest of the week."

"You tell me a place, and I'll meet you. Normally, I'd come by and pick you up, but I have a meeting that morning that will probably run right up until lunch. Would twelve thirty be convenient?"

"Twelve thirty is perfect. The Whistle Stop Tea Room serves a great home-cooked special on Saturdays and is right downtown on Montgomery Street. Do you think you can find it?"

"I'll be there," replied Keith. "See you Saturday."

"I'll look forward to the visit. Have a safe trip."

"Will do. Good-bye now."

As Abbie hung up, she glanced at her daily calendar reading. "Delight yourself in the Lord, and He will give you the desires of your heart."

Across town, two heads were bowed as petitions were raised on Abbie's behalf. The ticking of a clock on Beulah's mantle serenaded a long silence.

"Lord," Audry began softly, "continue to heal the wounds in Abbie's heart. Do You have someone else in mind? Another man who can love Abbie like she deserves to be loved? Please, Jesus, bless our girl and make Your way clear to her."

The creaking from the runners of the old upholstered rocker and the ticktock of the mantle clock formed a gentle rhythm, accompanying powerful prayers to heaven's door.

Chapter Thirty-Two

"Oh, fiddle," said Abbie aloud to herself as she flipped through her closet. "Surely I can find something to wear. This is lunch and a glass of iced tea, not dinner and the opera."

Finally arriving on a selection she could live with, Abbie dressed quickly and hurried off to meet Keith at the Whistle Stop. The last part of this week had been so busy that she hadn't had time to think about this rendezvous.

As she drove down Montgomery Street looking for a parking space, Abbie felt the butterflies rise in her stomach. *Ridiculous*, she thought as she turned off the ignition. *How hard can this be?*

She spotted Keith's tall frame through the front window of the café. He met her at the door and pushed it open for her. A shiver of uncertainty went through her, but Abbie put on a brave face, hoping her smile looked convincing.

Keith asked for a booth in the back corner of the restaurant. Bright sunlight streamed in through the window next to the booth. Just beyond the panes, the leaves of a Bartlett pear swayed gently in the October breeze.

It didn't take long for the pair to make a decision. They both ordered the blue plate special, which on this Saturday included roasted pork loin, candied yams, green bean almandine, hot baked fruit, and cornbread or rolls. Keith ordered the blueberry pastry for dessert; Abbie selected the pudding.

Almost as soon as the waitress had taken their order, she was back at the table setting down plates brimming with food. "Hope you enjoy it," she said as she disappeared into the aisle of the crowded restaurant.

The delicious smells set Abbie's stomach to growling. She was greatly relieved when Keith asked to say the blessing.

He lifted his fork afterward and looked across to Abbie. "Shall we?"

Keith buttered half of his cornbread muffin. "So what did you think about Camp 4Ever?"

Abbie finished a sip of sweet tea. "Oh, I loved it, Keith. It was the most fun I've had in a long while. I felt like I really made a difference, if only for a few children. That's more fulfillment than I've had lately."

"Having second thoughts about your current job?" Keith speared a slice of yam with his fork.

"Some days, yes. Other days, no. Something's missing. I just can't quite put my finger on it."

"I know what you mean." Keith took a long sip of tea. "That's how I felt when I was in pharmaceutical sales. I'm what you call a late bloomer in educational circles."

"Really? I just assumed you'd always been a coach."

Keith grinned. "I only wish Coach Jamison, my college basketball coach, could see me now. I played four years for him at Reserve Eastern. Science was my major. It was something I had a natural bent for. Let's just say, one thing led to another, and before I knew it, I was making a really handsome paycheck selling drugs. The legal kind, that is."

Abbie grinned and put down her fork.

"If you looked at Genny and me, you'd say we had the perfect life, but we didn't."

"Yeah, people used to say that about Joe and me."

Keith looked at her for a long moment as her voice took on a hard, edgy tone at the mention of Joe's name.

"By every worldly standard, I was successful. I was making so much money that I couldn't see straight, but the job took me away from my family. Genny began to resent raising two children virtually on her own. Over time, I developed an awareness from somewhere deep inside that I was missing something, that I ... perhaps we ... had made a wrong turn on life's road."

Keith rambled on but after a while it was apparent that Abbie was not following him. She was watching his face all right, but she was lost in thought miles away.

"Hey," Keith said, "I know this is pretty boring. Enough about me."

His interjection snapped Abbie back to real time from wherever she had gone.

"Oh, no, Keith. Your story's not boring at all. I'm just sitting here thinking how ironically similar our lives have been in many respects." She took a sip of her tea. "You've told me where you started from. Now tell me how you got into education."

"Are you sure?" asked Keith a bit hesitantly. "'Cause it sure seems like I'm doing a lot of talking."

"I like listening to you talk." That and her warm smile were all the encouragement Keith needed.

"Well, Genny kidnapped me one weekend. We took three days to do some serious soul searching. It became obvious that we both wanted the same things. The money and lifestyle had medicated us, numbing us with the ease and comforts that often come with an abundance of material possessions." Keith adjusted the position of his iced tea glass.

"Genny was a straight shooter. She always had the ability to nail me with a hard question, especially when I was getting too big for my britches. She asked me that weekend what was something I had always wanted to do, regardless of the pay. Coaching high school basketball was it. I didn't even have to think about it. Once we got home, Genny encouraged me to go visit Coach Jamison."

Keith sorted through a pile of memories, deciding which one to share next.

"After a three hour heart-to-heart with Coach, I knew without a doubt what I wanted to do, touch the lives of young people like Coach had touched mine." Keith reached up in an unconscious movement to run strong fingers through his hair. "Over the next few years, I kept my pharmaceutical sales job but worked on the side to complete my alternate route certification. It's kind of a back door to get into education for people who were not ed majors. Fourteen years later, here I am."

"What a great story." She reached for her dessert. "What's

really amazing is how little difficulty you seem to have had with the transition."

"I guess it was because coaching was something I wanted to do, a dream finally fulfilled. It's never felt like work."

Keith changed the subject. "Given any thought to Don's offer?"

"Well." Abbie picked at her banana pudding. "Quite a bit, actually. It's just that a move like that would require changes I'm not sure I can afford."

Keith realized she was referring to the financial predicament in which Joe had left her.

"Even though things are better now, I still feel I've got to be extra careful, especially where finances are concerned. The loss of our savings isn't all Joe stole from me. Financial security is something I'll never take for granted again."

"I wish I had some great advice." Keith wiped a stray bit of blueberry popover from the corner of his mouth. "I'll pray for you. I know personally that Don would be delighted to have you join the Timothy House staff."

"Thanks. I certainly appreciate your kind comments and your offer to pray for me. Tell Don I'm seriously considering his offer."

Keith nodded in agreement. He leaned against the padded back of the booth and gazed across at Abbie, taking in each curve of her face as she talked. *She has no idea how beautiful she is*, he thought.

"If you don't mind me asking, what brought you to McHenry today?" Abbie's asked.

He hoped she was as truly interested in him as she seemed. For a split second, he entertained thoughts of telling her that he drove all this way just to see her. Keith told Abbie about his meeting earlier that morning with Chuck Hawthorne. A McHenry businessman and valued Timothy House board member, he was also a generous contributor to the scholarship program.

Keith glanced down at his watch and was amazed to find that it was already 2:30. *How could two hours have flown by so quickly?* he thought.

"Well, Abbie." He folded his napkin and placed it on the table. "I hate to break up this pleasant afternoon, but I have to get back on the road to Robbinsonville. We've got a function tonight on campus that I'm expected to attend."

He couldn't be sure, but it looked like Abbie was as disappointed as he was to end this luncheon date.

After settling up at the front counter, Keith followed Abbie out of the Whistle Stop. A gentle breeze blew a few brightly colored leaves down the sidewalk. *How I wish this time didn't have to end*, thought Keith, watching the sunlight play on Abbie's hair.

"Keith, thanks for a delightful lunch. I thoroughly enjoyed it," Abbie said. "It was so good to see you again."

Keith smiled. "I'm glad we could get together." He clasped her soft hand warmly in a firm handshake. "Know that you'll be in my prayers, Abbie." He released her hand.

"Have a safe drive back to Robbinsonville and tell Don I said hello."

With a wave, Abbie turned and was gone down the sidewalk.

Keith headed off in the opposite direction, grinning to himself all the while. He turned back to glance at her when he reached the corner of Montgomery and Broad and caught sight of her getting into her SUV.

"Take care of her, Lord," he prayed as he turned the ignition in his Explorer. "Abbie Richardson is a very special friend I don't want to lose."

Chapter Thirty-Three

Visitors spilled out of packed pews as the annual Timothy House Christmas Pageant ended. The performance was adorable, touching, hilarious, and poignant. The cast and crew received a standing ovation. Chloe had spotted Abbie immediately in the crowd. By now, the little girl was firmly entrenched in Abbie's heart.

"Miss Abbie! Miss Abbie!" Chloe's exuberant voice called out from the platform as Abbie made her way through the crowd to the front of the chapel.

Chloe was dressed as an angel, and her homemade gossamer wings quivered as she jumped up and down, unable to contain the excitement she felt.

"Sweet girl." Abbie wrapped Chloe tightly in a huge hug. "I have missed you." She stepped back and held the small girl out at arm's length. "Let me have a look at you. You've grown a foot since July."

Chloe beamed. "I've missed you, too, Miss Abbie." She pulled up the white floor-length choir robe that served as her angel's garb and dug around in the pocket of her blue jeans until she came up with what she was searching for. With a bright smile, she held out a small, crumpled piece of fabric in the upturned palm of her hand.

"Merry Christmas, Miss Abbie!"

"Oh, Chloe, thank you." Abbie took the offering.

"I made it all by myself," the little girl said.

Abbie tenderly unfolded the wrinkled square of muslin cloth and found a hand-sewn embroidered heart with "Miss Abbie" stitched in the middle. The bright colors of thread, placed unevenly on the cloth, were a testament to Chloe's tutelage in Doris' craft class.

"Chloe, it's wonderful!" exclaimed Abbie as she held the piece of cloth up to her heart and then held it out in front of her to look at it again. "It's the best Christmas present ever."

Abbie reached in her purse. "I've got a present for you, too." She pulled out a colorfully wrapped package.

She watched with delight as Chloe excitedly ripped the paper. Inside was a small photo album containing pictures of the week at Camp 4Ever. The last page contained a hand-lettered paraphrase of one of Abbie's favorite Bible verses: "Watch out and see how God will answer your prayers beyond your wildest hopes and dreams."

"This is neat, Miss Abbie." Chloe carefully turned the pages. "Wait till Donnie Gail sees this."

Just at that moment, the choir director motioned for Chloe to leave the chapel.

"I hate to break up your visit, but we have to get ready for bed."

After another huge hug, Abbie watched the small girl disappear out the side door of the chapel into the winter night.

Abbie, Lane, and Eric had enjoyed a leisurely drive up winding mountain roads to Robbinsonville this December Friday. A first snow two days earlier had dusted the woods and the mountain highway with a light sprinkling of white as if some holiday culinary elf had been overzealous with a sifter of powdered sugar. Don and Doris had invited the trio to be their guests for the entire weekend.

After the pageant, the Fieldings hosted coffee and dessert for a small gathering of faculty, including Keith. Abbie hadn't told him that she was coming. She enjoyed their lunch in November. He had called her once more just to check in and say hello, but other than that, they hadn't had any contact. He spotted her earlier at the play and spoke to her at intermission. Abbie was surprised how glad she was to see him.

Now familiar with the Fielding home, Abbie made her way over to the large sideboard, brimming with desserts.

As she was pouring herself a cup of hot cider, a familiar voice greeted her. "Abbie, this is certainly an unexpected surprise."

She felt a blush rising on her cheek as she turned to see Keith standing beside her.

"Hello yourself, Keith." A bit nervous, Abbie took a sip of the steaming liquid. Her bright eyes, however, never left his.

"How have you been?" Keith moved a little closer to her in the crowded room. "Did you drive up with the Wyatts?"

"Yes, we arrived late this afternoon. We were lucky to find a seat in the chapel. Weren't the kids terrific?" She took another sip of the cider.

"They were." Keith reached past her to select a cookie. "In fact, I've heard Chloe ask Don several times over the past few days whether you would be here tonight."

He turned around for a minute as if looking for someone. He turned back to Abbie. "You need him to tell you what she said. You've made quite an impression on that little girl."

His kind words and bright smile warmed Abbie's heart. "I'll try to do that." She noticed how his piercing dark blue eyes rarely missed a detail of any encounter or situation.

"Look, I'm really sorry I haven't gotten in touch with you since our last visit. These last few weeks have flown by."

Abbie sensed the look in Keith's eyes revealed the sincerity of his words. "Don't think a thing about it. I of all people know how the school year flows."

I wonder if he thinks about me just as much as I have been thinking about him, she thought.

Several faculty members in search of refreshment joined them at the sideboard, forcing a quick end to the conversation.

"Look." Keith moved out of the way of another guest. "Are you staying the weekend?"

"I am. Doris is taking Lane and me shopping in the morning, but we'll all be at the vesper service tomorrow night."

By now, Abbie and Keith had gotten separated as several guests filled the space between them. Strains of "White Christmas" could be heard faintly above the murmur of lively conversation.

"I'm glad you're here, Abbie. I'll catch up with you later." Keith waved a hand toward her and then disappeared into the crowd.

As she talked with several other Timothy House faculty members,

Abbie found herself replaying the impromptu conversation just shared with Keith. For a moment tonight, she'd felt like the belle of the ball. She smiled to herself as she remembered her nervous excitement at seeing him.

Once more before the evening was over, Abbie spotted Keith across the Fielding's living room, his towering frame a head above the crowd. She couldn't help but notice how strikingly handsome he was and how nice it was to have a man pay attention to her again. He certainly was comfortable to be with.

In almost the same instant, Abbie wondered why she was attracted to this particular man. If she were totally honest with herself, she'd have to admit that she had in fact spent a great deal of time thinking about Keith Haliday. Her emotions concerning him flip-flopped this way and that. *What if Keith turned out to be like Joe? Dishonest and deceitful?* she thought.

As soon as this thought crossed her mind, Abbie recognized it as a defense mechanism, a protective shield she'd forged around her heart. How much easier to push someone like Keith away rather than let him in to the hidden chambers of her heart. *I blindly trusted Joe,* she thought, *and what good had that done?*

As Abbie said goodnight to Doris and Don, she caught one last glimpse of Keith across the room. She stepped out onto the front porch into the crisp December night to wait on Lane and Eric. An unexpected wave of anger and frustration chilled her like the night air, casting a damper on her spirits.

She knew now that she had some serious work ahead regarding Winnie's encouragement to "Aim small; miss small." She wrapped her arms tightly around herself and silently prayed that God would free her heart from this prison and give her the courage to trust others again. If she didn't, a relationship with Keith or any other man would surely melt away like the December snow.

Chapter Thirty-Four

On Saturday, Doris led Abbie and Lane through several antique shops, their wares ranging from near-museum quality to shabby chic. They ate a late lunch at a diner on the main square of Robbinsonville, catty-corner from the courthouse. Abbie afforded herself a rare luxury, a nap, later that afternoon. In the evening, Eric, Lane, and Abbie shared a light dinner in the kitchen of the cottage. Around 6:40, they started out across campus for the vesper service. The air was cold and crisp.

Stars hung like jewels in the night sky as the group walked quietly to Peter's Chapel. Named in honor of Jesus's beloved disciple, Marie O'Ferrall, the founder's wife, had painstakingly designed this building in 1939. She believed the children of Timothy House needed exposure to beauty as well as knowledge. Toward this end, she had imported the antique windows from England while the chapel was under construction. This night, their panes were ablaze with muted jewel tones, mirroring the glow of hundreds of candles lit around the room.

This prayer service, much like the Christmas pageant, was another Timothy House tradition and had become popular with local townspeople as well as with families of students. Tonight marked the formal end of the first semester. Early tomorrow morning, the kids would head home for a two-week break. The atmosphere in the chapel was sacred and solemn.

Of all the endless holidays she had weathered alone since Joe's death, Christmas was the hardest. It had always been Abbie's favorite holiday of the entire year. She had made an extra effort in her own marriage to make every Christmas as special as possible, perhaps since she had been so emotionally starved in her own childhood. She only wished the holiday had meant the same for Joe.

Joe had been all about appearances, constantly demanding that the house be decorated to perfection, especially during December. At the time, Abbie just thought it was part of the perfect life plan she and Joe had been living out, the perfect house and the perfect decorations. She was beginning to understand that Joe's focus had been primarily on the secular aspect of the holiday. Her heart ached with the knowledge that Joe totally missed the heart of Christmas, the real "reason for the season."

The vesper service was moving. The homily drew the listener straight to the Christ Child who came all those thousands of nights ago. "O come, let us adore Him. O come, let us adore Him. O come, let us adore Him. Christ the Lord." The strains of the Christmas hymn faded away as the service ended. Abbie quietly blew out her candle and placed it in the rack on the pew in front of her. She looked around the sanctuary. The room was warm and intimate in the candle glow. The dimly lit stained glass window over the altar cast a luminous glow over the room.

Abbie turned to pick up her coat and saw families hugging and embracing, sharing smiles and tender looks. Wistfully, she remembered similar moments with her own family. She blinked back tears and drew in a deep breath, squared her shoulders, and stepped into the aisle. *No matter,* she thought. *Drew will be home soon for the holidays.*

Keith had seen Abbie when he first arrived for the service and purposefully sat near her. As he watched her stand and gather her coat from the pew, he saw tears in her eyes. He totally understood. He had been blinking back some of his own. He walked to the back of the chapel and waited for her near the last pew. Abbie, deep in thought, almost walked right past him.

"Merry Christmas, Abbie," said Keith quietly.

She looked up. "Oh, Keith." Abbie gave him a soft smile. "Hey, Merry Christmas, yourself. I'm sorry. I didn't see you."

"I spotted you when you came in, but I didn't want to bother you." He took a deep breath. "Look, I know this is really on the spur of the moment, but would you like to grab a cup of hot chocolate? Gravlee's is

134

the local hangout, and they serve the best cocoa. I don't know if you have plans already with your friends or not." Keith stepped back into the pew so Abbie could make her way out the door.

"I'd like that very much. Let's just find Eric and Lane so I can tell them, and then we can go."

He smiled to himself and thought, *Way to go, big guy! One point for the home team!*

Chapter Thirty-Five

On the drive across town, Keith and Abbie enjoyed small talk about a variety of subjects. The main focus of their conversation tended to center around their work. As he listened to Abbie talk, Keith thought about how comfortable it was to be with her.

Gravlee's was a popular gathering place in Robbinsonville. The menu featured a blue plate special served, of course, on blue china. That night, the dessert was "to die for" chess pie, served warm right out of the oven. Keith ordered two large slices and two cups of Gravlee's famous hot chocolate from his favorite waitress.

Teencie Curtis made it her business to learn every steady customer's name by heart, and she had taken a good-natured liking to Keith as soon as he became a member of the Robbinsonville community. She knew the sad tale of his great loss. After serving dessert, she busied herself at the counter and gave the couple some space.

Keith and Abbie enjoyed a few minutes of polite conversation as they savored the pie. Once they finished, Keith's tone lowered, and his look became more serious. "Abbie," he said gently. "I couldn't help but notice your tears in the chapel tonight. I'm sorry that Christmas is such a hard season for you. If it makes any difference, I know how you feel."

Abbie sat quietly for a long while. For a minute, it looked like she would burst into tears, but after a few swallows and a sip of her hot chocolate, she seemed to regain her composure. "Thank you. Knowing that is a great comfort."

Keith stared down at his mug, lost somewhere far away from this time and place. Finally, in a voice barely above a whisper, he said, "It's been seven years since they died, and it never gets any easier." He looked up to meet her gaze, and his piercing indigo eyes swam with tears. "Do you mind if we get out of here?" he asked in a husky voice. "I need some fresh air."

Abbie nodded her consent. After settling up with Teencie, the pair headed out into the crisp December night.

"Let's take a walk." Keith led her down the sidewalk. "I want to show you something."

They walked in silence. Puffs of air now visible from their breath accompanied the sound of their footsteps. Keith led Abbie across the street to the county courthouse, the centerpiece of the Robbinsonville main square. They made their way to a gazebo located in a corner of the building's snow-dusted lawn. Large, sweeping oaks sheltered the small structure beneath their strong arms.

After sweeping away a bit of snow accumulated on one of the benches, Keith motioned for Abbie to sit down. Once she was settled, he took a seat beside her. "This is one of my favorite spots. It's a great place to come at night, especially when I need to think. The trees practically obscure this place from the street. It's like being in a tree house, only you don't have to climb."

Abbie looked around at the old, wooden structure. It was octagonal in shape, and its weathered timbers had surely witnessed many encounters, whispered conversations, and stolen kisses. Delicate gingerbread trim served as walls. Three benches provided ample seating room under a tile roof.

They sat silently for a while. The words unsaid were suspended like snowflakes in the night air around them.

"I know it's a bit chilly. How are you holding up?" Keith asked.

Abbie rubbed her hands together briskly. Her gloves made a muffled swatting sound. "I hate to ask you this." She blew her warm breath over her chilled fists. "But could we go sit in your car? I'm afraid I'm turning into Frosty."

Keith grinned. "You're a whole lot cuter than Frosty." He stood up and reached down to help her stand. "Race you to the car."

They half-walked, half-ran the short block to his Explorer. Once inside, Keith cranked up the motor. "Let's drive around for a bit until you thaw out."

They exchanged small talk as Keith drove the pair through the streets and back roads of the small town. A thin layer of powdery snow covered their surfaces. Their short journey ended where it began, in a parking space near the gazebo on the Robbinsonville town square.

"Just seems right we finish swapping stories where we began." He reached behind his seat and got a wool blanket. "Spread that over you, Frosty Girl."

Abbie grinned and took the warm coverlet from him. Keith helped her wrap it around herself.

"Sorry about leaving the café so abruptly." He turned to face her. "There are just times when the memories come out of nowhere. Taking a walk seems to help." He took a deep breath. "I need to tell you about my family."

"Keith, you don't have to tell me anything," broke in Abbie. "I understand." She shivered slightly and drew the blanket up underneath her chin.

Keith looked Abbie squarely in the eyes and smiled. "I know you do, Abbie, and that's exactly why I want you to know about Genny and our kids."

Keith stared down at his gloved hands, rubbing them back and forth as if vacillating between two hard choices. As he began, he looked not at Abbie, but out into the night beyond.

"This time of year is really hard for me," he said softly. "Christmas Eve is a time when families are supposed to be together. Instead, I found myself attending my family's funeral on a Christmas Eve seven years ago. I guess you could say we were together, sort of.

"We were living in Chancellors, a little bedroom community just outside Richmond, Virginia. I was the varsity boys' basketball coach for Mountain Laurel High School. Our team, the Cougars, traveled to Dodson, about seventy miles away, to play Stanton Academy. The game was really tight. We won seventy-four to seventy-one in double overtime, which put us in first place for the district playoffs."

Keith looked back down at his hands again. "Genny, David, and Amanda were waiting for me outside the locker room after the game.

They were so excited! This was one of my first really big wins at Mountain Laurel. I had promised the players we'd go get ice cream if we won the game.

"I kissed Genny and hugged the kids. They had a long drive home, and I wanted them to get back on the road. That was the last time I saw them. Why didn't I invite them to come get ice cream with the team?" His voice faded off.

Abbie waited wordlessly until he could continue.

"A drunk driver hit them head-on about twenty miles outside of Chancellors."

Tears spilled over Abbie's lashes and dripped silently, slipping off her knitted scarf onto the blanket drawn around her.

"The driver who hit them was a twenty-seven year old with a suspended license and three previous DUI convictions. The Breathalyzer registered an alcohol level two times the state limit. The guy walked away with only a few bruises and scrapes."

As Keith unloaded more and more of his story, Abbie occasionally reached up to wipe her eyes.

"I still can't remember much about the days after the wreck. What I do remember was sobbing for hours on end, days at a time, and asking God why. Every time I closed my eyes, all I saw were Genny and the kids."

"How old were your children?" Abbie asked gently.

"David was seventeen. He was a junior that year. He was a football guy himself, but he never missed one of my games. Amanda was fourteen. She was so beautiful. They were in the prime of their lives." Keith stopped again and stared out onto the courthouse lawn. After a long while, he turned to look at Abbie.

"How did you ever finish the school year?" she asked softly.

"I'm really not sure, to tell you the truth." Keith laughed. "My assistant coach was terrific and coached my guys through the district tournament. We'd have been sunk, for sure, without him.

"As spring came, I knew there wasn't any way I could remain at Mountain Laurel. I saw my kids everywhere. I heard their voices constantly. I finally told my principal in March that it wasn't fair to the team or the school for me to stay on when my life was in such a mess. Telling my guys good-bye was one of the hardest things I've ever done.

"For a time, I went back to the job with Buechner. I ran into Don at a men's retreat, and he eventually led me to Timothy House." He took a deep breath and expelled it in a long sigh.

Abbie's quiet voice broke the silence between them. "Thanks, Keith. It means a great deal that you trust me enough to tell me. My ordeal with Joe pales in comparison to what you've endured. I just wish there was a way I could take away some of the awful pain you feel."

Keith reached for Abbie's hand. He looked for a moment at her small hand nestled between his two large ones and then gently placed it back on her lap. He looked back into her eyes. "You already have, sweet Abbie. You already have. Now tell me about Joe."

Chapter Thirty-Six

For the next half hour, Abbie opened up a part of herself to which only a few other people had been allowed access. Tentatively at first, she shared with Keith the details of Joe's heart attack and the numbing grief of the days that followed.

"I battled a pretty desperate bout of depression, although I never went to see anyone about it. I had a teenage son depending on me. I simply couldn't afford to fall apart. I knew I had to keep going somehow for Drew. When it all got too heavy, I'd get in my car and drive for hours, up through the mountain roads above McHenry. One afternoon, I thought to myself, 'How hard could it be to just miss a curve and sail down to the valley floor below?'"

They were both silent for a long while.

"What kept you from doing it?" Keith finally asked.

Abbie hesitated for a moment. "You're the only person I've ever told this story to, but in some strange way, I think you'll understand. For a split second, I contemplated driving my car over the brow of Little Piney Ridge. Then I heard a voice say to me, 'I have plans for you, my child. Do no harm.' I've never heard the voice before or since, but it was loud enough to cause me to pull off the road onto the shoulder and pull myself together. Do you think I totally lost it?"

Keith looked her square in the eye. "No, Abbie, just the opposite. I think you found it. I think you heard God's voice on the mountain that day, and I'm so glad that you listened to it."

"Well, some days I'm not so sure. This year has been a year of searching for me, of trying to put all the pieces of my life back together. One of my good friends suggested I focus on just one small part at a time." She smiled as she thought of Winnie and her no-nonsense approach to life.

Abbie described how hard it had been to make ends meet financially for her and Drew, of how sobering it was knowing that she was now the sole financial provider for Drew and herself and not knowing where that money would come from, of how alone she had felt.

After she finished her story, Keith said quietly, "Abbie, the man you've just described to me is not the Joe Richardson I knew in college. I don't know what happened to him."

Abbie replied after a long silence. "I don't either. If you had told me twenty-one years ago that I would be sitting here telling someone this story of my life, I would have never believed it."

"Satan must have somehow gotten his hooks into Joe because the Joe I knew at nineteen was so on fire for the Lord." Keith shook his head. "What a tragic ending to such a promising start. How's your son holding up?"

"Amazingly well. Thanks for asking." Abbie smiled and thought of Drew's bright spirit. "Drew was seventeen when Joe died, and he took it really hard. He was just finishing his junior year. God has provided a terrific group of adults who have rallied around Drew through these last years and helped him get back on track. He's set to graduate from college this next May."

Keith waited silently for Abbie to continue.

"Drew's still trying to sort out how he feels about his father. I can tell he's still dealing with anger issues. He feels like his dad betrayed him. Drew was forced to tough it out alone in a season of life that might otherwise have been a great adventure. Funny now that I think about it." Abbie brushed her hair back behind her ear. "Joe really abandoned us both years ago. Drew never knew what it was like to have a dad's wisdom, a shoulder to lean upon."

Abbie looked somewhere far out into the dark night that surrounded them. "I grew up in a very dysfunctional family with an alcoholic parent, and because of that, I've worked especially hard over the years to make sure my relationship with Drew was secure, that he never for one minute doubted my love or commitment to him. I'm just sorry his father didn't do the same. Drew's such a great guy. Sometimes it's hard to believe he's really my son. I'm very proud of all the effort he's made to put his life back on track."

"All I can say," Keith said, "is Drew is very lucky to have such a courageous woman for a mother."

For a long while, neither Abbie nor Keith spoke. They were both aware that something sacred and special had passed between them, and they didn't want to disturb the moment.

"Abbie," Keith said, "I really enjoyed tonight. You're so comfortable to be with. Just knowing that you understand what I've gone through means a great deal to me. I hope you and I can be friends. I certainly feel that we already are."

Abbie, touched by his words and his honest, forthright manner, looked down for a long while at his strong hands and struggled to gather her thoughts before responding.

"I welcome your friendship. It's been a long time since I've felt like I had someone who could empathize with me. The lack of relationship, especially with a spouse, has always been the hardest part of this time of year for me to deal with emotionally, especially in light of all the damage Joe caused. I'll be praying for you during this holiday season."

"Thanks," said Keith with a wistful smile. "I'll pray for you, too. While we're on the subject of prayer requests, what are your thoughts about Don's job offer? He's talked with me at length about the possibility of you joining us here at Timothy House."

"I'm seriously considering it. Wow!" She brushed a wisp of dark hair from her face. "That's the first time I've said that aloud to another person. I have, though, spent lots of time talking to God about it. Moving here would mean major changes in my life, the most I've had to deal with in a few years. I promise you'll be one of the first to know when I reach a decision."

"Sounds fair to me." Keith slapped his hand on his knee. He glanced at his wristwatch. "Gee, I didn't mean to let the time slip away from me. It's almost eleven forty-five. I'm sure Eric and Lane are wondering where you are." He cranked the ignition and let the vehicle idle for a minute before backing the SUV out of the now-deserted downtown street and heading toward the Timothy House campus.

The pair rode in silence through the wintery night, the only sounds that of the motor and snow crunching beneath sturdy tires. The sound of roadway soon gave way to that of crushed gravel as Keith turned into the school's driveway and headed through the campus to the guest cottage.

He slipped out of his side of the Explorer and came around to open her door. He offered his hand and helped Abbie out. Once they reached the cottage door, she turned to tell him goodnight.

"Keith, thanks again for a lovely evening. I really enjoyed the visit. I hope you have a merry Christmas. Be sure and get some rest over the holidays. You deserve it."

Keith reached for her hand and took it gently in both of his. "Abbie, I enjoyed tonight, too. I hope you'll let me call you soon."

"I would like that." Keith brought her hand up to his mouth and kissed it lightly. "Merry Christmas, Abbie Richardson. You take care of yourself."

He released her hand and stepped back down the stone steps to his vehicle. As Abbie opened the door to the cottage, her last glimpse of Keith was of his smile and a hand raised in a wave good-bye.

Chapter Thirty-Seven

Abbie had practically bitten off Jacob Wooster's head near the end of first period.

"Mrs. Richardson," he had asked, "what's our homework for tonight?"

Abbie fought to maintain composure as she repeated to him what she had already explained to the class at the beginning of the period.

Melanie Simpkins received a withering glare, earned as a result of turning around to talk to Jill Satterwhite during fifth period. *Those two girls*, Abbie thought, *are going to be the death of my patience.*

Abbie made a mental note to herself to change the seating chart for that particular class. Even as she thought about rearranging her students, Abbie was painfully aware that what ailed her had nothing whatsoever to do with a seating chart. The disquiet lay deep within her soul.

At the end of the school day on this Wednesday afternoon, Abbie collected some stray pens, two paper clips, and fifteen cents in change from under the last desk in the fourth row of seats. Weariness pulled at every muscle and joint in her body. The cold, dreary January days were interminably long. Patience was wearing thin.

For weeks now, Abbie had been wrestling with the issue, trying desperately to come up with answers, though they continually eluded her. Did the Lord mean for her to keep teaching at Kent? Was this disquiet God's way of nudging her gently out of a nest that was too comfortable and familiar? How Abbie wished she could get to the bottom of what was troubling her.

Earlier in the week, Abbie and the rest of Kent's faculty received forms that would indicate a desire to be reconsidered for a teaching position for the upcoming school year. Commonly referred to in educational circles as intent-to-teach forms, they were due in early March. At the same faculty meeting, Mr. Patterson told the faculty that contracts would be in the mail by the end of March. Time was marching on. Abbie knew she needed to make a decision, one way or the other.

If Abbie were brutally honest with herself, her greatest discomfort, however, came from the mantle of discouragement settled over her spirit. She suffered from a divided heart. Joe's betrayal had stripped her of self-confidence and greatly impaired her decision-making abilities. Nothing made sense to Abbie anymore. Nothing was as it had been before, and it seemed it might never be the same again. It was as if she had waked up in a strange new world.

Abbie realized dissatisfaction with all aspects of her life had been slowly working its way to the surface over the past four years. Once Joe's dishonesty surfaced, doubt reached a fever pitch. Part of what wore Abbie down was the shame she felt due to Joe's financial misdeeds. McHenry was a small enough community that everyone knew everyone else.

Places and associations that had once been familiar in Abbie's world—church, school, community organizations, and social settings— now seemed alien. Too often she felt unwelcome and unwanted. Many people who had always before been friendly and outgoing now seemed distant and a bit standoffish. Perhaps it was only her imagination, but Abbie felt down deep in her heart that others blamed her somehow for Joe's wrongdoings.

The particulars of a lawsuit filed by a company who sued Richardson, Reynolds, and Wyatt for embezzlement were never reported publicly in the local newspaper. The damage, nevertheless, was done. "Richardson" was discreetly dropped from the firm's name, and although Abbie's friendship with Lane and Eric remained healthy and intact, the other lawyers in Joe's old firm now barely even spoke to her.

The cacophony of thoughts rolling around in her mind drowned out all sane thought. *How could I have been so duped? How in the world had Joe hidden this secret life he created?*

In these four years, the wound in Abbie's heart continued to fester. It was finally time for healing to begin.

Abbie headed up the hall to see Winnie. She'd been working on the Patriot Plan, and she needed some target practice.

"Hey, friend, got a minute?" Abbie plopped into a seat in front of Winnie's desk. It was almost 4:30, and most of the faculty had already left for the day.

"For you," Winnie said with a wide grin, "I've got all the time in the world. How's it going?"

"Well, I've been following the plan." Even as she said the words, she felt a little foolish. "Winnie, are you sure this is clinical advice?"

"Oh, Abbie, of course not." Winnie giggled as she ran her fingers through her wavy hair. "That's just my nickname for a way of taking huge problems and cutting them down to a manageable size. Would you feel better if I gave you some sophisticated, psychological term for the same course of action?" She leaned back in her chair and waited for her friend's reply.

Abbie wasn't quite sure how to ask the questions for the answers she needed. For a few moments, she carefully considered how to phrase her query.

"I've been giving a great deal of thought to my work and whether or not I really enjoy teaching." She offered a tentative smile to her trusted colleague and friend. "After a great deal of soul searching, I know I really do enjoy teaching. At least that much I am sure of. I'm still trying to determine if Kent Academy is the best place to do that work."

"That's great. At least you've hit one target successfully." Winnie's enthusiasm gave Abbie courage to pose her next question.

"God's been showing me that I have to find a way to get a handle on all the anger that I've stuffed down inside over all these years. Instead of dealing with it, I've used anger as an excuse to build walls around my heart and my mind. Like a princess in a tower, I need rescuing, but the great irony is this is a jail of my own making." After this admission, Abbie felt like a great weight had been lifted from her soul.

Winnie leaned forward in her chair. "Wow, Abbie. For a novice, you're a pretty good shot. I'd say you've just hit a bull's-eye!"

Abbie could see pure amazement on Winnie's face. "But, Winnie, where do I even begin?" Frustration accompanied her every word. "There are so many things I'm angry about: the years I feel I wasted with Joe, the fact that my son has damage of his own to deal with, the fact I worked so hard to have a good marriage, the fact I didn't even recognize mine for the sham it was …" Her words trailed off.

"Abbie," Winnie said quietly, "remember the plan. 'Aim small; miss small.' Make a list of the places in your life where you need healing. Writing it down will help." Winnie paused for a moment.

"Commit yourself to dealing with those issues one at a time." Winnie reached up and pulled her glasses off her head. "Remember, Abbie, this isn't going to happen overnight. You have to be patient with yourself and God."

Abbie nodded, too emotional to speak.

"You'll be surprised how much strength you'll find as you become more aware of what's eating away at you on the inside. Make that list a matter of prayer. Ask for His help."

In a voice barely above a whisper, Abbie asked, "Would you promise to pray for me about this? I can't do this alone."

"Girlfriend, you can count on a steady blanket of prayer from me. Just remember. God promises His children that He'll always make the path clear. You just have to keep your eyes on the Shepherd."

Chapter Thirty-Eight

Arthur Patterson's retirement announcement caught Abbie and the rest of the Kent Academy family completely off guard. A bulwark of the school and the greater community, he followed in the footsteps of the school's first principal. The beloved leader had been at Kent longer than most of the current faculty and provided continuity and a keen sense of direction for the school.

Abbie took a cake to the Patterson home on the Saturday after the startling announcement was made. Lucille, Mr. Patterson's wife, greeted her warmly at the door. She invited Abbie in and put on a pot of coffee. The three of them shared a tender heart-to-heart conversation.

Lucille's "just right" drip coffee was the perfect accompaniment to Abbie's lemon pound cake, still warm from the oven. The afternoon minutes stretched into elastic hours as the three friends laughed, cried, and reminisced about all the good and bad times they had shared together as a part of the Kent family.

"Abbie," Mr. Patterson said while reaching over to take Lucille's hand in his, "I realized I was giving the best of myself to other people and bringing the leftovers to my dear wife." A long silence followed as her slender fingers gently rubbed the top of her husband's large, square hand.

"I've loved being at Kent, but in every life, Abbie, there comes a time—a fork in the road, if you will—when a person has to choose which way to go. Our daughter, Janie, and her family live near Charlotte, North

Carolina, and they've invited us to move near them. Who knows? Maybe I'll get back into education as a volunteer in my grandson's preschool."

Later that afternoon, Mr. Patterson walked Abbie out to her car. "Thanks so much for coming by, Abbie. Your support of my decision means a lot to me and Lucille."

Abbie reached into her shoulder bag to locate her keys. After opening the car door, she paused before getting in. "Mr. Patterson, this afternoon you mentioned forks in the road of life. I wonder if I'm not at one of those forks, trying to decide whether or not to join the staff of Timothy House. How did you know which road to take?"

Abbie looked into the face of this man who had been her boss, employer, confidante, and friend for the last twelve years. *What an anchor he has been in my life*, she thought. Tears welled up in her eyes as the frustration of her own indecision rose to the surface.

"Abbie," he said quietly, "you and I are children of the king. As such, we will know … if we listen … when His voice is speaking. Listen within the still places of your own heart. The Lord will meet you there. Look for the presence of His peace in your heart and in that still small place within you. You will know." He reached over and gave Abbie a gentle hug. He held the car door as she climbed inside and buckled herself in.

"Thanks, Mr. Patterson." Abbie wiped away a stray tear. "Pray that I'll know the direction I need to take."

"I will, Abbie. I will."

Chapter Thirty-Nine

On this particular morning after their prayer time, Audry walked Abbie from the den to the front living room. Audry and Beulah had been meeting with Abbie on Wednesdays for the past four months to pray with Abbie about the Timothy House job offer. Their younger friend had been welcomed into their 6:00 early morning discipline. Just before departing for work, Abbie was always given a thermos filled with piping hot tea and a brown paper sack packed with freshly baked cappuccino muffins.

As Abbie pulled on her coat, Audry asked her in a low voice, "What keeps you from jumping off, from just going ahead and telling Arthur Patterson that you won't be back next year? It seems to me that, now that he's announced his retirement, the choice for you is clear-cut."

Audry waited patiently and watched the younger woman as she wrapped a paisley silk shawl around her neck. After adjusting it and buttoning up her long camel-colored reefer coat, Abbie stood silently. "I'm scared." Barely audible, the words hung like fog in the air between them.

"Scared." Audry stepped closer to Abbie and reached out to take both her hands. "Scared of what, sweetie?"

Audry tried to suppress a giggle but was unsuccessful in preventing its escape. However, a quick glance at the tears glistening in Abbie's eyes put an immediate end to any further outbursts.

Audry was immediately awash with chagrin. "Oh, Abbie," said this mother figure in Abbie's life. She gave both of Abbie's hands a quick squeeze, still holding them within her wrinkled grasp. "You're the bravest person I know."

Abbie looked down and shook her head slowly from side to side in denial of the declaration. "No, Audry, I'm a huge coward. Ever since Joe's death, it's like I'm stuck in concrete. I want to step out in faith with God, but my feet just won't move. I'm terrified."

Audry stepped back and looked into the younger woman's eyes. "Listen, Abbie," she said softly. "Do you remember that story in the Old Testament where Joshua is named leader of Israel after Moses's death? The people were to take the Ark of the Covenant with them and cross the Jordan River into the Promised Land. The Lord told them first to wade into the water, and then they would see Him at work."

Abbie reached into her coat pocket for a Kleenex. "My problem is that I'm afraid that I'll drown when I step into the water." She wiped away a tear.

"Dear Abbie, God's got His life preservers all around you: hope, faith, and courage you don't even know you have. He'll keep your nose above the water line, you'll see." She gently patted her younger friend on the arm.

Abbie pushed the tissue back down in her pocket. "I'll try, Audry. I really will." She offered a slight smile.

Audry reached up a soft hand to lift Abbie's chin. "Stick your toe in the water, dearie. God may be waiting on you to make the first move, and then He'll show you the rest of the way."

As Abbie headed off to school, Winnie's words rang through her mind. "Aim small; miss small." She thought, *Maybe Audry is right. Perhaps it is time to get my feet wet.*

Chapter Forty

Tonight was the February meeting of Loose Threads, and it was Abbie's turn to host the group. While waiting for a cake to bake, she checked her answering machine. The first two messages were from telemarketers, the third was from a political campaign on the upswing, and the fourth was a cheery message from Beulah saying she'd be by early around six to help Abbie get ready for the get-together. The last message was from Audry. Her voice sounded tired and strained as she explained that she was feeling a bit under the weather and wouldn't be able to make the meeting.

Abbie spent the next thirty minutes tidying up around her house. Satisfied that all was in order, she returned to the kitchen. She debated whether or not to call Audry, but curiosity and concern got the best of her. After setting out plates and forks for dessert, Abbie picked up the phone and dialed Audry's number. She was about to hang up when Audry answered, her voice weak and diminished.

Her dear friend's frailty alarmed Abbie.

"Audry, it's Abbie. I hope I'm not waking you up, but I just had to check on you. The message you left concerned me."

"Dear girl," replied Audry, sounding a little perkier. "I feel better already just hearing your voice. This has been a slow day. I just haven't been able to get going."

"Do you need anything?" Abbie tucked the phone between her ear and right shoulder and opened the oven door to remove the cake. She set the pan down on a hot pad. A delicious aroma wafted through her kitchen.

"No thanks. I took an extra dose of Geritol earlier. I'm sipping on a cold glass of orange juice right now. I'll be fine. Please tell the gals I said hello."

"All right," said Abbie, not feeling completely convinced. "I'll call you tomorrow. You just promise me that, if you need anything, you'll call me tonight, no matter the hour."

"I will, dearie. Good-bye now." Audry signed off.

As Abbie hung up the receiver, she whispered a short prayer for her friend, "Dear Father, please be with Audry and restore health to her. You know how much I love her. Please protect her."

True to her word, Beulah rang Abbie's doorbell precisely at six. Punctuality was one of Beulah's many qualities that Abbie admired. Abbie opened the door and flung her arms around her older friend. "Come in this house!"

"What smells so good?" Beulah put her quilting bag down on Abbie's den sofa.

"Oh, just a cake made from a new recipe I found recently. I hope it tastes good. You know how recipes can deceive you." Abbie headed back into the kitchen.

"If it tastes half as good as it smells, it'll be worth lappin' a lip over," said Beulah.

Abbie grinned to herself. Beulah was full of quaint, unusual sayings that never ceased to both amaze and amuse her. After putting on a fresh pot of coffee, the two friends returned to the den. Once seated, Abbie in her upholstered chair and Beulah on the sofa, Beulah looked over at Abbie with a serious look on her face.

"Abbie, there's something I've been praying about on your behalf. Honey, even though you haven't said too much, I think you're trying to decide what to do with this Keith fellow and how to fit him into your life."

Abbie felt her face grow very warm.

"I know these last four years have been extremely hard ones for you."

Abbie grinned wryly.

"I've been praying that you can come to some kind of a peace about all of this so you can get on with the rest of your life. Until you do, I'm worried you're going to miss out on some really special blessings that God may have right around the corner for you."

Abbie looked down and fiddled with her watch. Beulah had nailed her, cut right to the heart of the matter. As she tried to formulate an answer, she knew she didn't have one. Abbie also knew she had just about run out of excuses for delaying the decision about Timothy House. Her heart, however, was still precariously situated on a very tall fence where Keith Haliday was concerned.

"Oh, Beulah," Abbie began slowly. "I know I haven't handled any of this very well. You probably think I've lost all of my decision-making ability."

"No, sweetie, I don't think that at all," said Beulah gently as her deep brown eyes seemed to encourage her younger friend to continue.

"I am seriously considering calling Don Fielding soon." Abbie tried to sound positive. "You know Mr. Patterson has recently announced that he's going to retire. He's not really come out and said it, but I think he thinks I ought to take the job at Timothy House."

"Well, that's great," said Beulah cheerily. She pushed on to the awkward subject still hanging in the air between them. "What are you doing about all the pain in your heart? All of Joe's dirty laundry?"

"That's where I'm stuck." Tears glistened in Abbie's eyes. "I've been trying to reconcile within myself all the anger and pain that I feel where Joe is concerned. Winnie gave me some really good advice that I've tried to follow, to tackle these issues one at a time. It hasn't been easy."

Abbie narrowed her eyes. "What still galls me is how duplicitous he was and how stupid I feel for never having figured out any of what was going on while he was alive. Joe was supposed to be a Christian, a godly man. How could he have done this to me?"

The words spoken felt like a thick hedge that had sprung up around her heart. Its dense foliage-covered branches hemmed her in. Its sharp, prickly thorns prevented her from making any progress.

Beulah's bright eyes met Abbie's and smiled gently. "We're all prodigals, Abbie. Some just wander a little farther off God's front porch than others."

Abbie fought hard to maintain her composure.

"Sweet Abbie, you're not responsible for Joe's actions. There was probably no way you could have stopped him. Addictions, honey, are incredibly strong and terribly hard to conquer. You are, however, responsible for your own actions, your thoughts, and your response to what has happened to you.

"The way I see it, you have two choices. You can hold all the anger and pain tightly in your heart and in your hand, much like a toddler does when grasping a toy, or you can unclasp your fingers, open your hand, and offer back to God all your hurt as a sacrifice. Give it to Him so He can put all those pieces together, working them out for good in your life."

Abbie nodded.

"God is a gentleman, Abbie. He won't force you to open your heart, but His cleansing, life-changing power can't operate deep within you until you do." Beulah's short sermon was finished.

The ring of the doorbell interrupted. The two rose, and Beulah wrapped Abbie in her arms.

"You talk to God, sweet girl," she whispered. "He'll help you lay all this to rest. God has really big shoulders. It's time you let Him carry this burden for you."

Abbie squeezed Beulah tightly. "I love you, Beulah Tanner. I don't know what I'd do without you in my life." She stepped back and wiped tears away with the cuff of her sleeve. "I better get myself together. The girls will wonder what's wrong."

"You run and throw some cold water on your face." As Beulah headed toward the ringing doorbell, she chirped, "I'll let in the thundering herd." Her silver-crowned head disappeared through the doorway.

Abbie headed quickly up the stairway, a silent prayer forming on her lips. She turned on the light in her bathroom, and she could hear faint voices and snatches of laughter from below. The cool water felt refreshing on her hot, tear-stained face. After a few quick dabs of color from her makeup bag, Abbie ran a brush through her hair. She drew in a deep breath. For the first time in a very long while, the air felt clean and fresh. She bounded down the stairs to the fellowship and friendship awaiting her with the gals of Loose Threads.

Chapter Forty-One

Abbie's life had been put on hold. Every spare moment had been spent at the nursing home since Audry's stroke on March 5. Beulah had called Abbie early on that Friday to tell her that the nursing staff at Shelter Cove had been unable to wake Audry. "Unresponsive" was the term the nurse had used.

Audry had only been at the assisted living home for about two weeks prior to suffering the stroke. Years ago, Audry had the foresight to establish a living will that stipulated "no heroic or extraordinary measures" be taken to prolong her life in the event of a life-threatening incident. As such, once Dr. Stephenson determined that Audry's unresponsive state was in all likelihood permanent, she was placed on oxygen, and the natural process of dying was allowed to progress.

Abbie rose from the tapestry-covered glider rocker and crossed the short distance to the bed where Audry lay. The only sounds in the room came from the steady hum of the window air-conditioning unit and the oxygen pump. She took out an ivory-colored hairbrush from the bedside dresser drawer and gently stroked Audry's silky hair. The shoulder-length strands gleamed like burnished silk around her face.

Tenderly, Abbie picked up Audry's withered hand and brought it gently to her lips. She continued holding Audry's hand in her own for a time. Then she placed it back under the sheets with great care. Abbie tucked the soft white cotton blanket up around this dear friend's shoulders and returned to her post in the glider rocker.

Abbie left Shelter Cove about ten that night. Around two the next morning, the ringing of the phone brought her up from a deep sleep. Audry's long battle was over at last. After placing the receiver back onto the base, Abbie slipped from under the covers to her knees to kneel beside her bed. Hot tears coursed down her cheeks as she thanked God for every remembrance of her dear friend, Audry McCormick. The digital clock was ticking off the minutes toward four when Abbie finally laid her head on the pillow.

☙

Two days later, Dr. Franklin preached a wonderful memorial service. The mainly older crowd made their way to Beulah's home afterward for a home-cooked feast many of them had prepared. Murphy Gates made his way across Beulah's living room as the crowd thinned.

"Abbie, I'm so sorry about Miss Audry's death," he said in a low, soothing voice. Murphy's solid stature and relaxed manner put others instantly at ease. "I know how close the two of you were."

"Thank you, Murphy." Abbie received his arm around her shoulders in a comforting hug. "There will definitely be a terrific void in my life, but I know Audry is safely in heaven now with Jesus and I will see her again. She would want us all to be happy about her homegoing."

"She certainly would." Murphy released Abbie's shoulder. "I hate to bother you at this time, Abbie, but there are some legal matters regarding Audry's estate that I need to discuss with you. Is there any way you could run by my office in the next day or two?"

"Legal matters? I'm afraid I don't understand." Abbie's brain was in a whirl.

"Well, Miss Audry left part of her estate to you. I know this is probably quite a shock, but I think you'll also be pleasantly surprised. Would Tuesday around four o'clock work for you? That should give you time to get finished with your school day."

"Uh, sure, Murphy," Abbie said. A wave of curiosity rose within her. "I'll see you then."

As she left Beulah's home later that evening, Abbie wondered to herself, *What ever could Audry have left to me?*

Chapter Forty-Two

Three days later, Abbie's SUV pulled out of Kent Academy's campus, and ten minutes later, she parked in front of a two-story, brick colonial-style office building. Murphy's office was on the second floor.

Wilma Jennings, Murphy's secretary, lit up when Abbie entered the office. She stood to give Abbie a hug as she rounded the corner of the reception desk. Abbie had taught Wilma's oldest daughter, Carly. Wilma often told Abbie that, whenever she ran into her, how Carly still talked about Mrs. Richardson, even though she was now grown with a family of her own. After exchanging a few pleasantries and updates on their children, Wilma escorted Abbie into a small conference room, tastefully appointed with antique furniture and oil landscapes. A Staffordshire bone china coffee service graced the sideboard.

"Could I offer you some coffee, Abbie?" asked Wilma as she crossed the room to the sideboard.

"That would be great, Wilma. Thanks." Abbie settled in a leather armchair at the far side of the rectangular conference table.

"What do you take in it, honey?" Wilma's hand held a small sugar scoop and paused for action over a porcelain bowl.

"Sweet'N Low and lots of cream. I like my coffee pretty blond." Abbie smiled at Wilma.

As Wilma turned around from the sideboard with Abbie's coffee in hand, the door to the conference room opened, and Murphy entered, appearing a bit flustered.

"I apologize for keeping you waiting, Abbie." Murphy pulled out a chair. "It's been a bear of an afternoon. More work than minutes." He placed a large brown accordion file on top of the table and sat down.

Wilma placed the floral-patterned porcelain cup and saucer near Abbie's right hand and patted her gently on the shoulder. She closed the door quietly as she left the conference room.

"No bother, Murphy. I enjoyed getting to see Wilma and catch up on her family news. I haven't seen her in a while."

"She certainly keeps me in line." Murphy chuckled. "If she ever retires, I'll be in lots of trouble."

Murphy picked up the file and slid the elastic cord from around its bulky girth. He folded back the flap, slid his hand into the pocket, and withdrew a small box, a sealed envelope, and a sheaf of papers. After placing the file folder on the table, Murphy slid the box over in front of Abbie. The sheaf of papers remained in front of him.

Curiosity tingled within Abbie. She clasped her hands together under the edge of the conference table, gently rubbing the palm of her left hand with her right thumb, a nervous habit developed years ago. She waited for Murphy to speak.

"Well, Abbie, no need delaying good news. I'll explain to you in layman's terms exactly what Audry has bequeathed to you. After that, if you have any questions, I can read directly from the text of the will, which I have here in front of me."

Abbie's heart pounded. A strange yet sure sense of calm surrounded her.

"In the box, Abbie, you will find the diamond ring that Miss Audry always wore." A small gasp escaped Abbie's lips. "I think you know her fiancé, Bill Norris, gave it to her. Miss Audry wanted you to have it."

Tentatively, Abbie reached out and picked up the small cloth box. The rich black of its velvet cover had faded long ago. Its hue was now closer to a dull red. The velvet fibers were worn off in several places on the box's domed cover, showing evidence of being handled frequently through the years. Abbie grasped the top of the box and carefully lifted the hinged lid. A carat-and-a-quarter stone caught the gleam of the overhead fluorescent office light and winked at Abbie as she pulled the ring from the box's white satin interior.

"I don't know what to say." Abbie gingerly held the ring between her forefinger and thumb. For several minutes, she could only look at it, turning it occasionally from side to side.

"Well," said Murphy, breaking the silence, "aren't you going to try it on? Miss Audry was really excited about passing this treasure on to you."

"I guess so," stammered Abbie, a bit embarrassed by the gift.

She tried it on her right ring finger, as she wasn't yet ready to place another ring on her left hand. She slipped Audry's special gift over the second knuckle of the finger. The antique filigreed silver band fit like a glove. Abbie could hardly believe it.

"It is so beautiful," cooed Abbie softly.

She fanned out her hand in front of her face, enjoying the old stone's fire. Her eyes glistened as she realized the enormity of Audry's generosity.

Murphy allowed Abbie a few minutes to collect her thoughts. After a while, he cleared his throat, the sound breaking the spell in the small conference room.

"Abbie," said Murphy gently, "Miss Audry left this letter for you." He slid a plump envelope across to Abbie. She tentatively brushed the parchment surface with her fingers, gently caressing her name written across the front in Audry's familiar scrawl. "Miss Audry specifically asked that you take it home to read at your leisure."

"Thank you, Murphy," was all Abbie could manage to say.

"There is one more bit of business to discuss with you, Abbie, and it concerns a stipulation of Miss Audry's will." Murphy picked up the sheaf of papers stapled together that lay on the table at his left elbow.

As he grasped the cover page, Abbie could read its title, "Last Will and Testament of Audry Rose McCormick." She waited, unsure of what was to follow. *The gift of the ring*, she thought, *was certainly too generous in itself. How could there possibly be more?*

Murphy withdrew a pair of horn-rimmed reading glasses from his coat pocket, placed them on his square face, and began to read. "I do hereby bequeath Abigail Ellis Richardson a monetary gift in the amount of two hundred and fifty thousand dollars. The said amount is to be used for purposes spelled out in accordance with this will within the letter she will receive." Murphy pulled off his glasses and waited for Abbie to speak.

All Abbie heard for a long while was the pounding of blood rushing through her temples. *Surely I have misunderstood. Two hundred and fifty thousand dollars? Where in the world did Audry get that kind of money?* she thought.

Tears that only threatened minutes earlier now appeared in full force and ran down Abbie's surprised face. "Oh, Murphy." Abbie reached in her purse for a Kleenex. "I don't know what to say. Why on earth would Audry leave this to me?"

Murphy settled back a bit in his armchair. "Well, Abbie." He ran both hands over the well-worn arms of the chair. "I don't know all the answers to the puzzle. I think the letter will answer most of the questions you have. When Audry brought it to me back in December, she said her gifts would make sense once you read the letter.

"As for the money, Audry was always frugal. She was a woman who lived well below her means, and as you can see, that lifestyle yielded great dividends for her. Of course, now," added Murphy with a smile, "those dividends will pay off for you as well."

"Murphy, I'm totally blown away. Surely there's someone in Audry's family, a niece or a nephew, who is more deserving of this money than I am. I'm not even related to Audry." Abbie dabbed away more tears escaping her soft green eyes.

"Don't you worry, Abbie. Miss Audry left her extended family well cared for. If she told me once, she told me a thousand times that you were the daughter she never had. I trust her words, better than mine, will properly convey how special you were to her."

Over the next few minutes, Murphy helped Abbie fill out a series of legal documents that would expedite the transfer of funds. Abbie felt unattached from the moment, almost surreal, as she signed her name across the bottom of the papers. After a few more minutes of conversation, she reached down to retrieve her purse. She carefully placed the velvet box and Audry's letter inside. As she rose from the table, Audry's diamond ring winked at her once again from her right hand.

As they neared the door, Abbie gave Murphy a warm hug.

After opening the door to the conference room for Abbie, Murphy stopped. "Abbie, you know to call me if you need anything or if any questions arise after reading Miss Audry's letter. I'm sorry for all the difficulties you've had to endure over the last few years, and it would be an honor to be of further help to you, should you need it."

"Thank you, Murphy. I appreciate it. I can never thank you enough for all you've already done. I still don't know what to say."

"Just say thank you," replied Murphy with a wide grin.

Abbie unlocked her car and got in. After placing her key in the ignition, she sat for a moment and basked in the warmth of the March sun. A very real sense of God's presence and the shelter of His loving arms surrounded Abbie. God had not abandoned her after all. She was acutely aware that her life had just taken a wonderful new turn. *But in which direction?* she thought.

Chapter Forty-Three

Abbie fought the urge several times on the way home to pull over to the side of the road and read Audry's letter. Driving across town, she kept thinking, *Surely I misunderstood Murphy. He probably said twenty-five hundred dollars.* Abbie talked herself into waiting until she got home. At least there, she'd have more privacy. She was actually surprised when she pulled into her own driveway as her mind had been so busy trying to absorb all that had just taken place. Abbie hardly remembered the drive from Murphy's office to her home.

Abbie put down a large stack of papers that needed grading on the kitchen table. Laying her purse down next to the papers, she gingerly removed Audry's mysterious letter from the inside pocket. Abbie walked into the den and settled down in her armchair. She sat for a long time while sifting through details of this momentous day. The faded, floral chintz upholstery was comforting next to Abbie's skin. This chair was her favorite spot for thinking and praying.

Maybe this is part of some fantastic dream, she thought to herself.

But the diamond ring on her right hand was real all right. This was no dream. She took a deep breath, turned the envelope over, and carefully opened the sealed flap. Abbie reached in and withdrew a bundle of folded pages. The date on the letter read August 11, 2002. *Why, that was last summer. How odd!* she thought.

Dearest Abbie,

I am smiling to myself as I write this letter to you. I hope you know how much I love you and how much joy you have brought to my life. Abbie, you were the daughter I never had. I want you to have my ring; Bill would have loved you as much as I do. When you look at the ring, always remember God's promises as clear and bright as a diamond's fire.

Abbie, easily moved to tears, already had to put the letter down and wipe away a few. After a moment, she continued reading.

Drew told me many times that he might like to pursue a seminary degree. To that end, I want $100,000 of the $250,000 to go to Drew for seminary tuition. If he decides that seminary is not the path God is leading him down, then this money is to pay for another graduate degree. If Drew decides not to pursue an advanced degree, then the money is to be given to him on his thirtieth birthday.

Abbie, I know Joe robbed you of financial stability. I also know that sometimes money, or the lack of it, can be a barrier to Christians getting involved in God's work. I never want there to be any barriers in your life. After Drew's portion, you are now left with $150,000. Like the man in the Parable of the Talents, I want you to grow this money for the kingdom of God. I'm not sure whether you'll be taking the job at Timothy House. I think you should consider it.

After reading this part of the letter, Abbie put down the pages, now damp from tears. She closed her eyes and prayed aloud. "Oh, Jesus, I'm not the woman Audry thinks I am. Please forgive me, Lord, for the way I've allowed the darkness of grief to block the light of Your love. I am so unworthy of this outpouring of Your generosity. I'm not sure I'm someone you can use, but I'm ready and willing. I want my life to bring honor to Your name."

The cleansing purge of hot tears continued for a while. Abbie reached for a tissue in her jacket pocket. She picked up Audry's epistle and continued reading.

> *Abbie, hold firm to your faith. Use what God has given you—your family, your abilities as a teacher, your love of learning, your compassionate spirit—to further God's kingdom here on earth. Bless others with what you have been blessed with. What God desires more than anything else is your heart and your availability.*
> *Now to Him who is able to do far more abundantly beyond all that we ask or think, according to the power that works within us.*
>
> *All my love,*
> *Audry*

Abbie put the pages of the letter back in order, folded them, and returned them to their envelope. In spite of what she'd just read, Abbie found it hard to believe that Audry's extravagant monetary gift was real. She wiggled the newly acquired heirloom on her finger and pondered a new question. *Lord,* she thought, *what are You up to?*

Chapter Forty-Four

The sound of the refrigerator icemaker broke Abbie out of her reverie. Totally unaware of how much time had passed, she noticed how dark it was outside the window. The grumbling in her stomach, ignored earlier, now demanded attention. After eating a plate of leftovers, Abbie caught herself glancing down at the new companion for her right hand. Oddly, the ring felt as if it had always belonged there. The insistent ring of the phone broke her concentration.

"Hey, son," exclaimed Abbie after hearing Drew's voice. "How's school?"

"Great, Mom," replied Drew.

Abbie thought to herself, *He's in an especially good humor.* She smiled to herself, thinking how much better that mood might become once he knew about Audry's gift.

After exchanging a few pleasantries with Abbie, Drew said, "I wanted to check on you. I've been praying for you and that job offer at Timothy House. Have you thought anymore about it?"

Abbie hesitated for just a minute, wondering whether to tell Drew about the afternoon's momentous events and the decision she had reached but decided instead to wait.

"Oh, Drew, as a matter of fact, I have. Thanks for your prayers. They have definitely made a difference."

A tingle of excitement ran through Abbie as she thought back over another bull's-eye she had made this very day. She knew she was going to take Don up on his offer.

"I know how unhappy you've been the past few years at Kent."

Abbie smiled to herself as she realized how grown up Drew sounded. "Honey, that's sweet. I did have a long talk about two weeks ago with Mr. Patterson." Abbie chose her words carefully as she didn't want to tip her hand just yet. "He's known since last fall about Don's offer and has given me until April 5 to give him an answer."

"Mr. Patterson only wants what's best for you. He'll understand if you decide to leave. Besides, he's leaving himself. What a great guy he turned out to be. He scared me when I was younger, being the principal and all. But that changed the year Dad died. I'll never forget how he really helped me. I would never have finished high school without his support. That's for sure."

As Abbie listened to her son, a wave of gratefulness for Arthur Patterson's friendship washed over her. *Heaven only knows where we'd be without it*, she thought.

Drew paused slightly. "That leads me to my second reason for calling. This has been a light week at school, and I won't have much studying to do this weekend. I guess the profs are taking pity on us seniors." He gave a light laugh. "I was wondering if I could tempt you to drive over to Stanton for the day on Saturday. You know that lake near campus? I thought maybe we could fix a picnic and brainstorm about your job offer. I've got one of my own I'd like to run past you."

Her son's thoughtful offer touched her, and she was excited to hear about some possible good news of Drew's as well. "Drew Richardson, you've got yourself a date!" Abbie gleefully replied. "Will you even give me a hint about your offer?"

"Nope," said Drew teasingly. "You'll just have to wait in suspense until Saturday."

Abbie decided to tantalize Drew with some suspense of her own. "Well, young man, I may have a bombshell or two of my own."

As she wiggled her right hand, Audry's ring glimmered in the light of the lamp. Abbie looked past the shimmering stone to the letter lying in her lap.

"Have you had another call from that Keith guy at Timothy House?" Drew's tone was protective.

Abbie knew she had aroused more than idle curiosity in her son, aware of Drew's attempt to step in as her protector and advisor.

"I've had a few. I consider Keith a friend." Abbie was surprised to hear her own affirmation of Keith Haliday. He was in her thoughts a lot lately. "But my news doesn't concern him."

"Come on, Mom. You're killing me! Don't make me wait. You know I hate that."

Drew's pleading voice reminded Abbie of earlier times when, as a small boy, he would pester her for hours as he tried to figure out his birthday or Christmas gifts.

"You started this guessing game, Drewby," replied Abbie. "You'll just have to wait until Saturday." By now, Abbie was using every ounce of self-control she possessed. Her excitement about Audry's letter was almost uncontainable.

Abbie changed the subject so she wouldn't let the news slip. "I'll make egg salad and bring some of the fresh roast turkey that you like from Turner's Grocery, and I'll also make turtle brownies. How about if you grab some Mountain Dew, a loaf of bread, and some chips? Oh, do you have plates and napkins at your apartment, or do I need to bring some?"

"I think I can cover the order. Is ten o'clock okay? That would give us until about three at the lake? You should be able to get home before dark."

"That'll be great!" Abbie was already looking forward to spending much-needed quality time with her son.

Abbie hung up the phone after enjoying a few more minutes of conversation with Drew and agreeing to meet at his apartment. *Who could think straight at a time like this?* she thought.

She thought for a split second about calling Lane but then decided against it. Drew needed to be the first to hear the news. Besides, too much had happened today. Her brain couldn't deal with any more complex thoughts or decisions to be made.

The grading wasn't finished, but Abbie decided it could wait until morning. Long ago, she'd cultivated the habit of getting up around five o'clock in order to take care of schoolwork that otherwise would have eaten into precious family time in the evenings. She had never regretted putting her family ahead of her career. She just wished Joe had done the same. Oh, how much heartache and pain could have been saved for all of them.

After a quick bath, Abbie donned her bedroom slippers and padded back to the kitchen to make a cup of hot tea. While the bag steeped, Abbie turned off the outside lights and armed the alarm system. After sweetening her tea, she carefully climbed the stairs back to her bedroom.

She climbed up into her four-poster bed, plumped several pillows behind her back, and pulled the coverlet over her outstretched legs. She reached over to pick up the steaming cup from where she had placed it on the bedside table and leaned back onto the soft pillows. One more time, she played back the events of this very unique day. *Surely tomorrow,* she thought, *I'll wake up and realize this has all been some strange dream.*

Abbie picked up her Bible and flipped through the thin pages to a passage of Scripture that Beulah and Audry shared with her years ago, one they said they were claiming for her, but one she had become convinced that God hadn't meant for her. The heartache of these past four years had somehow obscured the truth of God's word, preventing it from sinking in.

Reading the words penned millennia ago by the prophet Jeremiah, Abbie felt a strange sensation of familiarity as she read, "I have plans for you, My child."

She suddenly remembered she'd heard those same words, as clearly as if someone had whispered them directly in her ear, on a day when despair had almost gotten the best of her. Abbie continued as Jeremiah spoke of "a future and a hope," reading and rereading the passage with great care. *Surely Audry's gift is too significant to write off as mere coincidence,* she thought.

At last, Abbie laid the Bible on the table and turned out the light. She was worn out from all that had happened that day. One last thing she remembered as her head hit the pillow was the verse to an old hymn by George Matheson, "O, Love that will not let me go, I rest my weary soul in Thee. I give Thee back the life I owe, that in Thine ocean depths its flow may richer, fuller be."

"Thank You, dear Lord," she prayed as she drifted off to sleep, "for Your unfailing love. Please don't let me go."

Chapter Forty-Five

Even with little sleep, Abbie didn't need an alarm clock to help her wake up on Saturday. Abbie knew she and Drew would remember this day for a very long time. She didn't want to miss a minute of it. She pulled in to the parking lot of Drew's apartment a few minutes after ten o'clock. No sooner had she turned off the ignition than Abbie spotted Drew, bounding down the stairs from the second level of the older brick complex. Drew opened her car door and wrapped his mother warmly in a huge hug. After adding Drew's additions to the picnic basket, the pair piled into the SUV and headed off to Lure Lake.

Abbie couldn't remember the last time the sky looked so blue, when food tasted so good, and when she enjoyed time with Drew this much! Laughter and small talk accompanied the first round of egg salad and turkey sandwiches.

How is this possible? Abbie thought as she watched her grown son sitting near. *Drew was just entering high school a few years ago, and now he's about to graduate from college. Where did the time go?* She smiled and listened to more of his conversation.

Hungrier than she thought, Abbie spread mayonnaise and spicy mustard on four more slices of honey wheat bread and pulled out the last of the turkey from a plastic bag.

She passed the second sandwich across to Drew. "So tell me about your job offer."

"Just a minute, Mom," came a muffled response as Drew bit into the soft bread.

Abbie waited, trying to be as patient as she possibly could.

"Well," Drew continued, wiping his mouth with the back of his hand, "you remember Josh Hastings from Camp 4Ever? We had a great time together, working with the guys at camp. Josh graduated a few years ago from seminary, and he has been working at Timothy House for several years now. He attends Wright's Creek Church. I don't know if you remember, but they were one of the churches that provided night activities for the campers."

Abbie nodded.

"Josh and I have kept in touch this year. Mr. Don's been talking to the minister at Wright's Creek. Their church is going to be starting a youth mentoring program with Timothy House, and Josh is going to be in charge of it. He and Mr. Don want me to help with the program. The mentoring position is a part-time job. Mr. Don has also asked me to help with special sports programs that Timothy House hosts during the year. That would provide work to fill in the rest of my schedule. What do you think?" asked Drew with a bright smile.

"Drew, it sounds good. What about the salary? You'll just be out of college, and sometimes churches can't pay as well as other organizations."

"I've got this figured out. The job salary's decent. A lady at Josh's church is going to rent me a furnished garage apartment for a really low price, so my living expenses won't be that much." Drew took a sip of Mountain Dew.

"Son," she continued a bit tentatively, "what about benefits, insurance, and all that?"

"Both the church and Timothy House have a benefit package that comes with their offers. Between the two, I'll have coverage. Not the best, but enough to get me started."

Drew was silent a moment. "There's one more thing. I realize I won't be putting my business major to much use right now. That was really Dad's idea anyway."

Abbie couldn't help but notice the wounded look that momentarily filled her son's dark brown eyes.

"I'd still love to go to seminary, but I don't have that kind of money.

At least this job will help me decide if I'm cut out for the pastoring life or not." He took another sip of his drink.

"You'll use more of your degree than you think." Abbie silently acknowledged to herself that, with God's help, Drew was putting on his "man clothes." In spite of his ongoing emotional struggles where his father was concerned, progress was clearly being made.

"I've really been praying about this, and I believe it's what I'm supposed to do." Drew leaned his long, thin frame back on his elbows and waited for his mother's response.

"Okay," said Abbie, sounding a bit more confident. "Looks like you have all the bases covered. When would you start?"

"Well, Josh and Mr. Don both said they would allow me about three weeks between graduation and moving up to Robbinsonville. Think you could put up with me until then?" asked Drew with a sly grin.

"You better believe it!" She reached over to her son and patted his arm. "Oh, Drew, that's great. I'm so excited for you. I'm content knowing you've thought this through and have made it a matter of serious prayer. I trust your judgment."

Drew straightened to a sitting position and pulled his legs up toward his chest, stretching out his arms across his knees. "So, Mom, I've told you my news. Let's hear yours."

Abbie opened the tin of brownies and took out two, handing one to Drew and keeping the other for herself. She broke off a corner of the brownie she held in her hand, put the morsel into her mouth, and chewed thoughtfully. She swallowed the last of the small bite and washed it down with a swallow of Mountain Dew.

Quietly, Abbie said, "I'm going to accept Don Fielding's offer at Timothy House."

Drew reached over and hugged his mom tightly. "That's super, Mom." Then in the next instant, he suddenly pulled back to look at his mother. "But wait?" he said slowly. "What pushed you over the line? Because the last time we talked about this, you seemed so undecided."

Abbie recognized this train of thought as another sign of Drew's maturity. "Let's just say I've been working hard to follow the Patriot Plan." She couldn't help but giggle as she uttered the words.

The perplexed look on Drew's face almost made her laugh again. "The Patriot Plan?"

"That's just Miss Winnie's name for a way of looking at problems. Instead of allowing yourself to remain totally overwhelmed, you tackle life's troubles one at a time." She reached over and playfully poked at Drew's ribs. "It may sound silly, but her advice has made a world of difference for me. Once I applied the rule to this particular decision, a move to Timothy House was the obvious choice."

"Finally you're doing something for yourself."

Abbie laughed at his response. "What's that supposed to mean?"

"It just means that, for the last few years, you've cleaned up all of Dad's mess and helped me stay on track, plus do your own job at Kent. This last year, especially, has really worn you down. You deserve to be at a place where you're really appreciated."

"Oh, Drew." Abbie reached out to brush stray strands of blond hair out of his eyes. "I'm appreciated at Kent, honey. It's just that I believe that God has work for me to do at Timothy House. Besides, with Mr. Patterson retiring, it'll be the perfect time to make a break with Kent."

"Has that Keith guy got anything to do with you accepting the job?" asked Drew suspiciously.

"Yes and no. I have never met anyone like Keith Haliday before, and I've really enjoyed getting to know him over this past year. I don't know if I've told you, but his wife and kids died in a tragic auto accident years ago. He's been through a lot, just like we have."

"Yeah," said Drew. "Josh told me a little about that last summer, the week we were at camp."

"Keith's become a good friend."

For a minute, Abbie was unable to speak. This was only the second time she had voiced his status in her life. The proclamation surprised her somehow. Perhaps it was hearing the words spoken aloud. Surprising her even more was the wave of emotion breaking over her. She felt flushed and clammy.

"Mom," said Drew with a chuckle, watching the color rise in his mother's face. "You're blushing!"

"I am not." Abbie placed the palms of her hands on her now-flaming cheeks. "It's merely hot out here."

"Mom," continued Drew. "I've been around girls enough to know a blush when I see one." He reached over and pulled Abbie's hands away from her face. "You really like this Keith guy, don't you?"

Abbie was quiet for a minute. She steeled herself to meet her son's direct gaze, and she finally looked into his deep brown eyes and nodded slowly.

"I guess I do. He's not like any man I've ever met before. It's not like he's made some declaration of his feelings or stated his intentions. We've just had some really solid talks, and I'd like to have more of them. I like the way I feel when I'm with him, protected and safe."

Now Drew was the quiet one. "I have a confession to make." He looked a bit sheepish. "I asked Josh to check out Keith. I noticed his name started popping up in your conversation a lot, especially after Christmas."

"Joseph Andrew Richardson," exclaimed Abbie with mock disgust. "You did not!"

"I did, too." Drew rose to his feet and walked over to lean against one of the oak trees near their blanket. He faced Abbie. "I don't want to see you hurt, Mom, ever again. I just needed to make sure this guy was the real thing."

"So what did you find out?" Abbie's curiosity was definitely getting the best of her.

Drew grinned back at her. "Josh told me Mr. Don said Keith Haliday is one of the most solid guys he's ever met. He said Mr. Don thinks of him as his own son. I think he'll pass inspection for the moment."

A sense of pride welled up deep within Abbie. All she could get out was "Oh, Drew" as she sprang to her feet and ran over to where he stood and engulfed him in the tightest bear hug she could manage.

After a few minutes, Abbie collected herself. She loosened her grip on Drew, pulled back, and looked up into his handsome, young face.

"It's time you sat down, son, and listened to me for a minute."

Chapter Forty-Six

"Drew," Abbie began as she sat cross-legged once again on the quilt. "Miss Audry left some gifts for you and for me."

"You're kidding," said Drew in a surprised tone. "What would she have left us?"

"Well, for starters, she left me this." She reached down to unzip the pocket of her fleece jacket, pulled out the worn velvet jewel box, and held it out for Drew.

He took it from her hand, grasped the box, and slowly opened the lid. As he did, the early afternoon sun glistened along the top of the stone. "Wow!" he whispered.

"I know." Abbie smiled as she noted her son's reaction. "That's exactly how I felt." She ran her fingers along the quilted stitches on the faded red and brown spread.

Drew took the ring out of the box and handed it to his mother. Abbie slipped it gingerly onto the third finger of her right hand.

"It's a perfect fit." She extended her fingers out in front of her, admiring the new addition.

Drew interrupted Abbie, bringing her back to the present. "You said gifts, Mom. What did Miss Audry give me?"

She looked over at her precious boy, now almost grown up, and she could hardly believe what she was about to tell him.

"When you were telling me about the job offers at Wright's Creek and Timothy House, you also mentioned seminary. Would you still like to go?"

"Well, sure, Mom, if you've got some spare change lying around." The sarcasm was evident in his voice.

"As a matter of fact, I do." Abbie reached across the quilt and drew Audry's letter out of her purse. For a long moment, she held it tenderly within her fingers. Finally, she put the thick envelope down on the quilt at Drew's feet.

Drew reached for it and looked over at his mother for an explanation.

"Son," Abbie continued quietly, "that is a letter that Audry left for me. It will explain what I am about to tell you. Audry left you and me a very sizeable amount of money. One hundred thousand dollars of it is to pay for your seminary tuition, if you still want to go."

Abbie stood up slowly. She realized she was chilly, even here in the spring sun. She zipped up her jacket. "You'll need a few minutes to read Audry's letter. I know I did. I'm going for a walk. I'll be back in just a little while." She tousled Drew's hair and headed up the hill toward the lake road.

After a short walk, Abbie sought shelter under a large oak near the water's edge. She soaked in the beauty before her. The cool, clear waters of Lure Lake shone brightly. Sunlight coated the surface of the water like gold leaf that rippled slightly in the gentle breeze. Several ducks floated carelessly near the shore. A blue heron glided slowly past, carried gracefully on unseen currents of air.

Snippets of the last four years flew through her mind, flapping their wings like so many birds. She cringed remembering how much Drew had suffered at the expense of his father's sins. One particularly painful memory was of her overhearing some students at McHenry discussing Joe's gambling addiction in hushed tones.

Drew had finally opened up to his mother in his second year of college about the distance he had always felt between him and his dad. His revelation had helped Abbie to make sense of some of the uncharacteristic behaviors she had witnessed in her son: several episodes of heavy drinking in his freshman year, associations with several unsavory friends, lack of academic success, and apathy concerning his walk with the Lord. Drew's talk of becoming a minister had only recently reemerged.

Abbie glanced back down the shoreline to where her son was seated.

She had watched him read and reread Audry's letter three times. It had now been about thirty minutes since she'd left him on the quilt. By this time, he had walked down to the shore and was standing near the water.

Abbie made her way back along the lake road. Drew appeared to be deep in thought as she approached him.

Quietly, Abbie said, "God is certainly one for surprises, wouldn't you say?"

She slipped her arm around her son's waist and hugged him tightly. For a long moment, neither spoke. "Despite all we've been through, God has not abandoned us. More and more, He's showing both of us just how very much He cares for us."

"You're not kidding," said Drew, the wonder obvious in his voice. He pulled back from Abbie and shielded his eyes with his hand. A wide grin spread across his face. "All I could think after you gave me the letter was that there was no way you just told me Miss Audry gave me a hundred grand."

"I know, Drewby." Abbie reached up and tenderly brushed a lock of his hair back from his forehead. "I felt the same way."

She paused. "How about another brownie?" Abbie nodded in the direction of the quilt.

The pair walked back and sat down on the coverlet. Abbie opened the tin of treats and held it out to Drew.

Drew took a bite of the large brownie he had just selected as Abbie bit into hers.

"Mom," he said as he wiped his mouth, "what do you think I ought to do about seminary?"

Abbie held up her hand, a signal for him to wait until she finished chewing. "Perhaps you should just sleep on this for a while. Start the new job with Josh and Mr. Don, and see what you think about the work.

"Murphy said he could recommend the name of an excellent financial manager who can invest the money from Audry until we each decide what to do with it. You don't have to make a decision today," she said before nibbling one more small bite.

Drew stood up and brushed off the crumbs from his jeans. "Would you mind if we headed on back? I've got to call Jason and Jonathan." He grinned from ear to ear. "They're never going to believe this!"

As Abbie drove home to McHenry later that night, she laughed aloud, remembering the drive back from the lake. Drew had talked nonstop all the way. Audry's generosity was already breathing reality into his once-distant dream of attending seminary. She smiled and thought, *See, Joe, you didn't steal Drew's dream after all.*

As she pulled into the driveway of her house, a peaceful, restful feeling, one she hadn't experienced in a very long time, filled her heart.

Chapter Forty-Seven

Oh, joy, Abbie thought wryly as she pulled into Kent Academy's parking lot. *Today is April Fool's Day. I can't wait to see what the kids have planned.* Every year, some precocious student managed to stump her with a tall tale that she bought hook, line, and sinker.

"I'm ready," she told herself as she entered the school lobby. She squared her shoulders and headed down the hall to her room.

Mr. Patterson was coming up the hall toward her. "Good morning, Abbie," he said as she approached and turned to walk with her down the crowded hallway. "Can I help you?" He noted the full stack of papers Abbie carried in her arms.

"No thanks, Mr. Patterson," said Abbie, always touched by his fatherly tone. "On second thought," she said as they approached her classroom, "it would be great if you would open my door."

The principal located the master classroom door key from the jumble of metal on his key ring, unlocked Abbie's door, and opened it. The cheery jingle produced by the keys was like a welcome "hello" on this chilly spring morning.

"Stop by my office on your free period, Abbie," he said before leaving her classroom. "I have something I want to share with you that may help you with the decision you're trying to make."

Abbie leaned over to unload the stack of paperwork onto her desk and looked back toward the doorway. "Yes, sir, Mr. Patterson. I'll be by around eleven. Thanks again for getting me into my room."

"Anytime, young lady." The principal smiled. "Anytime."

Any energy that might have been spent trying to decipher Mr.
Patterson's mysterious comment was quickly transferred to corralling
a roomful of boisterous, energetic students. As the first period bell
sounded, Abbie opened her textbook and began the day. Before Abbie
knew it, the bell for the end of third period was sounding. Her free period
at last. As she tidied the room after the morning classes, she remembered
the appointment in the principal's office.

Rosie greeted Abbie with a bright grin as she entered the office
reception area. "He's expecting you," Rosie chirped and nodded with her
head toward the open door behind her desk.

A ringing phone was quickly intercepted as Rosie's calm, competent
voice hailed a greeting, "Good morning. This is Kent Academy. Rosie
speaking. How may I help you?"

Abbie knocked gently on the open door and announced her arrival.

"Come in. Come in," said Mr. Patterson with a wave as he thumbed
through a large file folder on his desk. "If you don't mind, Abbie, close
the door."

A strange sensation, a forewarning of important news to come, swept
over Abbie as she took a seat in front of the principal's desk.

"How's it going, Abbie?" Her boss settled back in his chair. At this
moment, he reminded Abbie of her father. "Have you thought any more
about Don Fielding's offer from Timothy House?"

"I have, as a matter of fact, but I've had some really heavy things on
my plate lately that haven't left me much time or energy for sane thought.
As you probably know, Audry McCormick died a few weeks ago. She
was one of my dearest friends and was like a mother to me in many ways.
I miss her very much." Abbie couldn't continue and swallowed hard to
regain her composure.

"I knew about Audry's stroke and have been meaning to say something
to you about it. I'm so sorry."

"Thank you." Abbie reached over to grab a tissue from the box atop a
table beside her chair. Softly, she continued, "You know, Mr. Patterson,
I've been thinking a lot about what you said about knowing when you've
arrived at one of those forks in life's road. Well, I think I may have
reached one."

"I'm all ears." He leaned slightly forward in his chair.

Abbie took a deep breath. "Miss Audry left me and Drew two hundred and fifty thousand dollars."

"That's great, Abbie," replied Mr. Patterson. "That's a really funny April Fool's joke."

"No, really, Mr. Patterson. It's no joke."

A funny grin appeared on the principal's face as the reality of Audry's generosity fully began to sink in. For the next ten minutes or so, Abbie told her friend about the providential monetary gift that had come her way. She also told him about the ring, slipped it off her finger, and passed it across the desk for him to examine. A low whistle followed as he passed the ring back to Abbie.

"Abbie, this is a God thing." Mr. Patterson motioned to the ring as she placed it back on her right hand. "What I wanted to tell you today is that I think you should take the job offer at Timothy House." He took off his wire-rimmed reading glasses and looked her squarely in the eye.

"You and Drew have had more grief and sorrow to bear than any two people should have to deal with. You're a very gifted teacher, Abbie, but you've lost your joy and passion for the profession, at least here in the Kent environment. Even bright lights dim at times. God may be offering you a fresh start at Timothy House.

"You owe it to yourself to see what God has in store down this new fork in the road. You can always return to Kent, but you may never have another opportunity like this again. Pray and listen. The Lord will let you know."

Abbie could hear the ringing bell announce the beginning of fifth period beyond the door. "Thanks, Mr. Patterson," said Abbie as she rose to leave. "I so appreciate your wisdom and your counsel."

"You're welcome, Abbie, but it's really God's wisdom, not mine. Just remember you only have a few more days. I will need an answer regarding your contract by April 5."

"Yes, sir, Mr. Patterson. I promise you'll have it."

As she left the office and headed down the hall amid a throng of adolescents jostling their way to class, Abbie felt an unexpected peace settle within her all the way to the very center of her being. She knew this was not an April Fool's joke. This was the gift of peace only God Himself could deliver.

Chapter Forty-Eight

Thoughts of her came to him, unbidden. They appeared out of nowhere, dancing around Keith's head like ornaments on a mobile. Why did these images of Abbie Richardson keep coming to his mind? More and more, Keith found himself meeting her in his dreams. Sometimes, it was Abbie's face; other times, it was Genny's that swam in his head.

Keith shook his head roughly from side to side as if to clear away some unseen cobwebs. He laughed at himself and muttered under his breath, "What would Abbie Richardson ever see in me, an over-the-hill has-been with nowhere to go? Well, pal, it may be time to find out."

Movement in the doorway of his office caught Keith's eye. Don leaned against the door frame. "Got a minute?"

"Sure," replied Keith. "What's up?"

Don settled his stocky frame in a worn-looking office chair in front of Keith's desk. He leaned back and ran his hands over his short-cropped gray hair. "How many more staff positions do we have to fill?"

Don, Keith, and several other members of Timothy House's administration had been working hard over the last few weeks to put together the employment puzzle that somehow managed to come together during this part of every year. Keith picked up a notebook labeled "Faculty Planning" from the corner of his desk and flipped through it. "Looks like math and science are taken care of." He turned over a few more tabbed sections. "Think we're covered in history as well."

Don nodded.

"Oh, yeah," continued Keith. "That new Spanish teacher will be a huge asset. She's also going to teach the mountain needle arts class." Flipping through a few more pages, Keith tried hard to appear nonchalant as he asked, "What have you heard from Abbie Richardson?"

"Really, not much." Don rubbed the palm of one hand. "Looks like she may have decided to stay at Kent after all."

Keith sat silent for a few moments. "I'll try to get in touch with her by the week's end," he finally offered. "How's that sound?"

"Sounds like a plan to me," said Don. "I'd really like to wrap up these faculty assignments by about April 10 or so."

Keith closed the notebook and pushed his chair back slightly from his desk. "I'll let you know if I'm able to reach Abbie."

"Great." Don rose to his feet. "Don't work too hard this afternoon. By the way," he continued as he stood to leave, "how's basketball coming?"

"Not too bad. This season, my girls really have seemed to gel. I hope we can transfer that momentum into next season. We only have two more weeks of afternoon practices in the gym. If I can get my guys to play as hard as my girls, we'll be in business.

"It's funny." Keith stood up behind his desk and stretched out all seventy-seven inches of his frame. "I've really enjoyed the slower pace here at Timothy House. The work with these students has been especially rewarding. Along with coaching them on the finer aspects of ball handling and feeding the post, I'm coaching them for life."

The older man looked back to glance at him. "Keith, you've become a stalwart on the faculty and an integral part of the fabric of Timothy House in the time you've been on board. Wish I had more like you."

Keith grinned at him slightly, not sure exactly how to respond.

"I'm very proud of the basketball program you've built here at Timothy House," Don continued. "Just let me know what Abbie decides." He tapped a good-bye on the door frame as he left Keith's office.

Keith sat back down behind his desk. For a long time he stared at the picture of Genny, Amanda, and David that gazed back at him from a bookshelf across from his desk. For months now, he had been struggling with himself, grappling with feelings about Abbie that he could no longer deny. *Lord,* he thought, *I feel so disloyal to Genny and all we had, but I can't keep living in this limbo I've created for myself.*

Totally overwhelmed by all that was in his heart, Keith swiped for his jacket that hung on the back of his office door and headed out of the building. Ten minutes later, he found himself on the far side of Serenity Cove. A flock of geese winged their way overhead, rising over the tree line behind Keith. He followed their ornithological leapfrog until they disappeared from view. Keith kicked at some pebbles with the toe of his loafer, picked up a few, and skipped their smooth, cold forms across the water's still surface.

A group of students coming toward the lake caught his eye, causing Keith to resume his journey. The last thing he wanted to have to do this afternoon was talk to students and other faculty. He needed a place where he could be alone and gather his thoughts. He quickly made his way to the chapel.

By now, it was close to 4:15, and the students would be heading back to their cabins, enjoying much-needed downtime until the evening meal. As the heavy paneled door to Peter's Chapel closed slowly behind him, the cool darkness of this sacred place enveloped Keith. He stood very still for few moments, adjusting to the dim light within the old building. He slowly made his way about halfway up the aisle and lowered his towering frame onto the bench of an oak pew.

Points of light, filtering through the jewel-paned windows, settled like brightly colored pieces of confetti around the small sanctuary. The only artificial light came from an old brass lantern. A large wooden cross hung in the front of the chapel, its hand-rubbed and oiled surface covered with hand-chiseled leaves and flowers indigenous to this part of the Tennessee highlands. Keith found himself transfixed as he gazed at it.

From out of the depths of his soul rose up a thought, "Take up your cross, and follow me." As darkness fell around Timothy House, Keith stared at the heavy wooden beams that formed the altar's adornment. He wondered how heavy this particular cross would be to shoulder. He wondered how heavy the cross was that Jesus carried to Calvary. He wondered how heavy the cross would be that the Lord would ask him to shoulder next.

Keith moved to the edge of the pew, leaned forward, and clasped his hands together as he bowed his head for this much-needed conversation with his Heavenly Father. Silently at first, Keith's lips began to move in prayer. As more and more words tumbled forth, they became audible in the quietness of the chapel.

"Lord, I need Your direction. I wasn't sure if I could go on living after I lost Genny and the kids." For many minutes, Keith said nothing.

"You've redeemed my life in so many ways, and for that I am grateful. This job and my friends, for starters. What would I have done without Doris and Don? Your great kindness has overwhelmed me through the love shown me by these dear people.

"I thought I was whole again or at least repaired to the point that I could make it on my own. You know that all that changed last summer when I met Abbie Richardson. I haven't allowed my heart to feel this way for so long, and now I can't get her off my mind. Is this some game I'm playing with myself, or is there some higher purpose for her presence in my life?

"I'm fine with the single life. Do I even want to put myself in a position where I could be hurt? I don't honestly know if I can deal with a loss like that again."

Keith was so lost in the holy conversation that the moisture of his tears caught him off guard. He wiped them away.

"I'm afraid, when Abbie sees me, that she thinks I'm like Joe. How can I break through all the barriers she's built around her heart? Do I even want to go crawling around on an emotional fence that may be topped with barbed wire?

"Lord, I only want Your will in my life. I need my heart and my mind to get some peace where Abbie is concerned. It's time to fish or cut bait. Show me, Jesus, how to take this next step. I'm so scared, scared of being hurt, scared of losing, scared of all the pain I'll feel if I have to peel the scabs off the wounds on my heart.

"Protect Abbie, too. I know You have plans for her, plans for a future and a hope. I need to know whether or not I'm to be a part of that future. Give me courage, Lord, to take the next step. Whatever lies ahead, I know You stand in the road before me. None of this has caught You by surprise. I ask for Your presence and Your power but, most of all, Your peace."

Finally spent, Keith let out a shuddering sigh and a whispered "Amen." The sound of the dinner bell at Covenant Kitchen broke the stillness. As Keith made his way toward the dining hall, a plan began to take shape in his mind. A plan for the next step.

All day long, thoughts of Abbie and Keith had burdened Beulah. By four o'clock, she could no longer ignore them. After unplugging her phone so she wouldn't be disturbed, she got her Bible and headed for the den. Settled comfortably in the prayer mobile, she opened to a favorite verse in the writings of the prophet Isaiah. The eternal truth of its message, carried through all the ages, reminded her that God indeed had a plan for Abbie and Keith, even promising to answer before they called out to Him. The creaking of the old rocker accompanied her fervent prayers, lifting a song of intercession and praise that continued long after the light of day waned.

Chapter Forty-Nine

The headlights of Keith's Explorer shone across the front of Abbie's house as he pulled up into the driveway of her house. *Thank You, Lord,* Keith almost spoke aloud, noticing the glow of the front porch light and another burning in the living room window.

As he quietly closed the door to his truck, the dial on his watch read 9:59. The impromptu drive from Robbinsonville to McHenry had taken him a little under three hours.

Keith climbed the front steps and knocked on the door of the house on Flaherty Road. After a few minutes, he heard Abbie's voice through the door asking, "Who's there?" Her tone was all business.

"It's me, Abbie. It's Keith," he replied through the solid hardwood door. "Keith Haliday," his voice continued. "I'm terribly sorry that it's so late."

Abbie's face appeared through the patterned lace panels covering the sidelights beside the door. Keith's imposing frame all but obscured the glow of the porch light. She quickly turned the lock and opened the door.

"Hey," said Keith, not moving from where he stood on the porch.

"Hey, yourself." Abbie grinned. "Don't just stand there. Come on in."

Abbie closed the door behind him and locked it again. Abbie turned to look up at Keith. "Are you okay?"

"Yes, Abbie." Keith raked a hand through his thick brown hair. "At least I think I am. I know I should have called first, but I decided to take a chance that you were still up. I just need to talk to you for a minute, if that's all right." Still holding his keys in his hand, he waited for her answer.

"Well, sure, Keith." He slid the key ring into the pocket of his slacks. "Come on back to the den. We'll be more comfortable there."

Keith had never been in Abbie's house before but instantly felt he was in a very familiar setting. The home possessed a personality of its own that was made him comfortable and put him instantly at ease. Abbie led him through the living room and back into the den. She settled into her armchair and motioned for Keith to take a seat on the sofa across from her.

For a split second, Keith was not sure he could finish this task he came to complete. He hesitated for a minute and took a deep breath to calm himself and still his pounding heart. He needed to appear to be in control of his faculties. Sounding controlled would be half the battle.

"Well," Keith started, looking down at the braided rug on the floor in front of him, "Don and I have been working really hard over the last week or so, going over faculty assignments for next year. We hadn't heard back from you, so I thought I'd check with you and see if you had reached a decision."

"Funny you should come by tonight. I know the deadline Don gave me is just a week or so away. I'm sorry it's taken me so long to make up my mind. Don's offer is extremely generous." She smiled at Keith.

Keith picked up the faltering conversation. "Yes, it is a very generous offer. Don is a very generous man and I ..." he stammered. "I mean, we are hoping you will accept the offer."

Abbie shifted in her chair and ran her tongue over her lips. "I must admit, Keith. You've caught me totally off guard." She took in a deep breath and sat up a little straighter. "You may tell Don Fielding that I am happy to accept his most generous offer."

What Keith really wanted to do at that moment was throw his hands up in the air and yell "Yippee!" What he actually did was to smile broadly and say, "That's terrific, Abbie. Don will be so pleased."

"You're actually the first person I've told, other than my son Drew." Unbound, Abbie's long hair curled softly around her shoulders. She tucked more of the loose strands behind an ear.

At the mention of Drew's name, Keith grew a little more serious. "What does Drew think about all of this?" He waited for her reply.

Keith was very impressed with Drew and surmised he had worked very hard to overcome a great deal of psychological and emotional scarring inflicted by his father. Instinctively, he also knew that developing Drew as an ally would be crucial if he were ever to have a chance with Abbie.

"Drew is all for the move. He's practically begged me to take the job."

That's my boy, thought Keith.

"Drew graduates in May and will be moving to Robbinsonville himself. Josh Hastings and Don have pieced together two part-time jobs that will dovetail beautifully together for him."

"Really," said Keith. "Sounds interesting."

Abbie interrupted the conversation. "Forgive me for being such a terrible host." She stood up and motioned toward the kitchen. "Could I interest you in a cup of hot tea or hot chocolate? I've probably got something cold I could fix for you, if you'd prefer."

Rising from the sofa, Keith stood and stretched, twisting his torso from side to side, flexing his arms. "Some hot chocolate sounds great. Excuse my stretching." He placed both hands in the small of his back and leaned back slightly. "I'm just a little stiff from the car ride down here."

Abbie nodded wordlessly. Keith followed her into the kitchen.

"Mind if I sit down?" Keith motioned toward her table.

"Help yourself."

Keith watched as Abbie puttered around her small kitchen. "Cozy" is the word that came to his mind. A faint scent of cinnamon and apple spice hung in the air. She took out two matching ceramic mugs and placed them on the granite countertop. Abbie filled a teakettle with fresh water and set it on the stove to boil. Then she joined Keith at the kitchen table.

"Can I tell Don about your decision?" Keith asked.

"It would be fine to tell Don, but I'll need to formally tender my resignation from Kent Academy with my principal, Mr. Patterson. If you and Don could hold this in confidence until April 10, the date we previously agreed on, I would be most grateful. There are several colleagues I want to tell personally about this decision, and it will take me a few days to get around to all of them." The kettle's whistle brought Abbie immediately up out of her chair.

Keith watched Abbie in quiet fascination. Here in her own home, in her own kitchen, she was in her element. Very comfortable with herself, she didn't appear to feel awkward in the least about the late hour and the interruption of her evening.

Abbie prepared hot chocolate for Keith and a cup of hot tea for herself. She carried the mugs to the table and rejoined her late-night guest. Neither of them spoke for a while, lost in the mesmerizing steam. As Abbie sipped the hot liquid, Keith studied her. Even though he had spent time alone with her several times over the last few months, tonight was somehow different. *Perhaps because my heart is now involved*, he thought. He took a deep swig of the hot chocolate in a last-minute effort to gather courage, prayed a silent prayer, and cleared his throat.

"I need to apologize for showing up here so late." He held the mug tightly in his hands and gained strength from its warm surface.

"There's no need. I'm glad to see you anytime."

"Please hear me out." The tone in Keith's voice sounded urgent and strained. He looked at her for a long while. "I needed to see you tonight."

"You've already told me that." Abbie put down her mug. "Don sent you here to get my answer concerning the job offer." She picked up her cup and moved her chair back a bit from the table. "Would you like another cup?"

Keith reached across the table and grabbed Abbie's left hand before she could get up. "Not now." The volume of his voice was now very low, his tone much more serious.

"There are some things I need to say to you." He continued to hold her small hand in his, slightly tightening his grip.

"Abbie," said Keith, swallowing several times, "my coming here tonight really didn't have anything to do with Don's offer." He hoped Abbie could see how much he cared by the look in his eyes. "All I've been able to think about these last weeks and days is you and your decision to come to Timothy House."

"That's so sweet. I've spent a great deal of time thinking about this offer myself. Getting to work with you would definitely be a plus." Abbie patted the top of Keith's hand.

Better help her out here, pal, Keith's inner voice whispered.

Keith could tell by her lighthearted response that Abbie didn't have a clue as to the direction of this conversation.

"I care about you, Abbie. I care a lot, and I think you care about me, too."

Keith watched the gentle flame of a blush fan itself into an all-out burn across Abbie's cheeks. At the same time, he noticed her stiffen slightly. She pulled her hands abruptly from his. Hot, silent tears coursed down her gentle face and dropped without a sound into her lap.

"Abbie," Keith said softly. "Oh, dear Abbie." In an instant, he was beside her and had wrapped strong arms around her. He pulled her close to him, comforting her. "I'm so sorry if I upset you." He felt Abbie struggle to free herself from his embrace.

"No, Keith. I can't," she said firmly, attempting to push back even further away from him.

Keith stood up and backed away to his side of the table. "Forgive me. I meant no disrespect. Abbie, can we go back into the den and talk this out? Please give me a chance to explain."

"Okay." She wiped more tears that had fallen. She stood up abruptly from the table.

Silently, Keith followed her into the next room. She folded herself up in the chintz-covered armchair, tucked her legs underneath her, and crossed her arms across her chest.

It doesn't take a rocket scientist to read that body language, Keith thought, maintaining an appropriate distance on the sofa across the room.

She watched from the safe protection of her chair, waiting for his explanation.

"Abbie, you know how I lost Genny and our kids."

She nodded silently.

"For years, I've built a fence around my heart and haven't allowed anyone to get close." Keith leaned forward and clasped his hands together with his elbows on his knees. "I'm not willing to live that way anymore."

Keith watched Abbie press further back against the chair.

"I thought I didn't need love and affection anymore. All that changed, Abbie Richardson, when I met you."

Abbie's eyes widened slightly. Her arms remained crossed.

"It was so unexpected, meeting you at camp. How ironic that Joe was a part of both of our lives."

Keith watched as Abbie's green eyes narrowed, the expression in them growing cold and hard.

"Abbie, I know Joe hurt you terribly. I wish I could change all of that, but I can't." Keith raked his hand back over his head, the frustration in his heart almost as smoky and dark as the color of his hair.

"I also know that the few times we've been together have been some of the best times I've had over the past ten months." His voice took on a husky tone. "I'm not blind, Abbie. Your responses to me haven't gone unnoticed. I've just been patient. That's all."

Abbie looked down and uncrossed her arms.

"Abbie, I've been where you are." Keith leaned forward and looked her squarely in the eye. "I'm an expert in anger and blame and feeling sorry for myself. Don't think you corner the market on those emotions.

"It's taken me a long time to trust God again and to realize that He didn't abandon me. He never abandoned me. It's just that all the pain in my heart knocked the very breath out of my soul and shut down my emotions for a very long time.

"I'm willing to open my heart in order to see where a relationship with you might go, even if it means getting hurt. I think you're worth the risk." Finished for the moment, Keith continued to hold her gaze. He hoped somehow she could see how much he cared for her.

Abbie looked away from him, wordless. "I wonder what Drew would have to say about a relationship between us, especially knowing you and his dad were once close friends," she said a bit sarcastically as she turned back to face him.

Keith's jaw tightened, and he tried hard to control the tone in his voice. "I've been around Drew, and he strikes me as a pretty levelheaded young man. I think he'll give me a fair shake."

Abbie shifted in the chair. "And what if he won't?"

Keith could see her green eyes narrow even further like shards of glass, hard and sharp.

"Look, Abbie. Drew knows I'm not the same kind of man that his father turned out to be. Furthermore, I think you do, too."

Keith looked down at his watch and realized just how late it had gotten. 11:45. He still had a three-hour drive ahead of him. It was evident this evening had gotten seriously derailed, and it was time to cut his losses.

"Abbie, all I wanted to do tonight was to bare my heart to you and be honest with you. I'm sorry you could not or would not do the same."

These words seemed to evoke a river of anger and wounded pride in Abbie that erupted in her voice. "Keith Haliday, you don't know me at all." Her words came in short, angry, staccato bursts. "Don't think for one minute that my decision to join the staff at Timothy House has anything to do with you because it doesn't. You needn't bother yourself with me."

Once he heard these words, Keith knew it was his cue to leave. *Evidently, there is nothing I could say to change her mind*, he thought.

"Thanks, Abbie, for setting me straight." The sarcasm in his voice was thinly veiled. "I wouldn't dream of bothering you further, and you can be assured that I will certainly respect your position on our faculty. I wish you the best in your new job." Keith stood up abruptly and headed toward the living room.

Mutely, Abbie stood and followed him to the front door. The single lamp burning in the living room did little to illuminate the gloom that now lay between them.

"I'll convey your message to Don in the morning. Thank you for your hospitality and your listening ear. I won't bother you again. Goodnight."

Keith opened the front door and bounded out into the darkness that lay just beyond the glow of the porch light. He might as well have been stepping into outer space.

Abbie waited until Keith pulled out of the driveway and until she could no longer see his taillights before turning out the living room lamp. Her heart had plummeted somewhere far below the pit of her stomach. Profound frustration gripped her. Agitated with herself at having made a terrible mess of the evening, she felt absolutely awful. Despite the late hour, sleep was out of the question. After turning out all the other downstairs lights, Abbie made her way back to the den. The glow of the back patio light gently illuminated the darkness of the room. She returned once more to the safe perch of her armchair, where she had sat during most of Keith's very bewildering soliloquy.

Abbie replayed the entire night over and over in her mind, trying to make some sense of all Keith had told her. She had intended to relish a rare reprieve from grading papers and had been looking forward to enjoying a quiet night reading Terri Blackstock's latest thriller. No sooner had she tucked her feet up underneath her when the doorbell rang. She remembered how she had summoned her best don't-mess-with-me-buddy tone of voice when answering the door.

"At ten o'clock at night? Are you nuts?" was what Abbie really wanted to say when Keith had told her he needed to visit with her.

She also remembered how fishy it sounded to come all that way just to wrap up unfinished business concerning a job offer. *How could I have missed all the signals?* Abbie berated herself. *Keith's impromptu arrival. The lateness of the hour. The thinly veiled excuse for the visit. The color she had observed rising in his cheeks.* From the very start, Abbie found this evening's time with Keith completely different from their other encounters.

Feminine instinct that had lain dormant in her for too long slowly awakened and began to clang wildly as the conversation progressed. When he held her hands, she felt like a bird in a cage, trapped with nowhere to go.

Tears welled up in her soft green eyes. Fear that had been pushed down deep within her for the longest time now clamored to make its way to the surface. Fear of losing her heart again. Fear of having someone she loved utterly disappoint her again. Fear she would fail at love a second time. Silent tears blazed a warm trail down her face and dropped into her lap. Abbie wiped them away in the darkness.

Keith's declaration of his feelings left Abbie feeling very exposed, like he could read her every thought. A part of her had wanted to melt, to succumb to his wooing, but the part of her that was in control tonight was reinforcing the high wall constructed around the parapets of her heart. She knew what a part of her heart wanted to tell Keith, but a storm of emotions raged within her. Abbie revisited hurtful memories of Joe, nursing the deep wounds that he inflicted on her soul. She realized there in the darkness of the room that she wanted to protect her heart from further pain. She couldn't deal with abandonment of that kind ever again.

Abbie thought back over her conversation with Keith and could not explain to herself what triggered her angry outburst toward him. How curt and insensitive her comments about Drew must have sounded. Abbie winced, feeling a pang of guilt, hearing in her mind's ear Drew's kind words about Keith shared on their recent outing.

The barking of a dog somewhere nearby in the neighborhood brought Abbie sharply out of her introspection. *Sleepy or not,* she thought, *I do have to get up soon for school.* The emotional mystery of Keith Haliday and where he fit into her life would have to wait until another time to be solved.

As Abbie headed up the stairs, a darkness blacker and deeper than the night settled all around her.

Chapter Fifty

Right after school, Abbie drove to Oak Hills Church and headed to the chapel after parking her SUV. She pulled open its heavy door and stepped in to the cool darkness of its sanctuary. The room was quiet and dusky as the afternoon sun filtered through the many beveled panes of the windows. This small, sacred room provided a retreat from the world when life got too hard and heavy. Over the past few years, she had logged quite a bit of time in these pews. Today Abbie and the Lord had a great deal of business to discuss.

The days since Keith's visit were spent thinking of little else but him. At school, Abbie kept to herself. In the evenings, she used her answering machine as a buffer with the outside world. Now alone in the chapel's sanctuary, Abbie attempted to navigate the labyrinth of feelings and fears concerning Keith.

Despite her hurtful comments hurled at Keith, Abbie was sure of her definite feelings for him, ones she both wanted to explore and run from. They absolutely terrified her. On the one hand, Abbie put up barriers to Keith merely because he had known Joe. It wasn't Keith's fault that Joe betrayed her, yet Abbie couldn't quite reconcile herself to accept Keith simply on his own merits. On the other hand, she felt herself inexplicably drawn to this man. That was another funny thing. In many ways, Abbie felt like she had known Keith all of her life.

Part of what drew her to Keith was that he understood her pain, the pain of abandonment and great loss. God had led him to the other side of his pain to a place of peace, of that Abbie was certain, but she couldn't figure out how to get to that place herself. She kept running into dead ends and walls constructed of anger and fear.

Abbie leaned forward in the pew and took a hymnal from the rack. She thumbed through the familiar pages several times until she found the words she was looking for.

"Abide with me, falls fast the eventide.

The darkness deepens; Lord, with me abide.

When other helpers fail, and comforts flee,

Help of the helpless, O abide with me!"

Henry Lyte's enduring words usually ministered to Abbie's soul, but only momentarily today. Tears stung Abbie's eyes. A deep sense of shame enveloped her. She remembered her tirade and knew she'd probably lost any chance at a relationship with Keith Haliday.

"Oh, Jesus," she prayed, "please forgive me for what I said to Keith. I know I hurt him. I'm so confused. Every time I think I've gotten over Joe and have gained a handle on my feelings concerning him, some new emotion rears its head. I'm so confused, Father, about my feelings for Keith. Is he a part of Your plan?

"Please help me find some peace within myself. If it's possible, please give me an opportunity to make things right with Keith. I need to be able to ask his forgiveness. Tear down the walls I've built around my heart. Please show me Your way."

Hot, salty tears coursed down Abbie's face as she sat in the pew. Loneliness and grief washed over her in never-ending waves. She was so tired. Tired of wondering. Tired of hurting. Tired of this lack of direction and purpose in her life.

After a while, Abbie reached for her dad's Bible. She'd tucked it in her satchel earlier that morning. One of her most prized possessions, it was her link to all that was good, decent, and honest in the world. The pages were marked with sermon notes, information on word origins and definitions, and dates of benchmark events throughout his life, giving silent testimony to God's faithfulness and loving care.

Funny how thirty-eight years after his death, Lin Ellis and his steady secure faith were still molding and shaping his daughter's heart. Her father was always such an encourager for Abbie, always knowing exactly what to say to lift her spirits. His words had always calmed her troubled heart, especially on days when his little girl couldn't make sense of her mother's erratic behavior. *Why can't Dad be here now, Lord?* Abbie thought. *He'd have the perfect answer for me.*

The cover to her father's Bible had slipped partially off, and as Abbie reached into her book bag to bring out the love-worn volume, a folded piece of paper slipped out from underneath the cover. Abbie could see her name printed neatly in her dad's precise handwriting on the front of a letter. She recognized it as one found among her dad's papers after his death. *How did this get here? I was sure I had tucked this away in a safe place*, she thought.

A small cry caught in Abbie's throat as she held this long-forgotten treasure. With hands slightly shaking, she gently removed the wrinkled paper from its hiding place. She unfolded it carefully and began to read.

Dearest Abbie,

If you are reading this, then that must mean that God has called me home. I trust our Heavenly Father is meeting all of your needs.

No man ever had a finer daughter than I did. Thank you for loving me and for making me the happiest dad ever. I pray that God will bless you beyond all measure and that happiness in your own marriage someday will be an evidence of His love. You certainly deserve that after all the sorrow you unfortunately witnessed between your mother and me in your short life.

I am so sorry for all of the pain that your mother's struggle with alcoholism has caused in your life. If you could have only known her as I did before all that started, it might have given you insight into the woman she has become. Even though she may not always express it or show it, your mother loves you very much. The day you were born was one of the happiest days of her life.

You are an incredible young lady, Abbie. There are no words available to tell you how extremely proud I am of you. I see such promise in you. Never forget that God is in the business of reclaim-

*ing and reshaping lives. All He asks is that we be available and
teachable. He promises to do the rest.*

*I pray love—a real love—will find you. You deserve every hap-
piness life can afford and then some. Know that I want you to be
happy and would never want you to live the rest of your life alone
because of bitter memories from our marriage or a sense of guilt in
finding happiness when we never were quite able to grasp hold of
it ourselves. In love, I release you, Abbie, to whatever God has in
store for you.*

*Most importantly, I trust God will give you His clear direc-
tion and presence in this next phase of your life. He will NEVER
abandon you. I will see you someday in heaven, but until then, my
love goes with you. May you go with God.*

All my love,
Dad

Abbie couldn't breathe, much less think cohesively. How many times
over the years had she read this letter? Until now, it had lacked any
specific meaning. She carefully folded her dad's letter and hugged it to
herself. It was as if her father had somehow come here today, to this
place, to prod Abbie forward toward something she knew lay just ahead,
but as yet could not clearly define or see.

One of the last rays of the afternoon sun danced toward her, breaking
through the darkness of her soul. Abbie stared at it for long minutes. The
gossamer shaft appeared to her as a ray of hope, piercing the shroud of
gloom cloaking her spirit.

At last, a peace settled upon Abbie's heart, surrounding her with its
comforting presence. For the first time since Joe's death, she relaxed. She
knew she didn't have all the answers, but she had enough to begin to put
the pieces of her broken life back together. Long after the last light of day
faded, Abbie remained, safe within the chapel's shelter.

Chapter Fifty-One

If Abbie didn't hurry, she'd be late to a 10:00 appointment in Robbinsonville. Don was meeting her at Gravlee's. He sounded genuinely excited when Abbie called him the day before, telling him that she was accepting the job. She asked him for an opportunity to visit with him in person about various aspects of the offer. The decision to accept the job at Timothy House was the right decision. Abbie was sure of it. Drew's enthusiastic endorsement of her acceptance sealed the deal, stifling any lingering doubts.

Gravlee's was her idea. She only hoped she wouldn't bump into Keith there. Abbie knew she needed to patch things up with him, but her plate was full enough for the moment. This was Good Friday, and Kent Academy was closed for the Easter weekend. Perhaps it was a divine coincidence, but Abbie felt a rush of hope and excitement on this bright spring morning.

Over a week had passed since Keith's late-night visit and their argument. Abbie felt just awful about how she had acted. She used a great portion of the three-hour journey to Robbinsonville to ask God for wisdom in how to straighten things out with Keith. Remembering the pain in his eyes, Abbie was not sure if he could forgive her. Her heart hoped that he could. Somehow. Some way.

After parking on the square in front of the courthouse, Abbie walked a half block to the café. The sun, already making its climb toward its midday arch, filled the April morning with a golden glow. Don, watching for Abbie, came out onto the sidewalk to greet her as she approached.

"Abbie," he said warmly, taking her hand in both of his. "It's so good to see you."

"Thanks, Don. It's good to see you, too." She returned the handshake.

Don held open the front door to Gravlee's and waited while Abbie entered first. The early morning breakfast crowd had already cleared out. A few older men sat on stools at the counter, reading newspapers and sipping coffee. A young waitress bussed two tables near the rear of the café.

"Teencie picked out a special spot just for us." Don pointed toward a booth about halfway down the long wall of the café.

As Abbie slid in to her seat, she saw Teencie behind the counter, putting the finishing touches on a chocolate chess pie just heading into the oven. The waitress flashed a bright smile and nodded. Abbie smiled back.

A half-filled coffee cup was already on the table at Don's place. Teencie appeared as soon as they were seated and nodded toward Abbie. "Hey, hon."

Teencie's naturally curly hair, cut short, stood out in soft red ringlets all over her head. The curls bounced as she talked, which she did quite a lot of in a very animated manner. She took an order for a cup of hot tea for Abbie. Teencie placed her pencil behind one ear and headed off to the counter. She returned shortly to the table with Abbie's cup. She also brought with her a pot of coffee and refilled Don's cup.

"I was so delighted that you called," Don began as Abbie took a sip of the steaming liquid.

"Don, I'm excited about this job and find myself terrified at the same time. I'm still not totally convinced I'm qualified to do what you're asking me to do." She took a deep breath and let it out slowly, suddenly realizing how much tension was pent up inside her. She clasped and unclasped her hands.

Don beamed. "Abbie, don't you worry. You'll be a very valuable addition to our community. Doris is so delighted about your news. She and I have been praying for you during this year. We realize what a momentous decision this is."

He reached over to pat her arm. "You won't be sorry. God's going to use you in a special way to touch many lives."

For the next thirty minutes or so, Don and Abbie discussed various aspects of her new job, including the daily routine during the school year and the specific duties of a house parent. The cottage she would be living in would be ready for her arrival by mid-June. Abbie thought she might be able to move by the end of that month. She had yet to put her own house on the market.

Don reached down beside him to retrieve a thick manila file folder. He opened it and pulled out a white envelope. He placed it on the table and slid it across to Abbie.

"Inside is your contract and benefits package. I don't need it signed right now. Just take it home and read through it." He folded his hands on top of the manila folder. "If you have any questions, call me. I need it back with your signature by the end of next week."

Abbie picked up the packet, nodded, and listened to Don's request. "I'll put it in the mail by Monday, Don. I can't thank you enough for all that you and Doris have done for me. I'm not sure why you want me, but I have a peace that this is where I'm supposed to be. It will be especially great to be near Drew." As she mentioned her son's name, Abbie's grin widened.

"To have both of you is more than we hoped for," Don remarked. "Josh is so excited about Drew's partnership in the mentoring program. He's talked about your son all year long."

Abbie felt her eyes light up with pride.

"The pastor at Wright's Creek church is a fine man and will be someone Drew will learn a great deal from. Josh has told me about Drew's dream to someday attend seminary. Perhaps this work will help him nail down that decision."

A wave of gratitude washed over Abbie as she thought back over the events that God recently orchestrated, which would turn Drew's dream into reality.

"Oh, I almost forgot." Don's comment brought Abbie back from her reverie. He retrieved a small, light brown envelope from inside the manila folder and handed it to her. "Keith Haliday asked me to give this to you today. I told him that we were meeting this morning."

For a split second, Abbie couldn't say a word. "Why, thank you," she stammered and took the offering from Don's hand.

Keith was the last person she thought she would see or hear from today. She needed time to get a response together. Abbie took another sip of her tea, which was cold by now. At least it gave her something to do besides look like a deer in the headlights.

After a few more pleasantries, Abbie reached for her purse. "Don, thanks so much for meeting me here this morning. Being able to talk this move over with you puts my mind at ease. I probably need to head home."

Abbie waited by the front door while Don settled up with Teencie at the counter. The waitress waved to Abbie.

After telling Don good-bye, Abbie walked the half block back to her SUV. Once inside, she took the letter from her purse and held it in her hand. She ran her finger across her name, written in Keith's strong, clear handwriting. She took a deep breath, turned the envelope over, and opened the flap. A folded sheet of nutmeg-colored stationery lay inside. Abbie pulled it out and opened it.

Dear Abbie,

Welcome to Timothy House! You will be such a blessing. I trust this will be a wonderful new start for you.

I know I have no right to ask this, but would you meet me at Peter's Chapel? I am so terribly sorry about the way that I upset you last Monday night, and I'd like to have a chance to explain myself further. I have not been able to think of anything else since last week.

If you won't come or can't come, I will understand. Regardless of your decision, know that you are very special to me.

Your friend,
Keith

All the angst and frustration of the last week spilled out in tears that trickled down Abbie's cheeks. She tasted their salty sweetness on her lips. Oh, how she wanted to explain herself further, too. Abbie gently folded the note and slid it back into the envelope. She reached up and adjusted the rearview mirror toward her face. She wiped away the last of the tears.

Filled with a sense of urgency and a wave of purpose and direction that surprised her, Abbie cranked her SUV and headed off to Timothy House. The campus was only a fifteen-minute drive from town. The woods were filled with budding trees, spreading their display of new spring finery. Sunlight danced amid various shades of green, painting a vivid landscape of regeneration and new growth. Abbie mused over God's redemption of so many circumstances in her life. *Could He redeem a relationship with Keith?* she thought.

Abbie pulled through the stone columns at the front gate, and a sense of belonging in this place overcame her. For the first time in a very long while, she was home.

Chapter Fifty-Two

The door to the chapel was heavier than Abbie remembered. Adjusting to the dusky interior from the brightness of full sun outside proved a real challenge. She stood quietly at the back of the chapel; multicolored panes caused the refracted light to dance around the small sanctuary. The creak of a bench somewhere ahead caught her attention.

Abbie could now see Keith kneeling at a pew near the front of the chapel. He must have heard her behind him because he rose to his full height and stepped quietly into the aisle. She started slowly toward him. Keith met her halfway down the aisle and wrapped her tightly, safely, in his strong arms. The distance between them was bridged in a few short steps. No words were necessary to heal the breach between them.

For the longest time, all Abbie could hear was the gentle silence of this holy room. She pulled back slightly from Keith's embrace. Tears welled up in her eyes.

"I'm so sorry, Keith. Please forgive me." She could say no more.

Gentle kisses calmed the approaching storm within her.

"Let's sit down." Keith led her into a nearby pew. He took both of her hands in his and looked down at them for the longest time. "Abbie." He finally looked back up at her. "I don't know how to begin. First of all, I want to tell you how sorry I am that my visit last week upset you. I should have been more sensitive to the fact that Joe's betrayal has caused you to be very distrustful, especially of me."

Abbie interrupted. "No, Keith. I'm the one who should apologize. I don't know why I said some of the things I said."

"You have been hurt and betrayed, and you have every right to be wary." Keith squeezed her hands gently. "Fear creates some pretty strong responses in people who have been hurt like you have. I've had some of my own."

"It's just that what you told me that night caught me totally off guard." Abbie's hands began to relax within his. "My life is changing very quickly, and I'm in a place I've never been before."

Keith kissed her hands tenderly, still held between his own. "I'm not sure that you're ready to hear this, but I love you, Abbie Richardson."

Abbie drew in a sharp breath. Her heart was pounding wildly. Her eyes were riveted to his, but for the longest time, she could say nothing. "Keith," she began softly, "the last thing I want to do is hurt you."

She pulled her hands from his and folded them in her lap. Caught off guard by his declaration, she was now in uncharted territory. Her eyes darted around the dark space beyond Keith and settled on a speck of dust that floated in a shaft of sunlight, piercing the darkness like a moonbeam.

Keith leaned forward. "I know you've been hurt so badly, but I'm willing to wait as long as it takes for you to get to the point where you can trust and love me."

"And what if I can't?" Abbie settled further against the back of the pew, almost too fearful to utter the words. "What if the damage Joe caused is too great to undo? What if I can't bring myself to trust a man again? I can't do that to you, Keith. I couldn't bear it if I broke your heart." She brushed back a strand of hair that had fallen around her face.

"Look, Abbie," said Keith with quiet solemnity. "Let's just take this one day at a time. That's all God gives us anyway. I'm willing to do that if you are."

"I think I could do that," replied a hesitant Abbie. "But it's not just my feelings that I have to consider. What about Drew?" A lump rose in her throat at the thought of her son having to endure any more pain.

"I certainly respect your concern for your son. I also think he is a young adult who is very levelheaded and able to fend for himself. He's probably a lot more resilient than you give him credit for." Keith looked down for a minute. He looked up. "Would you allow me to arrange a time to talk to Drew? Seems the fair thing for me to do is to get his take on the subject of our seeing one another."

A bit surprised, Abbie smiled slightly. "You would do that? You would consider his feelings as well as mine?"

"Of course I would." Keith reached over to hold her hands once again. "I know I don't need his permission, but if this relationship is to have any possibility of succeeding, we'll need all the support we can get."

Hope rose in Abbie's heart as she listened to Keith. Years had gone by since she had felt this tingling, the sensation that something good could actually happen to her, a realization that God might actually want her to experience a life full of happiness and joy.

"I know we've both been through a great deal of loss and pain, but God has not abandoned either one of us." Keith's grip tightened around her hands. "I trust Him to lead us both to the next step."

For the longest time, the two sat and talked under the cross of Peter's Chapel. Unsure of all that lay ahead, but certain of the great affection that bound them together, that was enough for a start. As Abbie listened to all Keith told her, she was reminded of Winnie's advice.

For the first time she realized that God revealed His will to His children one day, one experience, one step of faith at a time. Otherwise, it would be too overwhelming to comprehend. Receiving this gift was like unfurling a great spool of beautiful ribbon. You started with the part you held in your hand.

God had never abandoned either her or Keith. Abbie knew that now. A sense of peace, a coming to terms with the fact that there would always be some unexplained areas in her life, enveloped her. The words of the great hymn of Matheson came back to Abbie, "O Joy that seekest me through pain, I cannot close my heart to Thee. I trace the rainbow through the rain, and feel the promise is not in vain that morn shall tearless be." God's promise never to abandon them would guide them both in the days to come.

About the Author

Sherye Simmons Green is currently a teacher. She was Miss Mississippi in 1979 and still lives in Mississippi with her husband and two children. This is her debut novel.

CPSIA information can be obtained at www.ICGtesting.com
Printed in the USA
LVOW122333051112

305964LV00005B/40/P

9 781469 761282